For Bill:
My St Paul's buddy!
Love you
Francine

CRADLE OF LIGHTNING

A STORY OF BOTSWANA

Francine Walls

Published by
TrilliumSpring Press
Seattle, WA

Cataloging-in-Publication Data
(additional data furnished upon request)

____p. ____cm.

1.) Africa—Botswana—History 2.) World History—Africa—American—Rhodesian 3.) Wars—Vietnam—Rhodesian Bush 4.) Historical Fiction—Women—World 5.) Life-changing events—Romantic—Historical

Walls, Francine The Cradle of Lightning: A Story of Botswana
FIC Wa 2024 PS642 W85 2024

ISBN paperback: 979-8-9901002-0-6
ISBN eBook: 979-8-9901002-1-3

PCN: 2024903831

Cover Design by Tim Barber, dissectdesigns.com
Interior Design by Danielle H. Acee, authorsassistant.com

CRADLE OF LIGHTNING

For Chris

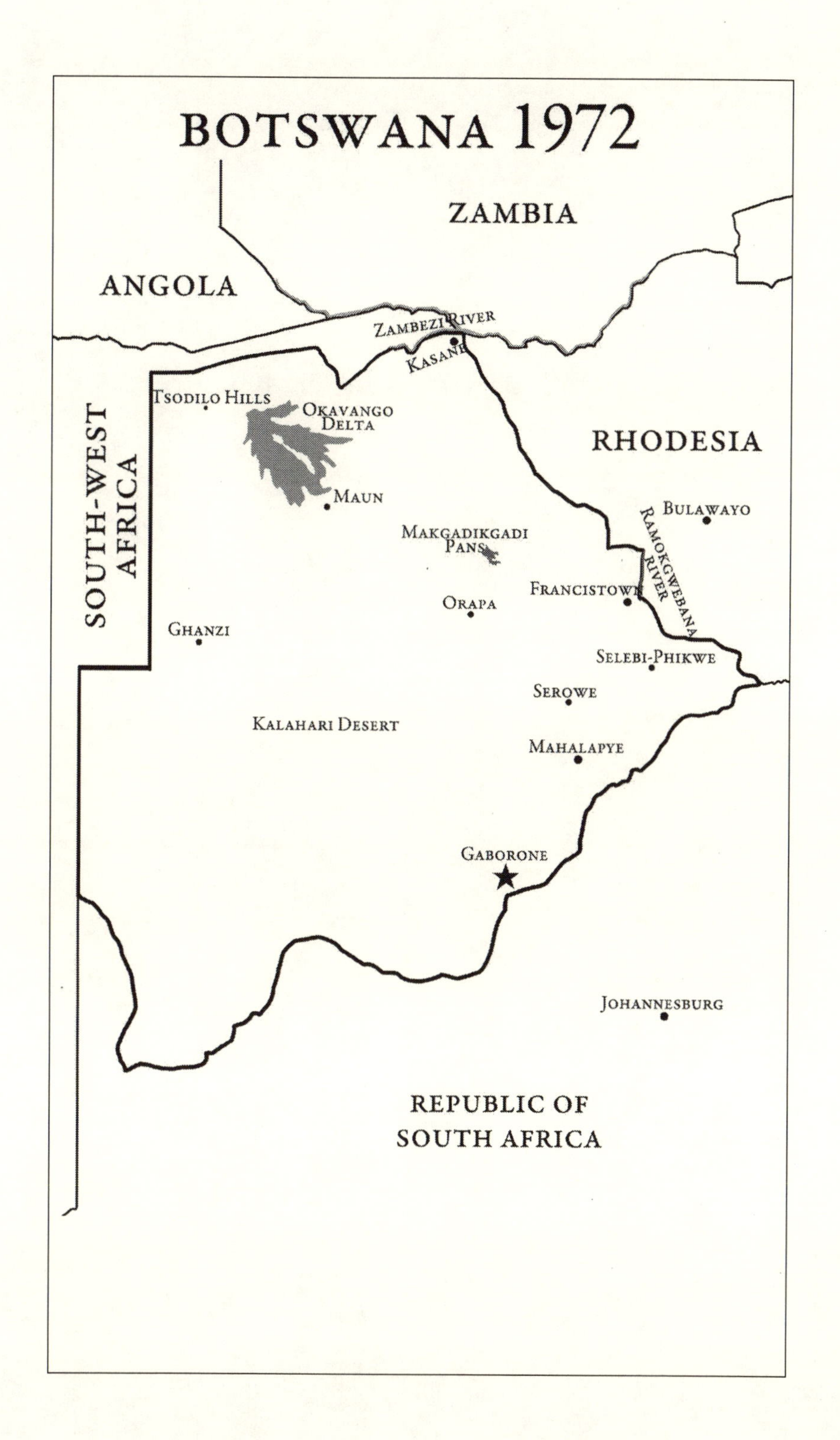
BOTSWANA 1972
ZAMBIA
ANGOLA
Zambezi River
Kasane
Tsodilo Hills
Okavango Delta
SOUTH-WEST AFRICA
RHODESIA
Maun
Bulawayo
Makgadikgadi Pans
Ramokgwebana River
Francistown
Orapa
Ghanzi
Selebi-Phikwe
Serowe
Kalahari Desert
Mahalapye
Gaborone
Johannesburg
REPUBLIC OF SOUTH AFRICA

Main Characters

Alicia Talbot: Teacher, widow of Eric, mother of Sammy, sister to Hannah, American

Balakile Mosweu: Member of a Police Mobile Unit, Motswana

Bronwyn Rhys: Teacher, mother of Geoff, fiancée of William, British

Chaparadza: Guerrilla commander, Rhodesian

Corley McClete: Teacher, Nigel's girlfriend, American

Dereck Kruger: School mechanic, South African

Dinizulu: Policeman, Motswana

Dorcas: Headmaster's wife, Motswana

Ellie Garcia: Teacher, Mick's girlfriend, American

Eric Talbot: Late husband of Alicia, killed in the Vietnam War, American

Fey Oakes: Teacher, nurse, American

Gaeyo: Head girl, Motswana

Geoffrey Mortensen: Son of Bronwyn Rhys and William Mortensen

Hannah Evans: Sister to Alicia, girlfriend to Lara, American

Hector Pierce, Col.: U.S. Military, godfather to Jake, American

Jake Hunter: Teacher, soldier injured in the Vietnam War, godson to Col. Pierce, American

Ketumile: Headmaster's son

Kgeledi: Head boy, football team leader, Motswana

Kgosi Monyame: Chief of Kukama Village, Motswana

Kunene Matlagodi: Headmaster of Kukama School, husband to Dorcas, father of Ketumile, Motswana

Kxoma: Student, Bushman tracker, Motswana

Lepetu: Student, football star, Motswana

Maria-Elena Pierce: Late wife of Col. Pierce, American

Mbengawa: Student, Motswana

Mick Cooper: Teacher, Ellie's boyfriend, American

Mr. Anand: Owner of the Snappy Mercantile, Indian

Mmegi: Student, Motswana

Mpule: Sammy's nanny, granddaughter of kgosi, Negotho's girlfriend, Glorianna's sister, Motswana

Mrs. Linchwe: Secretary to the headmaster, Motswana

Mubayi: Vice-principal of Kukama School, teacher in the Builder's Brigade, Rhodesian

Negotho: Student, suitor of Mpule, Motswana

Nigel Lennon: Teacher, carpenter, Corley's boyfriend, British

Ndona Leagajang: Farm manager, Motswana

Paul Winthrop: Teacher, American

Piet Van der Merwe: Shopkeeper, Afrikaner

Sammy: Two-year-old son of Alicia and the late Eric Talbot, American

Thale: Student, poet, Motswana

Tsau: Village boy, Motswana

William Mortensen: Teacher, fiancé of Bronwyn, father of Geoff, American

Glossary

Baas: Boss

Batswana: Citizens/inhabitants of Botswana (plural); Singular: Motswana

Biro: Ink pen

Bogadi: Payment by groom's family to the bride's family in cattle or cash

Botswana: Nation in southern Africa

Cuppa: Cup of tea

Dagga: Cannabis

DOA: Dead on arrival

Dumela: Hello, to one person

Dumelang: Hello, to two or more persons

Ee: Yes

Expat: Expatriate worker, a citizen of a country other than Botswana

Five by Five: Military term for "loud and clear"

Forms: Similar to "grades" in the U.S. Forms 1- 5 are similar to Grades 7- 11

Gabs: Gaberone, capital of Botswana

Headmaster: Principal

Jo-burg: Johannesburg, city in the Republic of South Africa

Kaiross: A rug made of hides sewn together

Kgosi: Chief of a village

Kgotla: Meeting place with kgosi, place for court of law, community council

Ko Ko: Said instead of knocking

Kopje: Isolated hill of boulders, uneroded bedrock

Kraal: Fenced enclosure for livestock, corral

Lima Charlie: Military term for "loud and clear"

Lorry: Truck

Matron: A woman who supervises students in a school

Mealie-meal: Cornmeal

Metsi: Water

Mikes: Military term for "minutes"

Mma: Woman, mother, ma'am

Motswana: Inhabitant/citizen of Botswana (singular); Plural: Batswana

Muti: Body parts used in witchcraft

Nnyaa: No

Pan: Craterlike depression

PMU: Police Mobile Unit, precursor to Botswana Defence Force (BDF)

POI: Person of interest

Prefects: Students who enforce discipline

Pula: Rain

Rand: Currency, Republic of South Africa

Rhodesian Bush War: 1964 - 1979, conflict in southern Africa

Rock rabbit: Rock hyrax, Dassie. Small mammal native to Africa, related to elephants

Rondavel: Traditional round hut with a thatched roof

ROTC: Reserve Officers Training Corps

Rra: Man, father, mister

Scarlet Pimpernel Fund: Fund to pay for the medical needs of students

Second Chimurenga: Rhodesian guerrilla war that led to Black rule in 1980, Rhodesian Bush War

Setswana: One of two official languages of Botswana, along with English

Shagging: Sexual relations

SOB: Son of a bitch

SOP: Standard Operating Procedure

Stile: Ladder over a fence

Torch: Flashlight

U.K.: United Kingdom

Uni: University

Phrases:

C'est moi: It's me.

Je ne sais quoi: I don't know.

Ke batla…: I want…

Ke itumetse: Thank you.

Sala Sentle: Stay well (to one staying); **Response:** Tsamaya sentle: Go well (to one leaving).

Te adoro, mi corazón: I love you, my darling.

Toute suite: Right now.

Tsena: Come, Come in.

Tswee-tswee: Please.

1
Botswana, Southern Africa
Sunday, January 9, 1972

At the sound of a distant rumble of trucks, Alicia Talbot opened the door of her thatched-roof hut and stepped outside. The heat was a slap in her face.

A few weaver birds flitted past the purple bougainvillea in her courtyard. Farther away, goats browsed in the brush and chickens scratched in the sand. Beyond the thorn trees on the southwest horizon, a cloud of dust rose from the dirt track that served as the road to Kukama School. As the trucks grew closer, one of the goats lifted its head and bleated. The chickens scattered.

Alicia's two-year-old son, Sammy, followed her outside, and he seemed to feel the tension. He raised his arms. She pushed back her long hair and picked him up. But she held him so tightly, he protested.

"Sammy *down*," he said.

"No. Stay still."

The trucks were close enough that she could read the word "Police" on their sides. The police could be as menacing as the

Rhodesian guerrillas on the border. She knew why the police were here. Yesterday, two machine guns were found under bushes in the school compound, something to do with the guerrillas, no doubt.

Carrying Sammy, Alicia stepped back inside her round hut, a rondavel. As she paced, she sang a lullaby to her son, yet he fussed.

"Hush. Mommy's here."

The police were from the small dusty capital of Gaberone, nicknamed "Gabs." Alicia did not want to imagine what they would do next. Maybe exams would be canceled, the school closed, the teachers declared "prohibited immigrants" and expelled from the country. She thought of her students, Negotho and Thale, for instance, whose parents sold all their cows to pay the school fees.

She pushed aside the curtains in her front window and peered out. Two policemen came up the lower path to her home on the western edge of the school compound. They wore uniforms and carried rifles. Her stomach churned.

Her rondavel was little protection. If she yelled for help, would her neighbors, William and Bronwyn, hear her from their home a hundred yards away? Would her friends Fey and Paul rush over?

The policemen pounded on her door. Alicia opened it a crack. One policeman was taller than the other. On his ebony face, a thin white scar zig-zagged from the corner of one eye to his chin. Despite the scar, he appeared dapper, his uniform new. The other man was shorter, with bits of straw in his hair, dressed in a wrinkled uniform.

"Dumelang," she said. Hello, everyone.

"Dumela, Mma." Hello, ma'am.

The tall one pointed to himself. "Dinizulu."

He gestured for her to leave. "Mma. Be away."

She grabbed a blanket, covered her son, and opened the door wider. The clanging of cow bells rang across the arid landscape. The insects hummed in the background.

Dinizulu grabbed her arm and pulled her out the door with such roughness she was thrown off balance. Recovering, she shielded her son with the blanket and walked across the clearing to her courtyard.

"Snuggle in, Sammy." He listened to his mother and pressed his face against her breast.

She heard a crash. Still carrying her son, she went back to her doorway and confronted them.

"If you're looking for weapons, I have none."

The policemen ignored her, overturning the cots and dumping her possessions on the floor.

At least they were staying away from the photographs of Eric taped to the walls. She touched her wedding ring.

Dinizulu opened her closet and swept the contents off each shelf. Her camera fell and hit the concrete floor with a sharp crack. He took down the large envelope on the top shelf and opened it.

Alicia flinched. "Take your hands off that." She kept her anger under control. She did not want to scare Sammy.

Dinizulu turned the envelope upside down. Eric's Bronze Star and Vietnam Service Medal fell to the floor.

"Get out!" she said.

The other policeman jerked his chin toward the door and pointed his rifle at her head. Holding Sammy close, Alicia bent over and picked up the five-pointed Bronze Star. The other medal was next to Dinizulu's feet. She did not dare pick it up, so she stood and walked outside.

She heard the men open the door to the Lizard Lounge, a small alcove built onto her rondavel. Her books hit the floor. Aware of something wet, she looked down.

Blood.

Blood dripped from her palm, streaking the yellow blanket with red. She felt light-headed at the sight. Sammy struggled to get down, but she held him up high enough to flutter her eyelashes on his cheek.

"Butterfly kisses, Sammy. Butterfly kisses."

He giggled, putting his arms around her neck.

She heard shouts in the distance. Without a word, the policemen left and strutted back toward the main gate.

Alicia stepped inside and set down her son. Books, papers, clothes, and mugs lay near the overturned cots. She smelled the soil from the house plants dumped on the floor. Scattered around were her mementos of Eric. She searched for his other medal.

Gone.

She gazed at the thatched roof, the wooden cross beams, the mud-brick walls, and her belongings jumbled on the floor. She longed for her home in Seattle and her flowering plum trees. Teaching in Botswana was her husband's dream, not hers.

With Eric dead, what am I doing here?

2

Jake Hunter's plane touched down at the tiny airport in Gaberone after an often-delayed trip from San Diego.

He stood up, rolled his shoulders, and rubbed the stubble on his chin. After wearing the same clothes for three days, he needed a shower, a shave, and a cold beer. He would not get them soon. His field work in geology kept him fit, but his wounds from the war in Vietnam bothered him. Dozing in an airplane seat left him in pain. He put on his hat and shouldered his backpack. A blast of heat hit him as he walked down the steps to the tarmac.

From London, the plane had flown down the entire length of Africa to Johannesburg. The sun rose over the edge of the continent, red as a beating heart. Mt. Kilimanjaro stood alone, a sentinel on the vast plain. Jake would have sat on the wing-tip for the view.

Colonel Hector Pierce, U.S. Army, stood in the sun outside the shabby terminal. A long-expected war in Rhodesia was heating up and spilling over into the eastern border of defenseless Botswana. Botswana, smaller than Texas, had a half-million in population, mostly illiterate. The country boasted less than fifteen miles of paved roadway.

Despite his exhaustion, Jake's anger swelled as he walked toward his godfather. They needed to have a serious talk. Pierce was dressed in civilian clothes. His short black hair was going gray at the temple, and his face was lined especially around his eyes. They shook hands, eying each other, neither smiled.

Jake spoke first. "Please accept my condolences on the death of Maria Elena."

Pierce gave him a curt nod.

Jake owed his godfather a lot, so he had turned down his dream job, doing research on the San Andreas fault. He would do whatever Pierce requested. When this mission was complete, he would return to San Diego, lickety-split.

Among a sea of mud-brick huts, Jake and Pierce walked single-file toward a ramshackle tavern, a shebeen. Women on the path carried pails on their heads to and from the water faucet, the standpipe. Barefoot, they wore ankle-length dresses with head cloths tied at the nape of their necks, their skin the rich color of mahogany. The hum of insects, the smoke from cooking fires, and the heat pervaded everything.

Both men ducked under the lintel as they entered the sweltering shebeen. The room smelled like beer. They sat down on either side of a decrepit table.

Jet lag and sleep deprivation took their toll, but Jake needed to orient himself to this new country without delay. He touched the backpack beside him. With the gear in his pack, he could survive almost any predicament.

Pierce asked the bartender, who had a cleft palate, to bring two lagers. In the U.S., the cleft palate would have been repaired in infancy, closing the gap between mouth and nose.

When the lagers arrived, Jake took a swig. Warm. Ugh.

He pulled out a handkerchief and wiped the sweat off the back of his neck.

Pierce spoke in a low voice. "This morning, the police tore into Kukama School, northeast, near Francistown. They suspect a hidden cache of weapons headed to the Rhodesian guerrillas."

"School?"

"You'll stride into Kukama School and volunteer to teach science. Independent boarding school. Six hundred students. On the eastern border with Rhodesia. Undercover work. The headmaster is desperate for teachers, so he would take the devil and probably has."

Jake took a deep breath. "I've never taught high school."

"You were a student long enough. Figure it out. Kukama is a key location to gather intelligence about guerrillas who hide in Botswana's hinterlands and go over the border into Rhodesia to attack."

"Their goal?"

"The guerrillas want to bring down the White-run government. They cut off the lips, ears, and noses of Black victims, and murder White families on remote farms. Rape. Murder. They bayonet babies."

Jake drank the rest of his beer, and set the glass down hard. "You know the nicest people."

Pierce shrugged. "The Rhodesian military fights against the guerrillas with mixed results. Batswana on the border get squeezed between the guerrillas and the Rhodesian military—misery sandwich."

Jake raised his eyebrows. "Botswana wants the U.S. to bolster its military?"

"No military here. Botswana's president wants infrastructure, not an army. He expanded the police force to three hundred men for the entire country and created Police Mobile Units, PMUs."

"Sounds dicey."

"Most policemen ride bicycles, unarmed. Few are equipped with modern rifles. No one has the expertise to defend the borders. Understand? We're here to act as trainers for the PMUs."

Jake pressed his lips together. "Another war," he whispered to himself.

Pierce sipped his beer. "Botswana is dependent on trade with South Africa and Rhodesia, both nations run by Whites. Botswana is almost entirely surrounded by countries in civil war. The U.S. wants Botswana to be the stable center of southern Africa."

"Can Botswana survive?"

"The nation's only hope of survival is to stay neutral and not support guerrillas in the liberation movements."

Under the table, Jake tapped his fingers on his thigh.

"Outside Francistown," Pierce said, "I have a compound and a small contingent of soldiers. Meet me there soon. On the weekends, you'll teach hand-to-hand combat, navigation, marksmanship, just like Ranger school. Botswana must prepare to defend its borders."

"How does the school fit into your strategy?"

"Near the border, a gunrunner channels weapons to the Rhodesian guerrillas. We don't know how. Machine guns found at the school might help us figure that out."

Jake waved the flies away from the table. "I'm not an investigator. Why am I here?"

"You're a geologist, top-notch cover story. Geologists found diamonds and mining started at Orapa south of the Makgadikgadi Pans last year. All diamond pipes run dry in the end."

"Sounds like a powder keg, Pierce. Just your style. Don't get me blown up. Rehab is hell." He stood up, stretched his cramping muscles and sat back down.

"The school's soccer coach left," Pierce said. "'Soccer' is called 'football' here. Volunteer to coach. You'll go to matches in various villages, acquire more intelligence."

Jake gave a hard laugh. "We didn't play soccer when I was a student." He shot an air-ball into an imaginary basket. "But at basketball, I'm a magician."

"It's a ball game. You excel at ball games. Read a manual."

A cockroach scuttled over Jake's boot. Donkeys brayed nearby.

Pierce frowned. "Confidential mission, don't get your throat slit. On the positive side, I hear beautiful women teach there. Pick a good woman this time."

Jake almost went over the table at him. Instead, he focused on his mantra: Stay calm. Stay alert. He stood up, put on his hat, and swung his backpack onto his shoulders.

"I'll hitchhike to the school. 'Rangers lead the way.'"

3

Alicia's rondavel was tidy once again when Fey Oakes pushed through the door carrying her black satchel.

"How you doing, Missy?"

Sammy dropped his crayon, knocked his coloring book to the floor, and ran to Fey.

"Auntie! Auntie!"

Fey set down her satchel and picked him up.

An energetic brunette, Fey, wore a neon-yellow muumuu that made her look like a daffodil, although in personality she was more like a Venus flytrap. She exuded competence and confidence. Armed with her satchel, she was ready for most medical emergencies.

"Did the police order the school closed?" Alicia asked.

"No more weapons found," Fey said, cuddling Sammy. "But the machine guns found yesterday enraged the police commander. Makes the school seem corrupt, as if we're complicit in running guns to the guerrillas."

Alicia sighed.

"One more cock-up," Fey said, "and the commander will close the school. They tore apart a few rondavels including yours to make their irritation known."

The school survived. Alicia was surprised at how relieved she felt.

Still in Fey's embrace, Sammy leaned toward his mother. "What I do, Mma?" Mother.

Alicia retrieved the coloring book and took Sammy from Fey.

"Would you like to color some more animals, little one?"

Grinning, Sammy displayed his perfect baby teeth. Alicia set him back on his chair at the table with his coloring book. She inhaled the familiar, waxy scent of the crayons. Sammy selected one and began to color a giraffe.

"Hard job cleaning up?" Fey asked.

Alicia nodded, recalling her decision to scrub out the fireplace. A month ago, she had lit a fire and smoke spread throughout the room. Dereck Kruger, the school mechanic and a friend, had sealed it off. Today, she stored a few items in the now-clean fireplace and moved the freestanding closet in front of it.

Fey grabbed Alicia's hand. "What's this? Blood?" She pointed to a cot. "Sit." She picked up her satchel, opened it, and pulled out a glass bottle and a cloth. "Around here, cuts go septic quicker than envy in a bitter heart. Did the police injure you? If so, I will raise hell with our embassy in Gabs."

"I cut *myself*."

Fey poured liquid on the cloth, and dabbed Alicia's bloody palm. "Tick-bite fever, bilharzia, and amoebic dysentery. You've had one disease after another since you came here. Don't get sick or injured again. I forbid it."

Fey looked over at Sammy. "Regardless of your apparent death wish, my honorary nephew glows with health. He's growing up."

Alicia smiled at her son, busy coloring.

"Your lovely smile is back," Fey said. "Now for the confidential gossip. Mick hurt Ellie again."

Alicia's body tightened. "No!"

"Ellie said she took a fall, but the wounds were not consistent with one. Do not make a ruckus. The last time Mick injured Ellie, you tried to get him canned. His cruel streak has an elephantine memory. Beware."

"Last time, he broke Ellie's arm." Alicia looked out the window. The clouds threatened more rain, thunder, and lightning. The cicadas and grasshoppers kept up their chorus.

"The headmaster will not fire Mick," Fey said, "not over what he sees as a domestic matter. The local policemen and our esteemed chief, the kgosi, will do nothing. They quibble about the size of the stick acceptable for wife beating."

Alicia did not want to hear any more. Sometimes the gossip from the bush telegraph was too graphic. "Did the police from Gabs bother you?"

"The headmaster deflected them. He won't jeopardize my unpaid nursing, especially since blood makes our matron faint, kind of like you. Anyway, he thinks I gush money. He's not aware of our secret stash, the Scarlet Pimpernel Fund. Also, he kept mum about the sabotage." She finished bandaging Alicia's palm and put her supplies back in the satchel.

Alicia hugged herself. "Will he call a staff meeting?"

"Soon. Maybe. But he won't invite the board members. They will have heard about the machine gun kerfuffle. If a man shoots a lion, everyone knows within a fifty-mile radius in ten minutes. Most board members won't risk the journey in the rainy season. The dirt track from Maun must be knee-deep in muck."

"Machine guns," Alicia said. "Is this too dangerous for Sammy? Should I stay or leave?" She bit her lip. "Dinizulu, that damn policeman, stole one of Eric's medals. I have so little of Eric."

Fey snapped her satchel shut and stood up. "Could be an omen." She peered at the photographs of Eric on the walls, interspersed with prints of Degas, Cezanne, and Pissarro. She tapped a photo of Eric with his curly hair, tie-dyed shirt, and bell-bottom jeans.

"Put this photo away. On second thought, put them *all* away."

For a moment, Alicia inhaled the salty air of Seattle, and heard the plaintive, long call of a seagull gliding overhead. She felt the light sprinkle of rain on her upturned face. With a start, she came back to the present. Fey stared at her.

"Photos?" Alicia said. "Can't take them down. My cockroaches crave hiding under them from the heat."

"They're not the only thing hiding here. Put yourself in the way of healing."

Alicia gulped. "What?"

Fey opened her satchel again and brought out a tin box with an eagle on the lid. She set it on the table. "Put your mementos of Eric in this."

Alicia moved to stand by the open door. "Dinizulu tears apart my home, takes Eric's medal, and you want me to stop grieving for my husband." She snapped her fingers. "Just like that?"

"Discombobulation fuels changes. If you wait, the status quo returns. Get a move on."

Alicia rubbed her hands on her jeans and fluffed out the cotton blouse sticking to her back.

"Eric's death disoriented you," Fey said. "The moments you and Eric shared will never be lost. Let him go."

Alicia objected to the arrogance, the presumption. The problem was, she knew Fey might be right. She clung to her memories, talking to Eric every night.

"You're meddling in the most intimate—" Her grief threatened to overwhelm her.

"Put your wedding ring, his poems, and all these photographs in this tin. When you talk to Sammy about his father, bring it out. He'll adjust."

Alicia looked at Sammy. He was picking out a crayon to color a hyena.

"Your son understands birth and death," Fey said. "He sees donkeys mate beside the path, a male up on the haunches of a female with a foal beside them. Our friend, Ndona, slaughters pigs, goats, and chickens at the farm. Sammy takes it all in. Most of life is out of your control. Control what you can, accept what you can't."

"Enough." Alicia's voice trembled. She pointed to the doorway. "Please."

Sammy colored the hyena blood red.

☆ ☆ ☆

That afternoon, the chickens clucked in the tall grasses, hiding from the sun. Goats perched in the thorn trees, munching on leaves. The faint rhythms of gumba-gumba music floated over the air from a distant shebeen. At an insistent knock, Alicia stopped writing in her journal, and put her biro, her ink pen, on the table. Were the police back? She opened the front door with apprehension. Geoff whizzed past her toward Sammy, napping on his cot.

"Play me!" Geoff hollered. He tugged on Sammy's arm.

Bronwyn Rhys, Geoff's mother, trudged up to the door. She was five months pregnant, out of breath, with a cloth bag on her arm. Her hair was a mass of short auburn curls. Sweat beaded on the hairline of her freckled brow. Five years ago, Alicia and Bronwyn sat next to each other in a Chaucer class in Swansea. Alicia studied at the Welsh university during her junior year abroad. They had become close friends.

Bronwyn pointed at Geoff. "The tiny terror got here before me, sorry." She stroked the curve of her abdomen. "My baby's dancing a jig on me bladder. I need a lie down. Can't get much kip with all the commotion inside."

Sammy jumped down from his cot ready to play with his friend. Sammy, an easygoing child, was eager for the chaos Geoff always brought. Alicia loved to watch the boys together, fair-skinned Sammy with blond ringlets and Geoff with black hair and brown skin.

Geoff's father, William Mortensen was a Peace Corps volunteer. Bronwyn was pregnant with their second child.

William and Bronwyn wanted to marry, but neither could face the bureaucratic complexities involved.

The boys ran out the front door to where Dereck had built a sandbox. An old truck tire sat beside it. The boys raced the toy cars around the sandbox, roaring and nattering in a mixture of English and Setswana. With nannies who spoke little English, the children learned the local language fast.

To watch over them, the women followed the boys outside and headed to the small courtyard in the clearing. Low mud-brick walls formed the courtyard a few yards out from the hut. Planter boxes of flowers sat on the walls. Mimosa trees grew behind the boxes. The fence around the courtyard was formed by chicken wire nailed to wooden posts at the four corners. A small gate provided access.

A net over the courtyard supported vines of honeysuckle and bougainvillea. The vines lowered the heat by a degree or two.

Alicia paused to examine the vines before she entered, on the alert for snakes. A deadly boomslang could blend with the foliage. Nothing lethal moved overhead, so they sat down.

"Did the police tear your place apart?" Alicia asked.

"No one plays silly buggers with William. He stood in our doorway, immoveable. Like a pyramid. Threaten his family at your peril. Handy with a knife, he likes to say. A Howard Uni grad to boot." She chuckled, hand over her heart. "My sweet William." From her bag, she pulled out a pack of Camels along with a box of matches. She lit a cigarette, took a drag, and exhaled.

"Ah, needed that."

Alicia frowned. "Didn't you promise Fey you would not smoke during your pregnancy?"

Bronwyn looked away. “She’s not *my* boss.”

Alicia ignored the barb. “What about your high blood pressure?”

Bronwyn exhaled smoke up into the vines. “My babe will pop out perfectly, like Geoff.”

“What about your sister? You told me in Swansea that—”

“Don’t be cheeky.” Bronwyn grimaced. “No worries. Got it? All is hunky dory.”

“Hope so.” Alicia saw the darkening clouds above the cigarette smoke. “Yet more rain on the way. Better grab Geoff and hustle.”

4

Jake hitched a lift on a truck piled high with crates headed toward Francistown. The dirt track was pocked with ruts. He wedged himself and his pack between crates labeled "Black Beans."

The truck halted to let people off or get on. More men climbed on top with Jake. The engine noise prevented conversation. The driver drove fast to skim over the tops of shallow ruts, and slower to negotiate the deeper ones. The smell of diesel was thick in the air.

Tracking the rain clouds, Jake opened his pack and pulled out his poncho a second before the torrent hit. Chagrined, his pack stayed dry, but he was drenched. The other men sat soaked, too. The truck drove on through the storm.

When the rain tapered off, the dust was gone, and the world sparkled. In the distance, hillocks of massive boulders dotted the landscape. They were "kopjes," Dutch for "little head."

A wooden cart pulled by a donkey took up the middle of the road. The truck swerved around the cart; the crates shifted and threw the passengers off-kilter. Unconcerned, the driver of the donkey cart waved merrily as the truck passed him.

After the road dried, clouds of dust engulfed them. Jake pulled out his canteen and took a swig. He was low on water.

An elderly man sat near him. A walking stick lay across his lap with a thin loop of leather nailed at the top. He sported a gray mustache and a short beard. He wore a knit cap and a spotless white shirt. His trousers were patched with swatches of red, green, and yellow fabric. Jake held up his canteen to the man who declined with a quick shake of his head.

They passed a group of gray-haired men who sat in conversation under a tall tree, no young men visible. Small boys herded goats, throwing stones, or hitting them with sticks to keep them together. Baby goats climbed up into the thorn trees.

Without a word, the elderly man slumped, collapsing. Jake reached over and checked for a pulse. The man was alive.

Jake pounded on the top of the cab. The truck kept going, and Jake kept pounding. He would pound until Easter, if necessary. A man's life was in danger.

The elderly man was sweating, losing moisture. The other men appeared distressed but did not volunteer to help. The truck pulled in front of a one-story building with a tall tree beside it. On the front were the words "Bottle Store," hand-lettered in red paint. Grassland savanna surrounded the store with a few huts scattered nearby.

Jake hoisted his pack, scooped up the unconscious man, and carried him to the back of the truck. He set him down on a crate and climbed down to stand on the tailgate. He picked up the man and stepped to the ground. "Stay calm. Stay alert," he said under his breath.

Jake carried the man to the tree and laid him on the sand. As the sun neared the horizon, an owl called from the tree. The man vomited.

Jake pulled his handkerchief from his pack, wiped the man's mouth, and shoved the now foul-smelling cloth into an exterior pocket. Children surfaced out of nowhere and gathered around them, eager for the drama. The man seemed to shrivel.

"Doctor," Jake bellowed. "We need a doctor!"

As the sun set, Sammy fell asleep. Alicia had read only to page three of *Red Fish, Blue Fish*. After the upsetting police invasion, they both needed an early night.

The night-music swelled outside. She lit a mosquito coil, blew out the lanterns and lay down in the nude, too hot for a nightgown. The corn husks in the mattress rustled as she tried to get comfortable. She watched the shadows in the room and went into a waking dream.

She saw Eric in the jungle. Sunlight glinted off the broad leaves of trees overhanging the trail. He and his men searched a poorly thatched hut, the roof held up by thin logs. An overturned pot stained the soil black. They paused, alert to every noise. When Eric moved into the dense foliage, his men followed in silence. Alicia tried to scream a warning, but she was too late. The jungle exploded in flames and bursts of gunfire. Eric lay dead on the trail.

Heart pounding, she struggled to breathe. At last, she caught her breath and grew calmer.

I have to stop this.

Sitting up, she twisted off her wedding ring. Eric had inscribed her ring with five words, "Time cannot alter my love."

She made a decision.

Putting on her sandals, she got out of bed. As Sammy slept, she took down every photograph of Eric. Fey's tin box was still on the table. She opened it and put in the photos and the envelope with Eric's poems, letters, and Bronze Star. With a pang, she added her wedding band and closed the lid. Fey was right. Eric was gone.

Dressed only in her sandals, she opened the front door and slipped outside.

She lifted her hands to the Milky Way in silent supplication, then pressed her hands over her breasts, and down to her belly where the skin puckered slightly, stretch marks from her pregnancy.

"Cradle of lightning" was what her Bushman student, Kxoma, called the Milky Way, a poetic image Eric would have loved. Eric's final poem arrived a week after his death. She recited it to the stars.

Let us lie down in the garden on a carpet of violets
amid the spires of hollyhock and foxglove.
No one will think to look for us there.

Rose petals caress us with their scent.
My kisses dapple your breasts.

Sleep will come easy.
Yes. Sleep will come easy, then.

5

Tsau, an older boy, appeared as Jake leaned over the unconscious man. Tsau said that no doctor lived nearby and the traditional healer was away. Jake asked the boy to carry his pack along with the elderly man's walking stick. Tsau agreed with an infectious smile, showing the gap between his two front teeth. While Tsau held the door open, Jake carried the man into the bottle store.

Light from a generator filled the room, which smelled of cooking oil. Flies were everywhere. Large, colorful advertisements for various beers and soft drinks covered the rough, concrete-block walls. A counter bisected the room. Beyond the counter, cockroaches ran over an old refrigerator, a cylinder stood beside it.

An overweight man with a bushy mustache leaned against the counter. Red capillaries streaked his bulbous nose. Dressed in a shirt, shorts, and knee socks, a safari suit, he stood by an ancient cash register.

"Velcoum, boyo." The Afrikaner sounded friendly despite his scowl.

The shelves behind the counter held bags of cornmeal, bars of soap, cans of fruit, squares of chocolate, and three-legged iron cooking pots. Jake laid the man flat on the counter.

The shopkeeper reared back. "Off."

"Sir, do you have ice?"

The shopkeeper grumbled. "No ice."

"You do have cold drinks, and I'll pay you for their use. Otherwise, this man may die, and, if he does, I will alert the authorities."

"Cooling the bottles costs money," the shopkeeper said. "Takes the tank. I need a deposit."

From his wallet, Jake pulled out a few rand, South African currency.

The shopkeeper grabbed the money.

Jake turned to Tsau. "Please, set my pack and the walking stick next to my leg. Bring cold cans to me from the refrigerator. Could you do that?"

Tsau grinned. He slipped under the counter, went to the refrigerator, and began his work.

Jake addressed the shopkeeper. "What is your name, sir?"

"Piet Van der Merwe." He straightened up and gave Jake a crisp salute.

Jake returned the salute. He took his canteen from his pack. "I need clean water and a fresh cloth, please."

"Extra fee." When he returned from the back room, Piet handed Jake the now heavier canteen and a grimy cloth.

Jake took off the shoes and socks of the comatose man, and the shopkeeper objected again, pointing to the bare feet. Jake ignored him, loosening the man's shirt at the neck.

The door opened with a squeak.

"Blimey."

"Either help or get out," Jake said in a loud voice.

"Steady on, mate. Nigel Lennox is me name. Carpentry's me game. England's me shame. Music keeps me sane. Corley's me flame. Me lorry looks like shite, but purrs like a Rolls Royce thanks to Dereck, best mechanic south of the Zambezi."

Jake turned toward Nigel, a short man with shoulder-length hair, a mustache, and a beard. His T-shirt read "Let Peace Rock and Roll" emblazoned over a treble clef. His jeans were torn at the knees. He wore sandals without socks.

They shook hands.

Nigel stared at the man lying on the counter and blinked several times. "What cha done to the poor bloke? He's the kgosi of the village near my school. You're in big trouble, baas."

"Kgosi?"

"Chief. Hereditary title. A kgosi is royalty. They don't wage war as warriors no more. They judge thieves and cheats in the villages. Flogging, fining, or jailing, that's the ticket. Never irritate a kgosi."

Jake took the cans Tsau brought over and put them next to the man's neck, armpits, and groin. He opened an orange drink, poured the liquid on the cloth, and dabbed the man's head and face.

Nigel stood beside them and sang one Beatles song after the other. For "Lovely Rita," he drummed on the counter with his knuckles. The children outside started to use the front door as a drum. Piet yelled at them to "bugger off," but they kept on with their play.

When the kgosi roused, Jake gave him sips of water from the canteen.

"Tsau, please ask him what he wants."

Tsau and the kgosi exchanged a few words.

"Talks crazy," Tsau said.

"Nigel, is there a clinic in the kgosi's village?" Jake asked.

Nigel nodded, studying the kgosi. "Hope he lives, old chap. The Batswana won't take kindly to you losing a chief."

Jake could hear Pierce shouting at him: "One day in-country and you've killed a chief? Good work!"

He lifted the man into a sitting position, put back on his socks and shoes, and tied the laces in a double-bow knot.

Piet used the stub of a pencil to add numbers on a piece of cardboard. He shoved it under Jake's nose. Nigel leaned in to take a look.

"Bollocks. The man's a cheat. You opened one can. Let's git."

Jake paid Piet what he asked, and added a small tip. The shopkeeper put the money in his cash register without comment.

Jake thanked Tsau and gave him several rand, the boy bowed and accepted the money with both hands.

Jake picked up the kgosi. "Nigel, where's your Rolls Royce of a lorry?"

Nigel took the backpack and the walking stick. Opening the door for Jake, he began to sing.

Lead on, O King eternal, the day of march has come.
Henceforth in fields of conquest,
thy tents shall be our home...

Jake laid the kgosi in the bed of the truck and covered him with his poncho. From the bottle store door, Piet called, "Come back any time, American. Bring more money."

As they drove away, Tsau and the other children ran after them, shouting their goodbyes. The tree by the bottle store was a silhouette against the crescent moon. A vulture landed on a top limb, and the entire tree shivered.

Nigel finished the hymn to the sound of shifting gears.

And now, O King eternal, we lift our battle song.

6

Later that night, far from any village, the gunrunner got out of his truck, leaned on the door and studied the sky. The rain had petered out.

"'Pula.' The Batswana call the rain 'pula.'"

He held a machine gun in one hand. With the other, he stroked his mustache and beard. In the moonlight, he kept his torch, a flashlight, turned off, but at the ready in a pocket. The sound of cicadas grew louder, faded, and grew louder again, as if an invisible conductor directed them. Close by, a civet cat leapt up at an angle and landed on top of its hidden prey. The victim let out a screech.

The gunrunner fretted. "The bastard's late. He'll never bring down the Rhodesian government with this incompetence. Dirty commies. I would murder the lot of them if I didn't covet their money."

He released the hidden latch on the secret compartment that held the AK-47s. Two years back, he had modified his truck to conceal weapons.

"Weapons are like water if you know where to turn on the spigot. A few more deals, and poof, gone to an island paradise. There I can relax."

A truck engine revved nearby. The grasses swayed in a breezeless night. He dropped to the ground and rolled under his truck. He lost his torch but kept his machine gun ready.

A loud voice with an upper-class British accent cut through the night. "You jumpy, Afrikaner?"

The gunrunner crawled out from under the truck, picked up his torch, and turned it on. The light pooled around his feet. An apparition in brownish-yellow khaki materialized.

"Everything here is either jumpy or dead, Chaparadza. And I'm an American, not an Afrikaner."

Chaparadza's scarred face was a puzzle with several pieces missing. One eye never moved. "What is happening at your school, Afrikaner? I need disgruntled students willing to abandon their studies to fight. When the world hears that Batswana students fight side by side with Rhodesian guerrillas, Botswana will be shamed into aligning with us. I will be rewarded for this masterwork of public relations. Minister of Justice, for certain."

"I *am* fomenting trouble," the gunrunner said.

"Yesterday, the Rhodesians followed us back over the border, hunted us down, obliterated one of my most able men. Two more of my men died from snake bites. Cape cobras, perhaps. I want anti-venom kits. You will bring them to me."

Chaparadza gave a signal and guerrillas surrounded the truck. They began to unload the weapons.

"Is this the weapon of the future?" Chaparadza touched the machine gun in the gunrunner's hands.

"Meet the AK-47. Fully automatic and stone-cold reliable. The Americans' M-16 can't hold a candle to it. Kalashnikov designed the AK-47 to be cheap and durable. I tested it out. This weapon is perfect for you."

Chaparadza sneered. "Nice to have an expert opinion." He took the AK-47 from the gunrunner and ran his hands over it, caressing it.

Someone screamed a short distance away. A bald man with a beaked nose walked over to Chaparadza and whispered to him. Two men came up, dragging a boy between them.

The boy hung his head. Blood dripped from a gash on his forehead. Chaparadza put his hand under the boy's chin and spoke to him softly. The boy came to life, pleading, gesturing to the east.

"Dirakan's his name," Chaparadza said to the gunrunner. "I plucked him from a village we passed. Others need less persuasion to join us in the fight, but this poor child is homesick."

He turned the boy around, and pushed him. The boy started to walk, then broke into a run.

"He tried to escape, wants to help his parents with their crops. Their only child." Chaparadza raised the machine gun and pulled the trigger. The gunfire deafened the gunrunner briefly.

The boy lay still.

The gunrunner swallowed his panic. The African night resumed its song.

7

At six o'clock the next morning, Mr. Kunene Matlagodi, headmaster of Kukama School, stood at morning assembly next to the flagpole near the front gate. The national flag had a light blue background with a large black stripe in the center framed by a thin white stripe. The headmaster often said that the stripes symbolized the peace and harmony between Batswana of African and European descent.

"We are builders of a great nation," the headmaster said.

Alicia stood with the students and other teachers. They all wanted to hear more about the outcome of the police invasion, not the headmaster's pep talk.

"Our nation is but a few years old, and we tend it with the care we give young children." Usually, the headmaster projected energy, and the students and teachers echoed it back. Not today.

The bush telegraph reported that the trustees wanted to replace Mr. Matlagodi with someone more malleable, less likely to drive the school so hard toward modern ideas. They blamed him for the discovery of the machine guns.

"What is our motto?" He scanned his audience. "Our motto is 'self-reliance, self-discipline, and cost-covering.'"

The headmaster's short Afro flattered his coal-black skin. He was darker than most Batswana, which may have hampered his career. Slim and clean-shaven, he dressed in a dark blue suit with a white shirt and gray tie, in contrast to the male expat teachers who favored shorts and T-shirts.

"Educated women are essential to our nation's future," the headmaster said, another view that did not endear him to the Board. "We have as many female students as male. Females are fed an amount equal to males. We have both academic and vocational training." He cleared his throat. "Not the normal way, indeed."

A graduate of Ft. Hare University in the Republic of South Africa, the headmaster wanted to modernize his nation, although he considered himself a traditional Batswana. He gave cattle to his in-laws on his marriage to his wife, Dorcas, a tradition called "bogadi." This compensated Dorcas's parents for the expense of raising a female.

"Derelict weapons found on school property threaten to undermine us. This must not happen. My students, please continue your education with dedication. Assistant Headmaster Mubayi will patrol the area to ensure that all proceeds correctly."

The much-shorter Mr. Mubayi who stood beside the headmaster seemed to swell in size at the mention of his name. One of his ears was smaller than the other, which made his head lop-sided. His face seemed fixed in a snarl. A large silver buckle shone on the front of his belt, gleaming in the rays of the sun.

After the headmaster dismissed the assembly, Mr. Mubayi clapped his hands and directed everyone to move along. Alicia watched the headmaster walk alone toward his office, hands interlaced behind his back. She hoped he and his school would survive.

The classroom seemed stuffy when Alicia entered her Third Form English class. She went to the windows, located on the east and south sides of the room, and opened them, hoping for a breeze. Then she stood before the wall-sized map of Africa and smiled at her students. She was tired, but to be a good example, she stood up straighter.

"Dumelang, most excellent class."

The students responded. "Dumela, Teacher."

Her students were dressed in Western-style clothing, a bit ragged and patched in places. They ranged in age from twelve to eighteen, all barefoot. Students started secondary school when their families scraped together enough money for the school fees. These students might be the only one of their siblings able to attend secondary school, and they represented hope for their entire family.

"Boipelo, please come and show us the location of both Botswana and Nigeria." Alicia beckoned her to come forward.

Boipelo wrinkled her nose, walked to the map, and pointed to Botswana. She took a moment to find Nigeria in northwest Africa. The student skipped a bit as she returned to her desk.

"Class, today we begin our study of a book by the Nigerian author, Chinua Achebe, called *Things Fall Apart*. The title of the book is from the poem, *The Second Coming*, by the Irish poet, William Butler Yeats. I gave you copies of the book and the poem last week. You've all read them, found the meaning of unfamiliar words?"

A few averted their eyes, others nodded.

"Launcelot, please read the poem for us." Launcelot was quite proficient in English. He jumped up with enthusiasm and began to read the poem.

Turning and turning in the widening gyre
The falcon cannot hear the falconer;
Things fall apart; the centre cannot hold...

When he finished, Alicia thanked him and turned to Mmegi, a footballer.

"What does the title, *Things Fall Apart*, mean to you?"

"Teacher, I did not raise my hand. I will be soldier. Soldiers do not take orders from women."

She walked over to him. "Will you be a better leader if you can speak with confidence? You will need to gain the trust of your men. How can you gain this skill?"

"I will talk with the elders about wars in Botswana in the past."

She nodded. "Botswana in the past was a complex place, as complex as it is today. Part of that past includes poetry called praise poems honoring the exploits of the great Tswana warriors. We'll talk about praise poems in a few days. Now what about the title of the poem?"

Mmegi stood up. "Teacher, you are a frail woman, but you gave birth to a son. I will speak. Things fall apart, like old huts that lose their thatched roofs. My parents say long ago the tribes warred against each other. Today, we have peace."

He glanced around the room. "Our paramount chief, Seretse Khama, is our first president. We are independent of British rule.

Our neighbor, Rhodesia, will become free because of guerrilla fighters. Guerrillas are heroes!"

As Mmegi sat down, he knocked his books to the floor. He picked them up, stacking them with precision on his desk.

Alicia wondered if he would give up his studies and his sport to become a guerrilla. She called on Mombazo. "What do you think about the title?"

Mombazo stood up with a sharpened pencil slanted behind his right ear. "It reminds me when the rains do not come, the maize refuses to grow. We go hungry, eat once a day, or starve. Our cattle get thin and die. Young men go to work in the mines in Johannesburg to feed the too many mouths in the village."

A movement outside caught Alicia's attention. She walked over to the southern windows.

A tall man opened the main gate and closed it behind him. His posture was ramrod straight, and he walked with an air of authority. Overdressed for the heat, he wore a long-sleeved shirt, trousers, and heavy boots. He carried a large backpack. She almost giggled when she noticed his hat. A Stetson, she was sure, wildly out of place. Must be an American.

When the man looked toward her, she smiled and lifted a hand in greeting. He waved back and continued on into the school. She brought a hand to her face. Had he reached through the window and stroked her cheek? He discomfited her in an unnamable way.

She whispered to herself, "Who is he, and what is he doing here?"

As she turned back to the class, Mombazo was saying, "Thousands of our men work in the mines. I fear it. Some die there. Many never return, forgetting their fathers, mothers, wives, and children. Our way of life falls apart like old cloth. At our school, someone does bad things. Not our way."

"Yes, Mombazo," Alicia said. "We have struggles in the school and in the country. But we can gain insight into Botswana when we study this novel, which tells of another country, Nigeria."

She pointed to the photographs she had taped on a wall of Nigerian women in elaborate, colorful dresses. "Women in Nigeria dress in a different way from those in Botswana. Their homes look different. But this story is about the human family, and it will be a part of your important examinations later this year. When we begin to study this book, what questions should we ask?"

Kante flirted with Chomie, the boy sitting next to her, touching his hand with her biro. Alicia called on Kante.

"I have not read it because I am too tired," Kante said with a slight lisp. "My mattress is stolen. I cannot sleep on concrete."

"No mattress? I will check into it, Kante. But let's return to our topic. Who can summarize this story? How about you, Monwela?"

"Ee, Teacher." Yes, Teacher.

Monwela sat up straight. "The main person in the book, Okonkwe, murders people. He murders one boy he loves. He murders one man by accident, and is exiled for years. When he returns to his old home, life changed. He kills one man who threatens his old way of life. He cannot accept the new ways with the outsiders. He commits the worst sin, he murders himself. His life fell apart."

"Yes. Now go further. Why did his life fall apart, Monwela?"

"The world changed, but not Okonkwe. In Botswana, many changes come with money from diamonds. We have wars on our borders. We have many tribes, and not all want to be one nation. Is this correct, Teacher?"

"Sadly, Monwela, that is exactly right."

8

The headmaster welcomed Jake to his school, delighted that a volunteer had turned up to expand his science faculty. The headmaster insisted Jake coach soccer, even without experience; he had no one else. Jake negotiated concessions on his teaching schedule, primarily Fridays off. Although there would be football matches on some Saturdays, he would have at least part of his weekends free.

The headmaster assigned Jake to a small rondavel near the northern perimeter fence, a hut with a concrete floor, two windows, a thatched roof, and no toilet or running water. The hygiene facilities were in ablution blocks and standpipes located around the compound. Electricity was available only a few hours a day. The generator was turned on primarily so students could study in the evenings.

Jake's hut was close to a stile over the fence. The path to Kukama village was adjacent to the fence. He planned to use the tree by his hut to run up an antenna for the shortwave radio Pierce would provide him.

In the distance, Jake saw hundreds of students in three long lines. The lines led up to gigantic vats sheltered by an immense roof. Jake retrieved his mess kit from his pack and headed up the path.

Each student carried a metal bowl but no silverware. Jake stuffed his silverware in a pocket and went to the end of a line. Lunch smelled good. He would try almost anything, even the mopane worms he had heard about, said to taste like potato chips.

He towered over the students. They greeted him cheerfully, wanting to practice their often-halting English. He asked them to teach him how to roll his Rs like they did. They preferred to ply him with questions about the United States. He asked the students about the police invasion the day before, but they had little new information.

Amid the chatter, a boy whispered to Jake that a guerrilla came late at night to recruit them to fight in Rhodesia. Jake wanted to hear more, but the boy was moved aside by an older, well-dressed student, no rips or patched clothing for him.

"Dumela, sir. I am the head boy. Kgeledi. You saved the kgosi. We give you our thanks."

"News travels fast."

"I am in my fifth year. First graduating class of this school. Next year, I hope to go to university and study engineering. We have too little water, too much sun, and not enough good land from which to feed ourselves."

He waited for Jake to nod, then continued. "We buy power from other countries. My uncle says there is a way to store the sun's energy and use it at night. Do you want to know my dream?"

Jake was curious. "Tell me."

"I will bring electricity to each home in Botswana. You are a scientist. You can help me."

"Have you heard of photovoltaic cells? The price per watt is falling. Gets more affordable each year."

Kgeledi pointed east. "We await you at four o'clock at the pitch for practice. A scholarship to university may depend on my success in football."

"While I'm skilled at many ball games, I've never played football."

Kgeledi's face fell. "You have nothing to teach us?"

"Call a team meeting for this afternoon, and we'll talk about my role."

Kgeledi walked away, his face glum. Immediately, another student introduced himself as Negotho. He told Jake he would become a doctor, flying in a plane from one remote clinic to another. His brother had died of an infected scratch in the bush, far from medical care. They chatted until Jake reached the front of the line. He held out his bowl to the woman beside the vat.

"Papa le nama," she said, ladling out the thick stew with the gamey odor of goat meat.

Carrying his over-flowing bowl with care, he sat down on the sand under a tree with a group of students. Like the students, he swatted away the flies and mosquitos as he ate. Students crowded around him, telling him their stories. Each student seemed to have a bigger ambition than the last one.

In an impoverished country, the odds were stacked against them. What were the chances any of these students would achieve their dreams? Upon reflection though, his money was on Kgeledi. He wondered how he could help improve the odds, but how?

9

The entire western sky was aglow in fluorescent pink. Alicia adored the flamboyant African sunsets. Everything was exaggerated here: the insects gargantuan, the storms apocalyptic, the heat nuclear. As she carried Sammy on her hip, she wished she would adjust faster.

The crescent moon would rise soon, but give scant light. She watched the moon phases with care, enjoying the full moons, but not the new moons. A full moon meant you could walk at night without a torch. A new moon meant the night was as dark as an underground cave. During a new moon, she kept her torch handy. You could easily step on a lethal critter.

She needed to deliver a welcome bag to the man who walked through the gate that morning. She found him holding a shovel and counting.

"Seven spiders, nine scorpions, eleven cockroaches, and one puff adder. When in doubt, quantify."

She came to a standstill before him as he stood to his full

height. He tossed away the debris. "Hello, Mrs. Alicia Talbot from Seattle. Hello, Sammy."

"You know our names?" She tipped her head to one side. He wore a blue and red plaid shirt, heavy trousers, and a five-o'clock shadow. His voice might be his best feature, melodious.

"Espionage. Under intense interrogation, your headmaster told me almost everything."

"Mr. Matlagodi usually runs quiet and deep," she said. "Thank you for saving Kgosi Monyame."

Were his eyes blue or green, she wondered.

"Heat exhaustion, not heat stroke. My minor medical education paid off." He propped the shovel against a wall, but it fell over with a clatter.

"Mister New Science Teacher, if you have only nine scorpions, you might want to explore further. A scorpion usually travels with its mate. Do you want to test my theory?"

She fished out her torch from the bag and handed it to him. She dropped a kiss on the top of Sammy's head.

"Thanks. I only have a pen light." Jake went inside with the shovel and torch. After the sound of clanging, he emerged with a dead scorpion on the shovel.

"Found it scooting up a wall, although a scientist can never draw a conclusion from one data point," he said, with a smile.

Jake tossed away the scorpion, and set the shovel on the ground. When he handed the torch back to her, she noticed a large scar on the back of his right hand.

Sammy squirmed in her arms. "Have boys?"

"Children? No children, Sammy, but you and I can play ball sometime. I need more playmates." He reached over and patted the boy, brushing Alicia's bare arm. She stepped back, her skin tingling.

She waved away a non-existent fly to hide her confusion.

"What a glorious sunset," she said, pointing to the horizon, now burning with waves of fire.

Jake gave the sky a fleeting glance. "Altocumulus, mid-level clouds."

"It's poetry! The trees become silhouettes against the sky, night erases them. Magic show." She twirled around with her son, and handed Jake the bag, keeping her torch.

"The Society for the Retention of Intrepid Teachers presents you with several items crucial to survive the first days on Planet Kukama. Fey, a nurse and teacher, assembled them for you. You'll meet her at dinner. Right now, she's having a clinic at her rondavel."

She pointed up the path where several students stood talking outside a hut.

"We're isolated, but our secret weapon is Mr. Anand. He owns the Snappy Mercantile in Francistown and imports essentials from Johannesburg. 'Jo-burg,' we call it. You'll find a packet of mosquito coils in the bag."

She shifted Sammy to her other hip. "If you light the mosquito coils, the incense from the coils will keep away the mosquitos. If you don't use them, tomorrow you'll have so many bites, you'll look like you have chickenpox. You have a few welts on your face already. Disease smorgasbord here."

"Malaria?"

She nodded. "Watch for snakes and other creatures that might lose their grip on the thatch. Keep the shovel handy. But you know this already?"

"Soldier in Vietnam. Bugs, torrential rain. Different here, though. Arid."

Sadness washed over her, thinking of Vietnam. She gave her body a shake.

"Tell me, why did you come here?" She opened her eyes wide, wanting an answer.

"I'm a paleoseismologist, someone who studies ancient earthquakes. In the past, at least one major earthquake occurred in the Okavango Delta. Not much research has been done here. I'm also interested in the kopjes." He pointed to her hand. "How did you injure yourself?"

"This bandage?" She touched her palm. "It's nothing. Come to dinner at the staff house around six o'clock." She pointed to the large rectangular building past Fey's home. "I'm eager to taste whatever our cook, Mma Sethunya, has created in her cooking pot. A wizard." She kissed Sammy's cheek and turned to leave.

"Wait," Jake said. "How about a tour? Tell me what goes on in the various buildings." His gesture encompassed the entire compound.

"Tomorrow after lunch?" He did intrigue her, and she could make a tour part of her duties as part of the informal welcoming committee. She caressed Sammy's back.

"Can you say, 'Sala sentle?'" Stay well?

Her son shook his head. No.

She set Sammy down and took his hand. "Shall we sing about the wizard of Oz?"

As she and Sammy walked away singing, Jake joined in a tenor voice. Alicia looked back, and her heart fluttered. A nearly handsome man, he looked capable of doing whatever he set his mind to do. You could park a Pontiac on that chin. He had that *je ne sais quoi,* charisma. But, for her? *No. I need no more soldiers.*

☆ ☆ ☆

Jake watched Alicia stroll off with her son. The faint scent of her perfume, jasmine, lingered in the air. He wanted to follow her, talk with her more, but he heard a cough behind him and turned. A man rushed toward him with an arm-load of bottles. He made a curious sight: mustache, goatee, long flaxen hair. The man wore a tuxedo shirt with a ruffled front and pearl buttons. A satin stripe ran down the side of his black trousers.

"Stop. Forget her!" the man exclaimed, slurring his words together. "I'm Paul. Sorry, can't shake your hand. Hand-shaking is an overrated ritual anyway. Spreads germs. Did you notice her ring finger? Someone said she took off her wedding band. Is it true? Did you notice?"

"No ring." Jake had seen only a white line on her ring finger.

"She's still married to her late husband," Paul said. "No one can compete with the idealized dead. Fey said she would help her get unstuck from the past. If she took off her ring, there's hope for me."

"*Late* husband?"

"Her husband was killed in 'Nam." Paul jerked his chin toward Jake's hut. "This yours? Hasn't been used in ages. The wildlife parties there at night. Did Alicia give you that bag? She's generous. You're not special."

"Thanks for the reminder."

Paul bowed. "My job as the token Boston Brahmin from Belmont is to cut people down to size. My ancestors came to

America from merry old England, some of the first colonists. I keep up standards. I eschew hardship wherever possible. 'Comfort and libations,' that's my motto."

Jake eyed the bottles, hoping for a cold beer. "About libations, need help with those beers?"

Paul nodded, and Jake took one.

"I have a trust fund," Paul said, "since I reached the age of twenty-five last August. My parents died when I was a child. Raised by my older brother. I have a propane-powered refrigerator. For the most part, the locals here have never seen refrigeration. They enjoy their meat slightly rotten, anyway. Worms intensify the flavor, they say—simply wash out the worms."

Jake knocked off the bottle cap on a boulder and took a long drink. He set the bottle down by his front door, and picked up the shovel again.

"Lucky for you," Paul said, "the best cook in the village works for us. No rotten meat for her. Kills the fatted goat herself. She's always pregnant, boatload of kids, and she's only thirty years old."

"The cook Alicia calls 'the wizard?'"

Paul studied Jake closely. "Say, buddy, you look military."

"Ex-Army. Vietnam."

Paul scowled. "Kill many babies?"

Jake threw the shovel down so hard it bounced.

"Not lately."

10

After lunch the next day, Alicia walked to the staff house where Jake stood under the overhang, out of the sun. He seemed at ease—a commanding presence. Her skin tingled where he had touched her arm the day before.

"Ready for the grand tour?" She felt a frisson of excitement in his presence.

He joined her on the path that ran down the center of the school compound.

The sound of tinkling bells floated in the air. A young boy herded the school-owned goats, each had a bell on its collar. Barefoot, he was on a quest for patches of grass. Insects whined. A bush shrike flew by, flashing its orange breast.

After her classes, Alicia changed into gray trousers and a pink tunic. She wore a broad-brimmed straw hat and left her wavy, blonde hair loose on her shoulders. She left behind the bandage for her injured palm.

Jake carried a daypack on his back. Once again, he wore a

plaid shirt and trousers. His hat was, indeed, a leather Stetson, well-worn with a braided cord at the base of the crown. He didn't roll up his sleeves in the heat. Odd.

As they passed, students called out to them. "Dumela Mma. Dumela Rra." Hello, ma'am. Hello, sir.

Alicia greeted two of her students, Thale and Boipelo. The two girls walked together, hand in hand.

"You'll hear lots of different local languages," Alicia said, "but the main one is Setswana, a tonal language. A few tips. One citizen of Botswana is called a 'Motswana,' two or more is 'Batswana.' You'll hear me called 'Mma Sammy,' which means 'mother of Sammy.' That's the tradition."

He asked so many questions during their walk, she objected to the interrogation.

"Just want to understand the situation," he said, sheepishly.

After morning assembly, students surrounded Jake, vying to talk to him. The girls touched his muscular biceps and giggled. He gave them all the same attention. He played no favorites and showed excellent instincts.

"Have you taught before?"

"T.A., teacher's assistant, in grad school."

"Takes a while to get used to the educational system here," she said. "The students must pass the exams in the third and fifth forms to continue with their education."

He swatted a mosquito away from his face. "Sudden-death exams."

They walked past the textiles workshop where girls spun raw wool into yarn, and then into blankets with geometric designs. The Snappy Mercantile sold them in Francistown.

"I have a stellar idea," Alicia said. "Let's climb the water tower."

"Is that risky?"

Alicia didn't care; she was eager for the vista.

When they reached the ladder to the water tower, a hand-lettered sign read, "No Trespassing. This Means YOU."

She recognized Dereck's handiwork and gave Jake a playful shove. "Race you to the top."

She began to climb the ladder, and he climbed after her. When she felt the sweat trickle down her back, she slowed down. He scrambled past her.

"Cheater!" she teased as he climbed above her.

They climbed until they reached the small wooden platform next to the metal water tanks high above the ground. Alicia's heart beat hard, from exhilaration as much as exertion.

Jake handed her a canteen from his pack. She took it with gratitude, took a few sips, and handed it back.

"Drink one gallon of water each day in the desert," he said. "Carry your water inside you, that's the rule." He tested a vertical support. "I see a bit of sawdust on the floor. Let's make this quick."

She gazed over the landscape. "Isn't this glorious? I love the blue dome of sky and the rolling grassland with its thorn trees. The river looks like a sparkling ribbon. Much of the water is from the rain upstream. By the time the rains end and the surface water disappears, water has seeped down into the sand. The river goes underground."

"Rivers like that are called 'ephemeral.'"

"Ephemeral. What a charming way to describe it. After the rainy season ends and the river dries up, the village women dig holes in the sand and wait for the water to seep in. They scoop the water into pails to carry home on their heads."

He stood close behind her and held a post with one hand while he wrapped his other hand around her upper arm.

She glanced back at him. Overprotective.

"Africa is the oldest continent," he said, "at over two billion years, maybe much older. Do you see how the river has changed course over the centuries? Ancient flood plain."

"Really? See the kopje in the far distance? Just beyond it is Rhodesia."

His voice dropped to a whisper. "We're that near the border."

"Fey told me to stay away from the kopjes as poisonous snakes live there. What do you know about them?"

"The kopjes are uneroded rock. Those boulders were harder than the ones that surrounded them and more resistant to erosion. See the top of those boulders? At one time, the land here was much higher."

"Showers and windstorms continue the cycle?"

He nodded. "The magma welled up from inside the earth to form what's called the 'Precambrian Basement.' Bedrock. The granitic boulders in the kopjes are very old."

"Can you imagine the earth as it changed over millions of years?"

"That's part of the fun. Geologists explore, too. Why don't you join me on my first trip into the wilderness? I'll teach you some geology."

"When I come up on the water tower, I feel like an explorer. I watch for changes in the landscape. Weird events happen. For example, dynamite was stolen from the shed at the rock quarry."

"Stolen dynamite? What else?"

Alicia told him about the fire in the supply room, water poured in the gas tank of the school van and other sabotage.

Jake looked at the sky. "Rain clouds headed our way. Let's go down."

"'Tis the rainy season. We get most of our rain between November and March." Alicia noticed something out of the ordinary to the north. "Do you have a pair of binoculars in your pack?"

Jake pulled out a small pair of binoculars and handed it to her. She trained them on the spot that puzzled her. "Beyond the path beside the northern perimeter fence is off-limits to everyone, headmaster's edict. Predators. But I see a change. Did a large tree rot and fall? I'll check it out later."

She handed him back the binoculars, and he tucked them away. "Take me with you when you go," he said. "No need to take unnecessary risks."

He put a hand back on her arm and another on a post.

"I've got first-rate balance," she said.

"Just want you to be safe." Jake kept his hand where it was.

In silence, they viewed the landscape. Only a few students were out in the afternoon sun.

At last night's dinner, Jake had studied each person in an unobtrusive way, his back to a wall. He stood up twice to stretch.

"You trained as a soldier, ROTC, maybe? My late husband was drafted. He loved his flower garden, corny jokes, and hitting the bulls-eye at the shooting range. Taught me to shoot."

Alicia put her hand on the railing. "Do you carry a hidden

weapon? A knife in your boot?" She frowned. "Did you come here like me, running away from something?"

He ignored her question. "Let's wrap this up, go down."

A gust of wind knocked her hat off her head. She pressed forward on the railing, reaching out to catch it.

Without warning, the railing broke away. She was falling, nothing to hold onto, nothing to stop her, no one to catch her.

11

Alicia saw Eric standing before her, a bright light surrounding him. He opened his arms wide, smiling in welcome. Elated, she knew they would be together forever.

Her body jerked, and Eric faded, then disappeared.

"No!" The loss was unbearable.

A voice said, "This will hurt."

Cloth ripped. Something moved her right shoulder and upper arm at the same time. The agony abated, but she was still in pain. She searched for Eric, but he was gone.

She wanted to tear out her hair.

"I did a closed reduction, put your arm back in its socket. We almost did a swan dive into eternity."

Rain and wind buffeted her, the words made no sense.

"The storm came fast. The clouds above us have lightning. The tower may get hit."

A hand was on her back. "Move to the ladder. I'll go first. Turn around, face the ladder as you descend. Hold your right arm across your stomach."

She shook her head. "No." She knew that Eric was *here.*

"If I carry you, the ladder will break. You must move."

"Never."

The rain fell harder. "Sweetheart, if you climb down the ladder, I will take you to Sammy."

How could I forget my precious son?

She knew where she was again and let Jake pull her up to a sitting position. She crawled toward the ladder, then stepped onto the first rung. He moved around her and down the ladder a few rungs and waited for her to descend.

The rain hit her like body blows.

Alicia moved down the ladder, rung by rung. She wrapped her uninjured arm around the outside rail to keep herself steady. Under the full force of the sleet, the ladder swayed. The rungs were slippery. The wind grew more violent. Her foot slipped off the rung, and she was falling again. Strong arms caught her.

☆ ☆ ☆

Alicia's shoulder throbbed, but she was out of the rain. She lay on a cot, covered with a blanket. She opened her eyes. Dereck's rondavel.

Dereck crushed out a cigarette in an ash tray. "Jake, you bloody idiot. Can't you read a 'No Trespassing' sign?"

Without a word, Jake opened the front door and went back out into the rain. Alicia watched him leave with trepidation. Would he abandon her?

Dereck touched her arm. "What's wrong with your shoulder, pet?"

"Relocated," she said. A wave of nausea hit, and she turned on her left side.

"Crikey. Did Jake get too friendly? He was a soldier, wasn't he? Soldiers are law unto themselves. Blighters."

"A railing broke on the water tower. I fell. He saved me."

"Broke? I examined the tower only last week. The ladder's rickety, but the rest is sound. A railing broke?"

Dereck struck a match and lit a burner on his hot plate. A cylinder stood beside it. After he put the kettle on, he took a towel from his closet and rubbed her hair.

"You like the view from the water tower, but in the future, either take me up with you or stay off. Do you promise me?"

"Promise you."

"Let's get you out of those soggy clothes, warm you up," he said. "You can wear some of my clothing."

They became friends months ago when Dereck was laid up with a back injury. She brought him plates of food and massaged his back. She surmised from his conversation that he preferred males as partners, not females.

She sat up, unzipped her trousers, and he pulled them off. He helped her put on another pair of trousers. He slipped a belt around her waist and cinched it. He covered her ragged tunic with one of his shirts.

"When your hat fell down, I knew you were up on the tower. I put it on my bookcase."

Dereck made a pot of tea. After he let the tea steep, he poured some in a mug and added milk. "Here you are, my girl. Cow's milk fresh from Ndona's farm. Hot and milky, the way you like it."

She took the mug from his hands and sipped tentatively. Too hot.

Dereck's face was the color of walnuts, weathered from outdoor work. His eyebrows were so bushy they grew together in a line. His hands were gray from working on various types of machines. He smelled of motor oil.

Before the school opened, Dereck worked with Nigel on the infrastructure. His expertise was in machinery, but his passion was politics. The South African police discovered *Das Kapitol* in his luggage when he returned from his studies in England. Evicted from his homeland for his political beliefs, he moved to Botswana to live in exile, seeing his parents rarely.

After a rap on the door, Jake walked back in and shut the door. He let the rain drip off him, then sat down on a chair. He frowned at the pieces of wood in his hands.

"Someone cut the railing in two places," Jake said. "The blade must be thin to hide the cut. A coping saw? Something felt off to me, but I assumed the railing was solid. 'Beware the fatal assumption.'"

Dereck walked over to Jake and touched the pieces of wood. He ran a finger along the cut edge. "Who would do this? Why?"

"Did you see anyone suspicious by the water tower?"

"The usual teachers, students. Fey joined me for a cuppa. Ellie waved as she passed."

"Who has carpentry tools? You?"

"You think I did this? You bloody Americans are so rude." Dereck looked at Alicia. "Except you, dear heart."

Jake's brow furrowed. "Not an accusation. Want to get the big picture."

"We teach carpentry here, ignorant man, including fine work. Part of the Brigades, our vocational training program. Nigel has a first-class set of carpentry tools. Other than his record collection, Nigel prizes his tools. He made my bookcase."

As she listened to the men, Alicia felt anger rise within her. Someone had cut the railing on the top of the water tower. Only she and Dereck climbed up there.

Worried, she wanted to return to Sammy too much to wait out the storm. After a few more sips of tea, she set down the mug and walked to the bookcase. She dismissed their advice to rest.

With her left hand, she reached up and took down her hat from the bookcase. Rows of Benson & Hedges golden flip-top cigarette boxes sat on the top shelf. Instead of cigarettes, they held nuts, bolts, and screws, all labeled in Dereck's hand.

A flag hung on the inside of his door. A hammer and sickle undulated before her.

Dereck put his rain coat around her shoulders, patted her back, and opened the door. "Take care of her, Jake."

Outside, the rain fell so hard it stung. Jake held her left arm to steady her. They walked together toward her home at a glacial pace.

No one was out. The earth smelled heavy, saturated. Lightning flashed again and again, illuminating the buildings. Thunder growled. Rain pounded the land, overwhelming it. Streams of water poured off the edges of thatched roofs. The wind blew the rain sideways, changing the world into a blurry landscape, an Impressionist's painting.

As they approached her home, Jake asked, "Shall I come in and check your shoulder?"

For a two-day-old relationship, he had touched her quite enough. She pulled away.

"Ask Fey to come."

"Sweetheart, at least, let me bring some ice from Paul's fridge."

A wave of anger burst through her.

"Do not call me 'sweetheart.' Only my husband calls me 'sweetheart.' You might as well stab me with that secret knife of yours. And if someone cut the railing to get me to leave, it will not work. No one will push me out of this school. I will leave when I am damn well ready."

12

The ice in the makeshift ice pack melted in minutes. Alicia threw the pack to the floor.

"I could have died! What about Sammy?" She rubbed her shoulder and fought back tears.

"No histrionics." Fey sounded stern.

"I want to be mature. Failing. Sorry." Alicia leaned back against her pillow.

Sammy sat at the table with his coloring book. Alicia suspected there were now navy-blue warthogs gamboling on the page. Her sister, Hannah, was Sammy's legal guardian if anything happened to her, but Alicia did not want that legal document used.

Fey picked up the wet cloth from the floor and put it on the table. "No broken bones. Jake, bless him, put the arm back in the socket the correct way. You did strain the tendons quite badly, though."

Fey sat down on a chair next to the cot with her satchel

beside her. "Paul wanted to bring the ice pack. I forbade him. Unrequited love, tad obsessive. Jake lent me his rain gear and walked me here. He seems decent, but I intend to find out more about him. Will he stay, I wonder?"

Alicia held her injured arm next to her abdomen, reluctant to think about her unreasonable anger at Jake.

"Ko Ko." Bronwyn opened the door and swept in, more pregnant than ever. "Heard you hurt yourself, love." She hung her coat on a hook by the door. "All copacetic?"

Alicia touched her injured shoulder. "Remind me why you insisted Sammy and I come to this abysmal place. One disaster after the other—"

"Bleeding hell, what cheesed you off?"

"No running water, lethal critters, and precious little electricity. I am tired of chamber pots, pit latrines, and sabotage at this school. Not to mention civil war in Rhodesia. Why weren't you candid with me about the dangers here? You're unrealistic. Worse, you're not even aware of it."

"Codswallop." Bronwyn put her hands on her hips. "Where's the girl I met at uni? That bird flew high. You're stuck, moaning for Eric, wallowing smack-dab in the past. Daft."

Alicia glared at her. "Don't insult me."

"Tosser!"

"Stop right there," Fey said. "Bronwyn, light a lantern."

Bronwyn made a face at Fey, went over to the table and lit a lantern. She began to talk with Sammy, patting his back and admiring his coloring work. A fine mist from the rainstorm came into the room through the space between the walls and the thatched roof.

Fey pulled out a pair of scissors from her satchel. "You tore your tunic beyond repair. Pity." She cut off the garment and stuffed it into her satchel. Alicia bemoaned the loss, although Fey would turn it into attractive bandages. Nothing went to waste.

"Bronwyn, grab a blouse without sleeves and with only a few buttons," Fay said. Her manner was imperious.

Bronwyn rummaged in the closet. "How's this?" She held up a voile blouse, burgundy. "Wear it to morning assembly and give the randy boys a chance to ogle your lily-white cleavage." Her eyes were joyful. The woman never held a grudge.

Hannah had sent the blouse. Low cut, it was not the sort to teach in. Lara, Hannah's girlfriend, designed costumes for a ballet troupe and loved to create her own clothes. When Lara tired of her outfits, Hannah boxed them up and mailed them to her appreciative sister. The clothes were inappropriate for most of life in Botswana, too delicate, too sexy. Nevertheless, Alicia hoped they would send her more exquisite castoffs in silky fabrics and luscious colors.

Bronwyn handed the blouse to Fey. Standing on either side of the cot, they helped Alicia put it on. Fey took out a long scarf from her satchel, cradled her patient's forearm with the scarf and tied the two ends together behind her neck.

"Promise me you will rest your shoulder," Fey said. "Keep the sling on for several weeks. Be judicious. Don't let your elbow freeze up. After a few days, start gentle exercises for mobility. Later, do strengthening exercises. Promise me?"

"No more promises." Alicia already regretted her promise to Dereck not to climb the water tower without him.

"Ignore my advice at your peril," Fey said. "Your shoulder will take months to heal. You're ambidextrous, but two hands are better than one." Fey pawed through her satchel, brought out a glass jar and unscrewed the lid. "Drink my anti-inflammatory herbal concoction. My new friend, Dr. Lekota, gave me the recipe. I will entertain no objections."

Alicia held the jar with her left hand and sipped the bitter brew.

"Now, tell me everything," Fey said. "No one else need listen."

Bronwyn was talking nonstop to Sammy and her unborn child. After the birth of Geoff, Bronwyn preferred motherhood and domesticity. Teaching was a sideline.

Alicia studied the thatched roof above her. "When I was falling from the water tower, I saw Eric."

Fey nodded. "You wanted to be with him. I understand."

Alicia clutched at Fey's arm. "I wanted to die, if that's what it took. Last night, I put my ring away, took down the photographs of Eric." She pointed to the denuded walls. "Today I saw him again." Tears ran down her face, unheeded. She cried until she gasped for breath.

"Mma? Mma?" Sammy abandoned his coloring book and climbed onto the cot with his mother. She pulled him to her and talked to him in a soothing way. Soon he relaxed and fell asleep beside her.

"What do I do, Fey?" Fey seemed to have all the answers.

"Sammy is the steel cord that ties you to life."

"I do want to live, even without Eric. I know that now."

"You're right on track. Bronwyn, find Alicia a handkerchief."

Bronwyn rummaged in the closet. She gave a hankie to Alicia, who dried her eyes, blew her nose, and put her hand on her heart.

"I'm volatile, but grateful for your help."

"You lived through Eric's death," Fey said. "When grief hits, accept it. Listen to your body's wisdom. Buck up. That's an order."

Alicia touched Fey's hand. "Don't ever change."

Fey wrinkled her forehead. "Why would I need to change?"

☆ ☆ ☆

"Gossip. Tasty gossip," Bronwyn said, as she walked into Alicia's rondavel later that evening with a plate of food. Alicia sat on her cot, dozing against her pillow. Tucked into his own cot, Sammy slept with an arm around his stuffed lion, Pinky, one of Hannah's gifts.

Fey had fed Sammy bread and cheese, stored in Alicia's canisters, before she left.

Alicia took a deep breath. "Sorry I snapped at you. But you did call me a 'tosser.' Harsh."

Bronwyn's smile showed her dimples. "Stop whingeing, you prat." She found a fork and handed it to her friend with the plate of stew. Alicia discovered she was hungry.

Bronwyn pulled up a chair. "The headmaster turned puce when we informed him of the booby-trapped railing, dark, dark purple. Nigel, our hairy lamb, was in high dudgeon. His nose turned red. 'Did you cut the railing, Mubayi? No porkies, you wanker.'"

Bronwyn, a natural mimic, captured the accent to perfection. "Mubayi shouted at Nigel. 'Expats are chattering monkeys.' Nigel barked right back at Mubayi. 'Piss off.' Remember that shiny buckle of Mubayi's? The buckle turns into a dagger. Mubayi pulled it off his belt and waved the dagger at Nigel, ready for a fight."

Alicia was glad she had missed the drama.

"Jake kicked the dagger out of Mubayi's hand," Bronwyn went on, "and Mubayi stormed out. Nigel started to follow, but Jake blocked him."

Alicia closed her eyes, speculating on what made Mubayi so angry.

"Wake up," Bronwyn said. "There's more. Nigel turned on Mick. 'Bloody hell, you never clean up your sawdust. You're no carpenter. Keep out of my classroom.' Nigel left with Corley close behind. Dereck stood up to Mick. 'If I find you cut that railing, I will strangle you with my bare hands.' Mick called him a 'fricking commie.'"

"No bloodshed?" Alicia asked.

"None. Paul watched it all from a safe distance. Mick turned on Ellie and dragged her out the door, calling her names. My William pulled out his knife and started after Mick, but I stopped him."

"You stopped William? He's as big as a tank and twice as powerful."

"Yeah, but I touched his arm."

"Of course. Silly me."

Alicia could not believe it. William, Mubayi, Nigel, Dereck, and Mick were at odds, Jake was referee. The fault lines among the male teachers were starkly visible.

Sammy whimpered in his sleep. Alicia stroked his arm.

"The headmaster came back to tell us he's called a staff meeting," Bronwyn said. "Friday evening. That new bloke, Jake, fancies you. Whatta hunk of delectable. Yum." Bronwyn took the empty plate and put it on the table.

Alicia winced at a sudden pain. "He saved my life, and I blasted him, both barrels."

By lantern light, they sat together in silence, listening to the night chorus. After a few minutes, Bronwyn put on her coat.

"Ta-ta. Going home to me blokes."

Alicia pondered the events of the day, thinking about Jake. He was a real soldier, not a press-ganged draftee like Eric. Eric had charmed her with his generosity, affection, and loyalty. But Jake? With him, she had felt safe, a rock-ribbed sense of security.

13

Alicia stood outside her rondavel the next afternoon, right arm in a sling. She needed a distraction from the ache in her shoulder, so she watched the sociable weaver birds in a thorn tree at the edge of her clearing. Fey said the male started with a long blade of grass and then made a half-hitch on a limb. From that, he built his nest with twigs, straw, and grass, all to attract a female. A true homebuilder.

With a chirp, a yellow and black weaver bird flew into the hole at the bottom of a nest. At the same time, Paul charged around the corner dressed in his usual attire.

"You and Sammy must fly back to the States for medical care," Paul said, out of breath. "A week should do it. I will pay for it. Don't worry about the Scarlet Pimpernel Fund. Why do you call it that? Never mind. I've arranged the details with the bank. The fund is yours to manage."

When Paul touched her left shoulder, she stepped back. His hand slipped off.

"Kind offer, Paul, but sorry, no. *You* go back to the States. You said you were in a boozy haze in med school. Give up alcohol. Earn your medical degree. Come back as a doctor. Treat the dreadful diseases here. You're an able English teacher, but your passion is medicine."

Paul moved toward her and rested his hand on her shoulder. "I'm a drunk. That's it, isn't it?"

She pushed his hand off. "No."

Paul's voice rose. "Is it the trust money? You think the money has muddled me up?"

"No."

"Did Fey tell you I'm wanted by the FBI?"

Her eyes grew wide.

Paul wailed. "Actions against the war in 'Nam. Bombs. Innocents injured. I am sorry." He pulled at his goatee.

"You made bombs?"

He pressed his hands to his forehead. "The feds will crucify me."

"You can't hide here forever."

"They'll put me in prison. What will happen to med school?"

"I'll always be your friend," she said, her voice soft.

"I want to be your lover, not your friend. You took off your ring." He pointed to her left hand. "Marry me!"

She spoke in a firm voice. "I'm sorry, but the answer is no."

"I'll get sober." His voice grew louder, more shrill. "I'll turn myself in. Marry me!"

"The answer is no."

He grabbed her left shoulder and leaned in to kiss her.

She slapped him.

Paul let out an anguished cry, turned and ran.

The birds fled her clearing.

14

Alicia arrived late to assembly on Thursday morning. She linked arms with Nigel. Corley stood on his other side. Paul was a few yards away. She tried to catch his eye, but he refused to acknowledge her.

Nigel whispered to Alicia. "You look knackered, love. Gutted, even."

She gave him a quick squeeze. "I love you a bushel and a peck."

She wore her burgundy blouse under a white shawl, her arm in the sling. Her long, black skirt touched the tops of her sandals. She had not combed her hair but fluffed it out with her fingers. Movement hurt her shoulder which made dressing slow.

Mr. Matlagodi glared at her, his body language clear. She must be on time and set a positive example.

After the headmaster dismissed them, Nigel walked away in an animated conversation with Corley over the influence of medieval church music on the songs of John Lennon. They were well-matched.

She searched for Jake in the crowd and discovered him behind her. He extricated himself from the girls who surrounded him and came up to her.

She had devised a formal apology to him, but when she saw him, she blurted out, "I ignored your intuition on the water tower. Forgive me?"

She studied the cerulean sky. "I get so focused, I forget others' concerns. To frost the cake, I yelled at you when you offered to help me. Bronwyn is missing her head, as I bit it off. I'm blushing all over. Can you tell?"

He raised his eyebrows. "Blush is my favorite color. Not your fault about the railing. I'm glad I was there to catch you. You can make it up to me."

"How?" She needed to tread carefully. He smelled faintly of aftershave which almost made her laugh. No other male expat here shaved, much less used aftershave. She predicted that he would give up shaving in two weeks.

"Desert exploration," he said. "Come with me next weekend. I'll have a vehicle by then."

"Cars are scarce."

"I'm a fast worker. Part of my industrial-strength charm."

She raised up on her tiptoes, certain that his eyes were twinkling. "The school girls have fallen for your charms. They want to join your harem."

"A harem could be an asset," he said, grinning. "If you explore with me, I'll teach you how to survive, if you're ever lost in the wilderness."

She shuddered. "Don't even joke about that."

"May I come over tonight, go over my plan?"

Her stomach did a somersault. He was beginning to look quite handsome.

A student walked by ringing the school bell. Jake headed toward the science lab. A bevy of girls who should have been in their classrooms followed him. Alicia watched him march up the sandy hill with his admirers trying to catch up to his long stride.

He was a stranger, but magnetic. If Nigel was Pan playing his flute, was Jake the Pied Piper?

Later that morning, Alicia walked in the door of her First Form English class. She glanced at the letters of the alphabet taped along the top of the blackboard and set her heavy bag on the teacher's desk. The room smelled dusty, although she and the students had cleaned it thoroughly before the start of the term.

"Dumelang, class. The barber has come to town, I see. Did he shave off every hair on your heads?" She had missed that fact at morning assembly, too focused on Jake.

The male students groaned and rubbed their newly bald heads.

"Let's start with 'Salutation to the Dawn' by the poet, Kalidasa. Who will lead us?"

Malebogo raised her hand. Alicia beckoned her, and the student walked to the front of the room.

"Repeat with me," she said. The students joined in reciting the ancient Sanskrit poem.

Look to this day, for it is life, the very life of life.
In its brief course lie all the verities and realities of our existence.
The glory of action, the bliss of growth, the splendor of beauty...

Alicia thanked Malebogo and took a quick peek at Mbengawa who sat by Negotho. Fey said cataracts caused the milkiness in Mbengawa's eyes. Negotho, one of her best students, helped him with his studies.

Negotho was the oldest in the class. His intelligence, kindness, and even-temper made him popular with the other students. He treasured a copy of *Grey's Anatomy* that a missionary doctor had given him. Before he came to Kukama School, he studied the book by lantern light at his family's remote kraal, a corral. Alicia had seen him walking with Mpule, Sammy's nanny, looking smitten. Would his interest in Mpule get in the way of his becoming a doctor? A pregnancy might limit his options.

"Class, I asked you to make a list of questions for your classmates during English practice time. Please get out your questions and move your desks to your practice group. Quietly. Assistant headmaster Mubayi is nearby. Let's not anger him with any noise."

Chairs scraped the floor as the students gathered into clusters around the room.

Alicia walked between the groups and encouraged them. To succeed beyond their villages, her students needed English. They did not have much opportunity to speak it, although it was one of two official languages, along with Setswana. Framing an interesting question that demanded an answer gave them a much better sense of the language than rote memorization.

In the group closest to the door, Dineo stood rooted to the floor.

"Please ask Florah your question, Dineo," Alicia said. "You can do this."

Dineo read from her paper. "The desert. When is our desert a most beautiful desert?"

Florah hesitated to answer the question. Alicia admired her hair, woven into braids running from her forehead back to the nape of her neck. Blotchy skin marred her face. Fey told her that Florah could have vitiligo, where the skin lost pigment, or she might have used a product to lighten her skin that damaged it. Skin color was important.

Florah closed her eyes. "Our desert is most beautiful when the antelopes lie in the bush and are loving the sun."

Before she could praise Florah, Baboloki, the class clown, waved his hands in her direction. "Teacher, teacher, my biro is refusing." His pen ran out of ink.

Alicia smiled at Florah and walked over to Baboloki. On the way, she picked up a biro from the desk drawer and handed it to him. He took it with both hands, bowing up and down in exaggerated gratitude until he got a laugh from his friends.

She walked over to a group of five girls and listened as Mapho asked her question to Malebogo. "What certain thing is the best thing about our school?"

Mapho's name meant "God's gift." Open sores covered her legs. Fey said the condition could be caused by long-standing malnutrition. "Send her to me," Fey said, when Alicia broached the subject with her.

Alicia agreed to do this, but she would do it with as much diplomacy as possible. Females often did not get enough to eat. The Scarlet Pimpernel Fund would pay for the necessary vitamins. Alicia named the fund after the classic 1930s movie starring Leslie Howard about a foppish man who was, in truth, a hero. To her,

Paul was a hero for creating the secret fund. Not the best name, she realized after learning about his bomb-making.

Malebogo answered Mapho's question. "The best thing about our school is we are now in the center of life and must not sit around chattering like rock rabbits or dreaming of days to come."

Eight of Alicia's high school and college friends in addition to Eric had died in Vietnam. Don, Fred and the others did not have "days to come." She brushed away the tear rolling down her cheek.

"Good job, Malebogo. Please ask Thale your question."

Malebogo spoke without hesitation. "Thale, how does the lightning look?"

Thale's cropped hair emphasized her radiant eyes and sculpted lips. She spoke in a serious manner. "In my mind, lightning can be the fringe on the cape of God."

Several girls in the group hid their giggles behind their hands.

Alicia had seen storms on the horizon with lightning strikes in dozens of places at the same time. Thale was right, lightning could be a kind of fringe. With that kind of observation, Thale could develop as a writer, if she could make it through school.

"Very nice image," Alicia said. The student ducked her head at the praise.

Alicia looked around the room. She suspected pregnancies in two girls. On Saturdays, Matron would sometimes line up the girls to manipulate their abdomens. A pregnancy meant instant expulsion. Fey told the headmaster to expel the boys responsible instead of the girls, but he refused. Educating girls lifted all boats, Fey said. But the headmaster responded that he was changing the school as fast as he could.

The school bell was due to ring. "Please put your desks back in their places." When the noise subsided, she went on. "We have talked about the meaning of biography and the lives of your leaders. Think about your own story. What is unique, particular to you? What about your life would you like to share in the next English practice group?"

Some moaned dramatically.

"I'll put some gifts on the chair by the door, courtesy of my sister. Leave me the list of questions you wrote for today." She pulled out the biros and butterscotch candies from her bag and set them on the chair. The students stampeded toward them.

Alicia called Thale over. A few days ago, Thale confided that she wanted to be a teacher of English. She wanted to read more books by African authors in English.

Alicia pulled out the books in her bag. "In our library, I found several authors you might enjoy. Here's *A Book of African Verse* that includes poems by a Nigerian woman. This one is a book of short stories by Bessie Head, a South African who lives in Botswana. Alan Paton, also South African, wrote *Cry, the Beloved Country*."

Thale picked up the books. "May I borrow?"

"May I borrow *them*, and, yes, you may. Since you write poetry, please write a poem about your observations, something special in your life, your culture. We'll try to get some of your poems published."

Thale clapped her hands, looking delighted.

Alicia knew that Thale's family sacrificed for her secondary education, unusual for a daughter. Boys usually took precedence.

She gestured to the storage cabinet in the corner. "Do you need extra paper?"

"Ke itumetse, Teacher." Thank you, Teacher.

As Thale left the classroom with a new pad of paper, she picked up a biro. Alicia heard the cellophane crackling as Thale unwrapped the candy.

A few minutes later, Alicia stepped out the door of the classroom sucking on her own piece of candy. Kxoma was waiting for her, his face heart-shaped, his skin brownish-gold.

She beamed at him. "Kxoma, your account of tracking a springbok kept my attention right to the end, riveting."

He cleared his throat. "Teacher, I cannot stay." He spoke in a monotone. He plucked at his shorts and stared at his feet.

"You cannot stay in school?"

His chin trembled. "We are at short ends."

"Kxoma, you can earn your Junior Certificate, I am certain."

He stood mute, his eyes dull.

"Talk to me before you leave," Alicia said. "Promise me?" If he dropped out, it would be difficult, if not impossible, to get him back.

She watched Kxoma as he walked away, shoulders slumped. He needed school fees. Kante needed a mattress. Mbengawa needed an eye operation. And what about Mick and his violence? She felt an invisible force pushing her from behind, insisting she move forward.

15

Alicia prepared herself mentally for her visit to the headmaster. She talked with him often about matters on which they both agreed, such as how best to prepare students for the exams they must pass. But whatever challenged his authority, he resisted.

At the headmaster's home, she sat with him in the living room. This was the only home in the compound with running water and an indoor toilet. His wife, Dorcas, brought in mugs of black tea. She was a large woman with pillowy hips and breasts. Her young son, Ketumile, walked behind her, holding onto her skirt.

Dorcas greeted Alicia, delivered the tea, took her son's hand, and walked into an adjacent room. Alicia saw Lepula, Ketumile's nanny, pick up the boy and kiss him with tenderness.

Alicia held the mug, feeling the warmth of the hot tea in the hot room. She and the headmaster sat in canvas-backed chairs made by Nigel and his students. She took pleasure in Nigel's craftsmanship, visible throughout the school. They were lucky to have him as a master builder and carpentry teacher. But yesterday, he had told her that he wanted to marry Corley and move to the U.S. She suppressed a sigh. Teachers were scarce, and she would ache for him when he left.

"Mrs. Talbot, you may commence." The headmaster leaned back in his chair, steepling his fingers.

"Sir, do you remember Kxoma in the First Form?" She would start with the easier request.

The headmaster lifted his chin in agreement.

"Kxoma," she said, "has both the intelligence and determination to help Botswana in the future. But his tribe is denigrated. The students avoid him, call him 'Bushy.'"

He took a sip of his tea. "I struggle with this issue. Beliefs learned in childhood are hard to change. Our Mr. Mortensen told me how Black men are treated in the U.S. Men in Georgia came in the night and took his father away. They saw him no more."

Bronwyn had told her the story of William's father. William would protect his family, no matter the cost. He watched for danger, on alert, like Jake.

The headmaster went on. "Our president tells us we must set aside the past and become one tribe—forget wrongs. Is this possible? In the past, White men kidnapped Bushmen children, enslaved them, shot Bushmen for sport and worse. How can we move forward with such a heritage?"

"Kxoma faces great obstacles including lack of school fees," she said. "Helping him would help the nation."

"Our kgosi asked me to give Kxoma a place here. He saw the poor education given to Bushmen children in Ghanzi—no books, no paper, no biros, one teacher for many children, no roof to protect them from the cruel sun. But I need school fees to keep the school viable."

"Sir, I want to ask Mr. Hunter to hire Kxoma and his father to teach him animal tracking. Perhaps he will pay Kxoma's school fees in return for this instruction."

The headmaster pursed his lips. "If Mr. Hunter agrees, he can arrange this with Kxoma's father. You have my permission."

"Another request is more delicate. Cataracts cover the eyes of Mbengawa, another of my students. I can arrange for an operation. Miss Oakes says the operation may improve his eyesight."

The headmaster stared at her, frowning. Alicia felt the sweat running down her back. He was worried about the price, no doubt. Money was scarce. She hurried to say, "An anonymous donor will pay for the operation."

"Mrs. Talbot, secrets are hard to keep. If you favor one student, he may face prejudice. You may have many requests for help. The kgosi will confer with the parents. They may refuse. Change is hard, even change for the better."

This was the best she could hope for. She forged ahead. "On another topic, someone stole the mattress of one of my female students."

The headmaster brushed a fly away from his face. "Always another problem with you. Talk to Matron about replacing the mattress. Too many pressing concerns."

Alicia thanked him, stood up and walked toward the door. The headmaster called her back.

"A teacher is angry that you give gifts to students. For those who believe others have more than they do, envy can turn to rage. I wish to avoid seeing you or your son as a target."

"Who objects, Headmaster? I was invited by you to come here. You tell me I'm an essential part of educating Botswana's youth. I will do whatever I can to help our students get the best education possible. If you do not want me here, I will leave." Her face flushed. "But if you do, I expect you to keep us safe while I do my job."

Once again, she headed to the door, but the mother-bear instinct rose within her. She turned back, went to her chair, and sat down.

"Headmaster. How long will you tolerate Mick's violence?"

16

That evening, Sammy sat on his mother's lap paging through his picture dictionary. A lantern illuminated the small courtyard, moths swirled around it. The fragrance of honeysuckle floated in the air. Alicia saw the flicker of a torch just before Jake called out, "Ko Ko."

When he sat down beside her, she had a question ready.

"The night sky seems much brighter here than in Seattle. Why is that?" She wanted to forget her tense conversation with the headmaster. Mr. Matlagodi glowered at her when she brought up Mick, but what would he do next to Ellie?

"Magellanic clouds."

His answer startled her. "Clouds?" She narrowed her eyes. "No chance."

"The 'clouds' are two galaxies that orbit the Milky Way. Those galaxies are only seen in the southern celestial hemisphere, they're named for Ferdinand Magellan. We're close to the Tropic of Capricorn here. In ancient times, astronomers recognized these galaxies even before telescopes were invented."

"You are well-informed."

"Scientists know great facts. Worth keeping me around."

"Oh, yeah?" she teased him.

"Not convinced? You told me about the on-going sabotage. With the headmaster's permission, I talked with several about how to protect the systems here, like the water pump, the generator, the food supplies, and the school vault. If the water line is destroyed, that would be a problem of a greater magnitude."

He grimaced, stood up, stretched and sat down. "Dereck called me a 'bloody interfering blighter,' but later relented. Mrs. Linchwe had no qualms. 'Get your ass in gear and bolt my safe down pronto.' She was speaking Setswana, but I got the gist."

Alicia chuckled. "Mrs. Linchwe will do whatever she can for the headmaster—total devotion."

"Nigel volunteered some lumber. William agreed to work with me. According to Mrs. Linchwe, Mr. Anand will procure the supplies needed."

He pulled out a map from his pack. "Are you ready to hear about our trip?" His eyes lit up. "We'll have more adventures than a visit to the Magic Kingdom."

Alicia remembered with pleasure a trip she took to Disneyland as a child with her parents and sister. She listened to the trilling song of nightjar birds. Sammy studied a lioness in his dictionary, tracing its body with a finger.

The sand squeaked a little as Jake moved his chair closer and unfolded his map. Warmth radiated from his body. He pointed to the Zambezi River.

"David Livingstone crossed the Kalahari. In 1849, he explored the Zambezi and tried to find the source of the Nile.

He opened southern Africa to commerce. Ambitious man. Big consequences."

She inhaled the woodsy scent of his shampoo. She wanted to run her fingers through his hair. Instead, she held Sammy tighter.

"The name 'Kalahari' means either 'the great thirst' or 'a waterless place,' depending on your source. No permanent surface water, and the temperatures are extreme. Humans survive in a narrow spectrum of temperature. We live by the consent of geology."

"Ke batla metsi," Sammy said. I want water.

"'Metsi' is the first Setswana word I learned. Allow me." He grabbed his pack and pulled out a canteen. Unscrewing the lid, he held it to the boy's lips. Sammy drank his fill, and Jake put the canteen away.

She kissed her son's cheek. "Can you say, 'Thank you?'"

"Ke itumetse," Sammy said, pronouncing the words carefully. He returned to his book.

"He speaks more Setswana than I do," she laughed. "Hey, you plan to go into the Central Kalahari often for your geology work, right? Want to hear my latest idea?"

He kept the map on his lap and cocked his head. He did not mention that her brilliant idea to climb the water tower almost killed them.

"Kxoma," she said, "one of my students, writes about tracking wild animals with his father. They are Bushmen. Expert trackers. Would you like to hire Kxoma and his father to teach you tracking?"

He looked up at the stars for a few moments before speaking. "I'm familiar with tracking in the Sonoran deserts. My godfather taught me that tracking is *observation.* He made me alert to the weather, the landscape, the direction of the wind. We would track a mountain lion for hours, sometimes on our hands and knees. Not to kill, but to understand. We got to know the mountain lion, tried to think as one."

He focused on her. "I'll talk to Kxoma, see what we can work out."

Alicia relaxed. "I cleared it with the headmaster."

He leaned closer. "Tell me why."

"I want you safe in the wilderness, of course. Kxoma needs the fees to stay in school, which I want very much. Is that selfish? Forgive me?"

"I live for your apologies."

He was close enough to kiss her. Was there a mutual attraction? He certainly was handsome.

Sammy's book fell to the ground. She picked it up and dusted it off.

"Thank you for agreeing to talk to Kxoma. We need to go in."

"Call me amenable, one of my most fetching qualities. I'll get the prep done for our trip." As he stood to leave, he said, "You have fortitude."

"Fortitude? No. Foolishness, more like."

He lingered for a moment. He seemed ready to say something. Instead, he turned on his torch and headed up the trail.

"Sammy, are you ready for our night-night song?" Alicia left a window open above their cots, maybe a breeze would find them. No more geckos raced across the walls, bedtime for them, too.

She lit a candle and blew out the lantern.

Siting together on Sammy's cot, she held the candle as they sang.

Go to sleep now tiny geckos,
racing faster than the breeze.
Jump down now, you little goats
eating in the thorny trees.

Stay well spiders in the thatch.
Listen to the singing grass.
Now let's blow the candle out.
Now let's blow, blow, blow the candle out.

At the end of the song, Sammy blew out the candle. She savored the scent of the candle and the wisp of smoke that rose into the rafters. After that, Sammy turned on his side, gave Pinky a big smooch, and fell asleep.

She pulled up his sheet, kissed him and listened to his steady breathing. She opened the window wider and lay down on her own cot, imagining tiny angels doing the polka around her head. She was almost asleep when a noise at the window startled her.

"Teacher? Teacher?"

When she recognized Negotho's voice, her fears dissolved.

"Ee, Rra?"

"A few older boys have anger," Negotho said. "They will attack teachers as they sleep unless the headmaster makes things better. Too many problems here."

"When will they attack?" She listened hard for his answer.

"Pretend no one tells you. I am dead if you tell others." His voice sounded strained.

Predators yipped outside the perimeter fence. The night chorus continued, but the student was gone.

Alicia lay awake, considering the threat.

What could I do?

17

Friday evening the teachers gathered in the sweltering staff house. Alicia sat down in the front row, a penlight stuffed in her pocket. Kgeledi sat on her right side, Fey on her left. Paul greeted Alicia and sat down nearby, friendly again.

Mpule stayed late to take care of Sammy. Glorianna, her sister, joined her. They would walk home together in the dark.

"Thank you for your courage," Alicia whispered to Kgeledi, who worried a piece of paper with his fingertips. After morning assembly, Alicia enlisted Jake in her plan. They talked with Kgeledi later in the day. With reluctance, Kgeledi agreed to attend the staff meeting and speak about the students' concerns.

Bronwyn and William came in the front door. Bronwyn, in the last awkward months of her pregnancy, leaned against a side wall. Mick and Ellie stood against the opposite wall, looking bored. Alicia craned her neck around and saw Nigel and Corley sitting with Dereck and Ndona toward the back.

Mubayi stalked in with Jake close behind. Alicia waved at Jake, and he came over and sat behind her, touching her left shoulder. She enjoyed his touch, but she tried not to make too much of it. Relationships at Kukama School often burst into bloom and faded just as fast. Bronwyn said some teachers came just to "smoke dagga and shag," and that wasn't far wrong. Jake might be interested in the shagging part, but Sammy was her top priority, and her son needed stability.

The headmaster entered the room and strode to the lectern. His dark suit, white shirt, and red tie sagged in the heat. "Come to order," he said. The room quieted. "Mrs. Linchwe will take the minutes of our meeting." He acknowledged the woman seated in a chair to his left, pointing at her with his chin.

Mrs. Linchwe was dressed in a crisp white blouse, black skirt, and ankle socks with lace-up shoes. Nothing sagged. A pair of eyeglasses perched at the end of her nose. A clipboard with a sheet of paper and a biro rested on her lap.

"We have several items on our agenda," the headmaster said. "First, Mrs. Talbot almost fell to her death from the water tower."

The room buzzed with conversation but not surprise, the bush telegraph had spread the news.

"A person cut a railing on the water tower so it broke off with a slight push. Who is that person? If you have information, please come to me. The police will continue to make inquiries."

Alicia suspected that detection was not high on the list of abilities of the local police. She stood up, "Sir. May I have permission to speak?"

The headmaster inclined his head slightly. "I recognize Mrs. Talbot."

"Let's move on to what we can solve," she said, "namely, the grievances of our students. Please allow Kgeledi, head boy, to present the students' pressing concerns."

The teachers nodded, murmuring in agreement.

"Mrs. Talbot, students do not attend staff meetings."

How do I convince him?

"At the kgotla, each person speaks freely," she said. "The kgosi listens to the ordinary person in order to understand how it is with his people. You are like our kgosi, and the staff meeting is our kgotla. Please let Kgeledi speak."

The headmaster stroked his jaw for a moment. "He may speak."

Alicia sat down, and Kgeledi went to stand beside the headmaster, facing the audience. His shorts revealed his bare quivering knees.

Kgeledi read from his paper. "Esteemed headmaster and teachers. The saboteur has not been identified which worries us. We find worms in our mealie-meal. Sick students are left without care. Matron ignores their ailments but denigrates Miss Oakes who is not a Motswana."

"Matron's a gold-plated nincompoop," Fey said under her breath.

"But a Motswana nincompoop," Alicia whispered back.

Kgeledi continued. "The vocational students have insufficient chairs, tables, and blackboards. Sometimes a teacher does not come to teach them. Worst of all, in Serowe, some students did not pass their examinations due to poor teaching. They became violent. They—"

"You have a duty to tell me of student problems." The headmaster's eyes bulged. "Why did you not come to me?"

Usually deferential, Kgeledi responded in a cold voice. "Death threats."

The teachers reacted, all talking at once. In the midst of the uproar, a male student burst through the doorway.

"You treat us like children!"

Startled, the teachers stopped talking. Lepetu, the school's football star, advanced on the headmaster, looking combative.

Jake leapt out of his chair and grabbed Lepetu, twisting an arm behind his back. The student struggled, but could not break free. Jake whispered to him, and the student went still.

"Headmaster," Jake said, keeping a firm hold on Lepetu. "This student represents other angry students. It might be wise to listen to him."

The headmaster frowned. "I object to this severe disruption." But sounding resigned, he nodded. "We heard Kgeledi, let us hear Lepetu."

Jake released him. The student took a breath, and addressed the headmaster.

"Our parents sell their favorite cows so we can study. All students work hard, studying and taking care of our school each day."

Alicia stirred in her seat, agreeing with Lepetu. The students did help maintain the buildings and the farm, essential work that kept the school open.

Lepetu turned away from the headmaster and pointed at Mubayi. "We call Mr. Mubayi the 'Cruel Beast.' For a minor infraction, he made me stand in the noonday sun until I fainted. His prefects make slaves of young students. Mr. Mubayi touches girl students. He—"

Mubayi leapt to his feet. "Ignorant boy! He speaks lies. Beat him and send him home to stink up the kraals." Growling, Mubayi moved toward Lepetu, hand raised. Jake intercepted Mubayi, putting him in a head lock.

Lepetu yelled, "We will destroy property, boycott classes, until you act on our complaints!" He ran to the front door and disappeared.

Pandemonium reigned.

"Order! Order!" the headmaster shouted. "Mr. Hunter, release Mr. Mubayi. He has his temper under control, I am certain. Harmony is our way."

Alicia was wide-eyed at the raw emotion. She was glad that Sammy was home with Mpule and Glorianna.

Before Jake released Mubayi, he said, "If you hurt Lepetu, you will answer to me."

Rubbing his neck, Mubayi hurried out the door.

Fey bounced up. "I ask to be recognized."

"You have the floor, Miss Oakes." The headmaster seemed glad for the diversion.

"I nominate Mrs. Talbot to chair a committee to address student grievances."

Alicia's idea for this meeting was spinning out of control. She rose to decline.

"Mrs. Talbot, you will be the chairman," Mr. Matlagodi said.

Alicia sat down, deflated. Thanks to Fey, she had another assignment. Fey was the one with chutzpah, she should do it. Alicia's shoulder throbbed with renewed pain as the sheer number of problems threatened to overwhelm her.

"Mr. William Mortensen, Mr. Ndona Leagajang, Miss Fey Oakes. I will add you to the committee along with Kgeledi, head boy, and Gaeyo, head girl." The Headmaster pulled out a handkerchief from his shirt pocket and patted the sweat on his upper lip. "Without doubt, someone will inform the Minister of Education and the Board of Trustees—sabotage, machine guns, potential rioters. Our donors in the U.K. and Scandinavia may reconsider funding us."

Without warning, the electric lights flickered and went off. The room went dark, and the teachers groaned. Alicia turned on her penlight.

18

As the teachers dispersed, William and Jake huddled together in conversation outside the staff house. Alicia, grateful to leave the oppressive heat of the room, talked with Bronwyn.

The two men came up to the women after a few minutes. William put his arm around Bronwyn, and she snuggled against him. Alicia envied their total peace with each other. She remembered that intimacy with Eric. With a pain in her heart, she forced herself to focus on what Jake was saying.

"We'll create a night patrol." Jake kept his voice low. "Head off any student violence."

"Three years I've been here," Bronwyn said, tears in her eyes. "Not one student fight. I worship the feisty buggers in my classes. Violence?"

"How may I help?" Alicia asked. She needed sleep after lying awake the previous night. But she was the one who roped in Jake and Kgeledi, so she felt some responsibility for the situation.

"Let us use your home tonight for a meeting," Jake said. "Can't use the staff house. Too many eager ears."

He touched Alicia's elbow. "I'll go recruit volunteers. See you in one hour."

When Jake disappeared, Bronwyn and William headed toward their home. Alicia walked toward Sammy and the babysitters thinking of saboteurs and rioters.

"Will the students be able to take their examinations in November, let alone pass? Will the school even survive that long?"

☆ ☆ ☆

Moths fluttered around the two lanterns that illuminated Alicia's home. She sat at the table next to Fey, glad that Sammy was asleep in the Lizard Lounge. Several small plants grew in pots on a windowsill. The bouquet of flowers on the table imbued a floral scent to the room.

When Jake walked through the open door, Alicia felt butterflies in her stomach. Her palms grew sweaty, so she tucked her hands under her thighs. Jake sat down on his haunches with his back to the door of the Lizard Lounge.

Dereck, Nigel, Ndona and several other male teachers sat on the cots. William came in last, closed the door and folded his arms. Bronwyn was at her own home, tending Geoff.

Alicia began the meeting. "Ndona told me that he chose students to replace Mubayi's prefects." She smiled at Ndona. "Thank you."

Ndona stood up. He was a wiry man with hands calloused from years of farm work. Like Mrs. Linchwe, he never seemed to notice the heat.

"For my nation, I will do *anything* to keep our school alive."

Goosebumps rose on Alicia's arms. Here was a patriot.

Ndona sat down, head held high, and Fey jumped in. "The headmaster acted swiftly. Unusual. Most students will be happy about the changes. Mubayi has some students on his side, his people from Rhodesia, the Matabele." She gestured toward Jake. "I worry about Lepetu. As his coach, will you talk with him?"

Jake gave Fey a thumbs-up.

"We need a few more men," William said, "including those from the vocational side. Forget Mick. He never volunteers."

Jake stood up and addressed the group. "For the next few weeks, we'll organize into teams, limit the shifts to two hours each, and change the time each team goes out. We need to catch the troublemakers red-handed. Expel them, if need be."

Jake seemed to take command in a natural way. Alicia figured it was his military training in tandem with his self-confidence. He identified a problem and worked with others to solve it, that was his style.

"William and I will create a schedule," Jake said. "We start tonight. Women are welcome to patrol, if they're partnered with a man. Sounds sexist, but 'safety foremost' is one of my rules. Comments?"

"No sidearms," Fey said. "We don't want to escalate the situation. Several of you wear concealed weapons. We're not a posse." She stared at William. "Think of yourselves as a stabilizing presence."

Fey scanned the room. "Kgeledi mentioned the violence in Serowe. Rocks were thrown through windows at sleeping teachers and some were injured. A group of students threatened their head boy with death if he warned their headmaster. Their head boy was too frightened to speak up. Not our Kgeledi. He's a gem."

A slender knife appeared in William's hands. He held it over his head. "The school is my family. Call me an eye-for-an-eye kind of guy."

"Put your knife away, William," Alicia said. "You're in my *home*."

William put his knife back in his ankle sheath.

"Nigel? No dagga," Fey said. "I want you sharp as a new saw blade."

"Blast." Nigel looked crestfallen.

"What happened in the staff meeting tonight may cool student tempers," Fey said. "But it won't last. We need real change. That's Alicia's job as chairman."

Alicia did not want the job. Lepetu had stirred up a whirlwind. Violence would be met with violence, not the improvements he sought.

The meeting ended, and the teachers filed out.

Jake sat down on the chair Fey vacated. "You failed to mention who came to warn you about the student upheaval," he said, "but you kicked up a fuss. Gutsy."

"And you failed to mention how you got Lepetu to calm down."

"Elementary, my dear Watson. The footballers chose a motto: 'We play by the rules. We play to win. We play as one tribe.' I told Lepetu that if he played by the rules, I would help him. If he did not, he was off the team."

He touched her hand in farewell, and her pulse quickened. Full of vitality, he seemed to throw off electric sparks. But did she need more complications in her life?

Absolutely not, she thought. *I need no more complications.*

19

At one o'clock in the morning, Jake, dressed in black, opened his door at William's knock. He emerged with his penlight on. Nigel popped out from behind the bulk of William's body and waved.

Nigel wore shorts, sandals, and a T-shirt that read, "Give Peace a Hug" superimposed on a teddy bear. While Paul was an outspoken opponent of the war in Vietnam, Nigel was against the war but not combative. After his recent trip to Francistown, Nigel shared the news that Nixon was pulling some troops out of Vietnam, a good sign.

Jake walked side-by-side with Nigel; William walked a few paces behind them. William had told Jake that he needed little sleep, and that he would often walk the compound at night while his family slept, keeping watch.

Nigel talked nonstop about Corley and music. For him, life was an endless cornucopia of pleasures. After a few minutes, Jake pressed a finger to his lips. Nigel stopped talking mid-sentence. The man could take a hint.

The three men peered into nooks, holes, and crannies. Nigel grinned when he pointed out the stubs of candles and used condoms in an unfinished rondavel. They did find a small pile of rocks, but that was it. Jake called off the hunt after two hours. Worried, he watched the men leave. The school was off-kilter.

At his hut, Jake took off his ankle sheath and put the knife under the rolled-up towel he used for a pillow. A few minutes after he lay down, a flashback pinned him to the cot.

He crouched in a trench on the firebase in Elephant Valley. His friend, Scottie, was beside him on his left. Below them, hundreds of enemy soldiers rushed toward the razor wire that surrounded the base. Mortar shells exploded. The radioman on his right was calling in reinforcements when he went silent. Jake glanced over; the man was dead.

Jake grabbed the handset from the radioman's hands. "Gold three six, Gold three six, this is X-ray one five. Incoming, we have heavy incoming and a visual on regulars in the tree line, three hundred meters to my front."

The reply was instantaneous. "X-ray one five, this is Gold three six, our time to your location is thirty mikes, over."

"Gold three six, I'll have enemy in the wire in one-zero mikes. I say again one-zero mikes." He reached for the handset tuned to air support. "Eagle nine, eagle nine, this is X-ray one five, over."

The reply came quickly. "X-ray one five this is eagle nine. I read you Lima Charlie, over."

Jake shouted. "Fire mission, fire mission, enemy to my front, tree line three zero zero meters. I say again, tree line three zero zero meters to my front."

"Roger, I copy three zero zero to tree line at your front. I have three fast movers on the way, drop will be danger close. I say again, danger close, do you copy? Over."

"Roger that. I read you five by five for danger close. Out."

Scottie moved forward. In a flash of light, he fell to the earth.

Jake dropped the handset and leapt out of the fox hole. He pulled Scottie back.

A blast slammed Jake, and he fell back, holding his friend. Numb, he grabbed the handset. "They're in the wire!" he shouted. "They're in the wire!"

He screamed to his men, "Incoming! Take cover!"

In front of him, their chaplain grabbed the weapons of a fallen soldier and, with a weapon in each hand, fired back at the onrushing enemy. Munitions from a warplane pounded the ground around them. Blackness descended. Jake could do no more.

20

Sunday morning, Jake walked the three miles from the school to the main dirt road beyond Kukama village and hitched a lift to Francistown. He was tired yet eager to see the town and meet up with Pierce.

Francistown was a hard-working, dirt-under-the-nails kind of place with no paved streets. The names of the businesses on the main street were painted on the false fronts of the one-story buildings: Snappy Mercantile, Grocery, Bank, Springbok Superior Hotel, and Lion's Dream Oasis Club. On the verandas, men with treadle sewing machines sewed shirts and dresses while their clients stood next to them chatting.

Inside the club, the entire continent of Africa vanished. No dust, no flies, no cockroaches and not one woman in the gentleman's club. Men of every skin color bellied up to the long, gleaming bar. The gigantic mirror behind the bar reflected the faces and the colorful liquor bottles. A uniformed bartender poured drinks. The manager stood at the door, debonair in his official livery, greeting each newcomer.

Fans blew a breeze from each corner.

Colonel Hector Pierce sat in an easy chair dressed in a safari suit. A glass of whiskey in one hand, he waved at Jake and pointed to the empty chair beside him.

Jake sat down and ordered a cold beer. Then he turned to Pierce and asked quietly about the shortwave radio, weapons, and vehicle he needed. Pierce replied that all was ready except for anti-venom kits. Short supply. Backordered.

Before searching out the bar, Jake had visited the local office of the Botswana Geological Survey and Mines Department. The English geologist, Dr. Trevor Cooke, had very few maps to offer him. He told him to contact the geologists at the copper and nickel mine at Selibi-Pikwe and the diamond mine at Orapa. Dr. Cooke arranged for an Aussie pilot to fly Jake along the border with Rhodesia later that day.

In the bar, Jake handed Pierce a list of teachers and staff for background checks and verbally made his report. He did not yet know why the machine guns had been hidden at the school. They may or may not be related to the incidents of sabotage and attempts at guerrilla-recruitment at the school.

As Jake downed his beer, a woman in a cranberry-red dress entered the room. She argued with the manager in a loud voice. Jake cursed inaudibly. This could not be a coincidence. Fey had followed him.

Fey held her satchel like a battering ram, refusing to budge. Voices rose even louder. Jake whispered to Pierce that they needed to leave. He walked toward Fey, arms wide open. He embraced her and maneuvered her out the door.

"No women allowed?" Fey fumed. "You should be ashamed of yourselves. Relic of a bygone era, discriminatory."

Pierce pointed Jake to the Lioness Lounge, the place for women and their companions.

Fey stopped her tirade and examined Pierce. Her tone changed. "Who is your rapturous friend, Jake, my man?"

Jake all but choked.

The Lioness Lounge smelled like a heavily perfumed woman had just left. Fey sat down and set her satchel on the floor beside her, poised and calm. The two men sat in chairs facing her with a low table between them. Jake formally introduced Pierce to Fey. A waiter appeared as if conjured. Pierce gestured for Fey to order.

"Gin and tonic with ice made from bottled water," she said to the waiter. The man put down a cloth napkin on the table and left.

"Now tell me everything, and don't leave anything out." She gestured for Pierce to speak.

"Jake and I are old friends from San Diego," Pierce said. "Botswana will emerge from the dark ages now they've found diamonds. Business opportunities abound. We're just two buddies swapping stories."

"You are a superb specimen, Hector Pierce, but a mediocre liar. Jake's story is chock-full of holes."

She beamed at Jake, and turned her gaze back to Pierce. "With the help of Mrs. Linchwe, our school secretary, I used the antiquated telephone system to talk with my contact in Washington, D.C. A thorough man. Turns out, Jake has a godfather named Hector Pierce, U.S. Army, and here you are. Imagine that."

The waiter brought her drink, and Fey took a healthy swallow.

"'Two buddies,' indeed," she scoffed. "Pull my other leg. By sending Jake to my school, the Army is poking in its big snout. Not on my watch."

Pierce stood, preparing to leave. "You are making an unsubstantiated accusation. Enjoy your drink, Miss Oakes."

She lifted her chin. "You will sit down, or I will announce Jake's undercover status Monday morning at assembly."

"Do that and you will lose an excellent teacher," Pierce said, his eyes flinty.

Her voice deepened. "Better than a spy in our midst."

"You would compromise a mission."

Fey's fist hit the table, spilling her drink and knocking the napkin to the floor. "I knew I smelled a rat."

Fey and Pierce glared at each other.

In a conciliatory manner, she said, "Instead of scrapping your mission, join with me. Your resources will come in handy with the troubles at our school." She opened her satchel and pulled out an envelope.

"My Alicia snaps pictures of students, staff, and their families. Last term, I borrowed her camera to take photos of teachers I suspect of nefarious deeds. Alicia is a helpful woman. Loves to plan, loves to teach, great mother. Not sneaky and suspicious like me. I ordered a double set of photos."

"Goddammit," Jake said.

"I left out the surreptitious photos when I gave her a set."

Jake jerked his head. "Did you destroy the negatives? If these photos are of certain people—"

"I said 'surreptitious.' Get a hearing aid, buster."

"You are without scruples."

"Me? Ha! If the shoe fits..." She spread out the photographs on the table.

Jake surveyed them. He pointed out one to Pierce. "Here's a math teacher, Mick Cooper, with his arm around his hapless girlfriend, Ellie Garcia. In this one, assistant headmaster Mubayi, a Rhodesian, glares at Dereck Chamberlain, our Marxist mechanic."

Pierce remained silent, looking grim.

"Hector," Fey said, gathering up the photographs, "why don't you visit me, check out the rest of the photographs for POIs? You want to find out who hid the machine guns, correct?"

Pierce put the napkin back on the table and sat down. Jake watched as Pierce and Fey continued to stare at each other, ostensibly in anger. Jake saw a shift in their demeanor. He thought that Pierce might be sucked into Fey's orbit, but dismissed the idea as ridiculous.

Pierce leaned toward Fey. "POIs. Persons of interest."

She tilted her head. "Imagine a pit bull lurking beneath my flawless complexion. If I sink my teeth in, I don't let go. Hector is the perfect name for you—a heroic soldier, smart, powerful. Your fate will be far better than your namesake in Greek mythology. We'll make the perfect team."

Her smile was incandescent.

A visible energy zipped back and forth between Fey and Pierce, feral and unquenchable. Pierce *had* succumbed to Fey's siren song.

"FUBAR," Jake whispered. Fucked up beyond all recognition.

21

Monday morning before dawn, Mpule knocked at Alicia's door, ready to care for Sammy. Alicia trusted Mpule to play with Sammy and keep him safe. Her shoulder felt a little better. Weary of her sling, she left it in the closet.

As Alicia was departing, Mpule said, "My grandfather, Kgosi Monyame, asks Sammy to visit."

According to Fey, Mpule's father was killed in a South African mine accident and her mother died shortly after of a broken heart. The grandparents took in Mpule and her sister, Glorianna, without hesitation.

"Ask Rra Dereck to lend you a wheelbarrow to carry Sammy," Alicia said. "It's too far for a small child to walk." She went on to give Mpule a list of instructions. Children did not sweat like adults did, so special care must be taken in the heat. Mpule agreed to cover up Sammy's head with a hat and take plenty of water. The nanny seemed glad for her to leave.

The extra fuss meant Alicia would be late to morning

assembly. Because of this she ran flat-out in her sandals. Rounding a bend, she came upon a large snake coiled in the middle of the path. The snake's scales were smooth and dull. From the dirty gray coils, the head rose flat-sided, coffin-shaped. The inky-black mouth was open wide. Her momentum thrust her forward; she could not change course. She leapt over the snake.

When she slowed down and looked back, the snake had vanished. She bent over, hands on her knees, panting. Their strike was swift. Without the anti-venom, the bite of a snake could mean paralysis and death.

Oddly enough, she felt braver for having survived the snake, a bit invincible. Something about the anomaly she saw from the water tower niggled at the back of her mind. She would explore the wilderness beyond the northern perimeter fence very soon.

First, though, she would be late to morning assembly.

☆ ☆ ☆

Early that afternoon, Jake stood on the veranda at the colonel's compound a few miles outside of Francistown. The new-to-him Land Rover made the trek from the school much faster than hitchhiking. Several gigantic sycamore fig trees grew within the compound. A lilac-breasted roller with electric-blue wings flew among the trees, its call harsh and rattling.

A wall around the compound enclosed Pierce's residence and office, a dormitory, a parking area, a guardhouse, and a large building that included a training facility, storage area, and a mess hall. Armed soldiers kept watch at all times.

Three Batswana men, Mokgweetsi Moreng, Mompati Keganne, and Balakile Mosweu, were driving away. The local head of police had recruited them from the national police force for a coveted assignment in a Police Mobile Unit, PMU.

Pierce explained to the three men that they would be protecting Botswana's eastern border to limit the operations of both the Rhodesian guerrillas and the Rhodesian military. Jake would teach the men Ranger skills. The Batswana and Americans would patrol together. When the Americans withdrew, the PMUs would be made up solely of Batswana.

Before the three men arrived, Jake had told Pierce that his late wife, Maria Elena, knew he had been unfaithful when he was stationed in Saigon. Pierce had paled. The arrival of the three men interrupted them. After they left, Pierce insisted he have his say.

They walked into the residence. Pierce pinched the bridge of his nose, and closed his eyes. "I broke my marriage vows. I regret…it."

"She told me you lost your way. She wanted me to help you. That's why I came." Jake's voice rose. "I told her I would honor her request."

Pierce looked haunted. "She handled my long deployments with grace and strength, a generous woman. Did she forgive me?"

"You didn't deserve her." Jake's voice broke on the last word. "If you want Fey, she is not a sweet-tempered woman like Maria Elena. Fey is focused, fierce, and determined. A warrior. Do not underestimate that woman."

They locked eyes.

Pierce broke the silence. "While you're savaging me for my shortcomings, what about you? Kath did not believe *you* deserved *her*."

"You're bringing up my divorce? Kath couldn't handle the extent of my injuries."

"Kathleen Ciara O'Connor was a faithless woman."

"Bullshit."

"I have contacts."

"You did not..." Heat flushed through Jake's body; his hands clenched.

"The day after your divorce was final, she married your former friend, Mark Catalbianco."

"That's news? She said she didn't have the strength to help me recover. She apologized. Cried even." Jake thrust his hands in his pockets.

"Total baloney." The vein under Pierce's left eye began to pulse. "She cheated on you the minute you walked down the corridor to board the plane for Vietnam. Probably before. Being unable to stand on her own two feet was her weakness."

Jake's jaw tightened.

"Deep down, you were tired of Kath, weren't you? She was beautiful, true. But she lacked integrity. Both Maria Elena and I saw it. Kath told me at a dinner party that she faked the footnotes on her research papers. She paid others to do tough assignments. She lacked inner strength, which you have in abundance. You were badly mismatched."

Jake winced. "Why do you want to hurt me?"

"You need to face some home truths. You're not naïve, yet you asked your pal, Catalbianco, to take care of Kath while you served in Vietnam. Why trust a man who slept his way through two sororities? He did check on her. Often. Believe me, those two belong together, and as far away from you as possible. She did not deserve you."

Jake tried to catch his breath.

"You came here," Pierce went on, "because Maria Elena asked you to help me? Well, she asked me to help *you*. You were mired in unhappiness over Kath. Despite being inundated with graduate work and physical therapy, you could not move on."

Jake ran his hands through his hair. "Is Maria Elena pulling our strings from the grave?"

"She loved us *both*," Pierce said. "When your parents asked us to be your godparents, I swore I would do my best. I love you like you're my own son. Please, forgive me." He held out his hands.

Jake turned away and headed toward his vehicle. The puzzle pieces of his life were snapping together, and he didn't like the picture.

As he started the engine, he muttered to himself. "Are we both stupid about women?"

Late that evening, Jake and Alicia sat side-by-side in her courtyard, talking by lantern light. When he arrived, he set his pack by his chair. Alicia had already put Sammy to bed. The waxing crescent moon shone above them.

Jake seemed lost in thought. He had not mentioned their upcoming trip into the desert. She hesitated to bring it up. Instead, she inquired about his progress with the football team.

From his pack, he pulled out the manual with the rules of football. He had found it in the school library. The name of the last coach was written on the page inside the cover, Andy Shepherd. Teachers donated their books when they left the school rather than haul them back to their home countries. Jake didn't want his team to be disqualified on a technicality, so he studied the manual.

"In terms of my own ability, I can move the ball up and down the field, but without real control. When there's enough moonlight, I'll go to the pitch and practice. The team won't be there to laugh at me when I fall on my keister."

He was determined to master the sport.

"The team cleared the pitch of weeds today. The goal posts are tree limbs. I worked them hard, doing complex drills. After practice, the team chose their team leader."

"Kgeledi?"

"He's a natural. He wants to know more about storing energy from the sun, a technology discovered in the last century, but only recently developed. Useful in remote places. No rioting for him. He won't jeopardize his chances for a profession."

Alicia took a deep breath, inhaling the scent of the trees and long grasses. She enjoyed being with Jake. She suppressed the urge to trace the shape of his eyebrows with her fingers. She recognized what she was feeling. Longing.

Jake took out his canteen from his pack and took a sip. "Lepetu stayed silent at our team meeting, he's simmering. That concerns me. The team wants to win, but they must learn to work together. We'll drive the school's van to matches, and the roads are rough. Lepetu needs to keep his temper in check."

He stood up, hitting a fist into the palm of his left hand. "Dammit. If a footballer knocks into him, I don't want a fight in close quarters. Could threaten the entire trip."

His sudden anger surprised her.

"Gotta shove," he said abruptly. "Have to finish a lab prep for tomorrow. Maybe I'll blow something up. That will get their attention." He grabbed his pack and headed up the path.

Mortified, Alicia felt the blood rush to her face. She had read his signals wrong. He wasn't interested in her, he was just being kind to the widow of a fellow soldier.

22

Early Saturday morning, Alicia was awakened by Jake's distinctive double-knock on her door. She opened her eyes and groaned. Still dark.

"Sammy stayed overnight with Geoff," Jake shouted through the door. "I know because I tapped into the bush telegraph. No smoke signals or talking drums required. Just talking. Yak, yak, yak."

"You're the big bad wolf who never sleeps."

"I'll count to five. Then, I'll huff, and I'll puff, and I'll blow this hut down."

Alicia crawled out of bed and grabbed her gabardine trousers. She tucked her hair behind her ears. After putting on a shirt and her sling, she stumbled out the front door, clutching her daypack to her chest.

She followed Jake to his Land Rover, put her pack in the back and climbed onto the front seat. Jake's jacket bulged on both sides. Before he got into the driver's seat, he removed his jacket, revealing a pistol in a holster on one side and a small black case on the other. Ammunition, probably. She wondered where he obtained the gear.

Outside the front gate, they drove for hours on rutted tracks. Heavy squalls passed through twice, but the Land Rover plugged along undeterred. Once the dirt track faded away, there was only wilderness. Jake stopped from time to time to check his compass and maps before moving on. They talked in spurts.

After a while, he stopped near a gigantic tree. The hanging fruit on the tree looked like fat, brown sausages. Fey had warned her about the "sausage tree," with fruit so heavy it could knock you out if the fruit fell on your head. Mokoro tribesmen used these trees to make the dug-out canoes they paddled through the Okavango Delta. Alicia hoped to visit the Okavango, take a trip in a canoe, and see the wildlife.

She noticed the metal bar above the top of her door and touched it. "What's this for?"

"That's called the 'Oh, Jesus!' bar. On crazy rough roads, you hang onto it and pray for divine intervention. This vehicle has a winch and lots of engine power for when we get stuck."

She gulped. "Thanks for the warning."

"I packed extra fuel, water, two spare tires, a first-aid kit, and a shovel. Just like I do when I explore remote regions in the States like Death Valley."

Alicia yawned. The larks and lovebirds sang in earnest, well past dawn. She climbed out, opened the back door, and picked up her pack. "I'm not at my best this early."

He grabbed his gear. "Never would I be so rude as to point that out. My mother raised a gentleman."

He pulled out another pistol from his pack. "You'll need to carry this."

She stepped back, startled.

He made a sweeping gesture at the sand and thorn trees. "The Kalahari Lion is king here, not us, and two pistols are better than one. Twenty-two shots each. Hands up! This is a stick-up."

She let him strap the holster and ammo pack onto her waist.

"Now you have a Colt .45, a semi-automatic pistol called the 'Commander.' It will stop a predator with a *well-placed* shot. I want you to practice today. Back at the school, I'll conceal the weapons so the headmaster doesn't confiscate them."

"Why is your backpack so large?"

"Water. Never assume you have enough water. 'Beware the fatal assumption.'"

"Fatal assumption?" She brushed the ubiquitous flies away from her face. "You've mentioned that rule before."

"The wilderness is indifferent to us. No mercy—zero, zip, nada. I consider each trip in advance. When things go wrong, I'm ready."

"You have too many rules." She crossed her eyes and made a face.

"Don't worry, Tenderfoot. Practice makes better."

He pointed in the direction she should walk. The air smelled fresh, not dusty like back at the school. She walked in front of him and picked her way along.

"Finding a trail between the brush and thorn trees is akin to threading a needle," she said.

"If you're in front, I know you're safe. Whining is forbidden by the management."

She kept any further complaints to herself.

As the sun rose higher, shadows flowed from the trees. Insects hummed in the background. An enormous bird with black and white plumage and a topknot like a quill ran past them.

She stopped. "What was that?"

"Secretary bird. Predator. Eagle on stilts. They hunt on movement. A rabbit is safe if it keeps still, even sitting right beside the bird's foot. If the rabbit moves, he's dead. The secretary bird is the only bird that stomps its prey to death. What's the lesson?"

"Keep your nerve?"

"Smart girl."

"Smart *woman.*" She started walking again. "Notice that, smart *boy*?"

He laughed. "You bet I did. I am the king of observation, if not diplomacy. I will update my vocabulary forthwith."

She walked a few more paces. "Remember on the water tower, a missing tree puzzled me? I went to check it out."

"The area forbidden by the headmaster?"

"Had to do it." She shrugged at his exasperated sigh. "A dying thorn tree was forced over, leaving a big hole. There were footprints but no tire tracks. Terrific place for a burial, but what?"

"'No unnecessary risks.' That's my rule. Next time, take me with you. Being helpful is a requirement. Scout Law." His voice had a smile in it.

"You were a Boy Scout?"

A giraffe emerged from the brush in front of her, and she stifled her surprise. The animal began to eat the leaves off the top of a thorn tree.

Jake touched her back and whispered. "Bull giraffe—too big for a lion to take down. He uses his horns in violent combat with other males for dominance." He pointed to hoof prints the size of dinner plates. "Kxoma's father says the story of animals, both predator and prey, is in the sand."

He beckoned her away from the giraffe. She wanted to stay and watch how their long tongues dodged the sharp thorns, but he was ready to move on. Her shoulder ached from carrying her pack.

"My committee met yesterday," she said. "Gaeyo and Kgeledi will make a list of students' grievances. The dirty ablution blocks are a problem. They're smelly and no one wants to clean them. We will hire a woman from the village. Terrible job."

"Some jobs are."

"Gaeyo caught the culprit stealing mattresses," she said. "The thief sold them over the fence to villagers, desperate for money, probably. Mrs. Linchwe ordered replacements from Mr. Anand. The headmaster expelled the girl, a sadness for her and her family, no doubt. Did you notice that Gaeyo has a fake arm?"

"Quite realistic."

"Gaeyo wants to help disabled children—blind, deaf, those with multiple sclerosis—get an education. She sent President Khama her ideas for a school that's easy for anyone with mobility problems. Nigel said he could make the adaptations, just needs the money."

"Aren't the headmaster and William on your committee, too?"

"William told me he'll be the 'enforcer,' whatever that means. The headmaster never attends, too busy." Alicia paused.

"Did you say you've been married?" She hesitated to question him, but she wanted to know.

"Did I? Can't remember." In a humbler tone, he said, "I was. After I returned from Vietnam, my wife, Kath, divorced me."

Alicia's face grew warm. "That question was too personal. I'm sorry."

"Apology not required. I have a question for you. Do you want another child?"

She could not believe it. He was asking her about her desire for children. Was he interested in her after all? She was a little bit thrilled.

"Wait," Jake said.

She stopped and turned around. He took off his pack, set it by a thorn tree and climbed up the trunk. She followed his lead. From her perch, she perused the ochre grasses.

She nudged him. "Herd of impala at two o'clock."

He pulled out his binoculars and peered through them. "Eagle eyes."

"My father writes books on the American frontier, like the Lewis and Clark expedition and the Oregon Trail. We both have sharp eyesight and excellent hearing. He says we would have been hunters in a much earlier era."

"When we run out of food and water, you can bag us an antelope."

"Speaking of food, the rainy season will end soon. No drought this year, a blessing. If there's a drought, starvation follows. The cattle die, wealth disappears. They treat their herds like a savings account."

The desert stretched out in all directions, seemingly endless.

A hornbill squawked as it flew by, its heavy yellow bill gleaming. Another hornbill followed behind. Perhaps they were a pair.

"See those ship funnels?" Jake gestured to beige columns. "Those are termite towers." He climbed down from the thorn tree, picked up his pack and headed toward them. She followed close behind him.

A portion of one tower had caved in. She peered in at the wriggling larvae.

"If you need protein, eat anything edible."

Thinking of eating larvae made her thirsty. She took out her canteen and drained it.

Jake gave her a questioning look. "Have you discovered how unprepared you are for the desert?"

"I'm prepared. Cheese, a hat, a folding knife, and my canteen."

"Your canteen is empty. The cheese will make you thirstier. Your folding knife would not deflect a mouse."

She touched her hat. "My hat is nice, though."

"Hand me your canteen." He refilled it from his own canteen without spilling a drop. "Do you have a torch? If we stayed overnight, you would need one. Where's your compass? If vultures swooped in and carried me away, could you find your way back to the Land Rover?"

She scrutinized the trees with their needle-sharp thorns. Everything looked the same.

"Can you read topographical maps? They tell you about the terrain. Can you light a fire? Gets cold out here at night, near freezing at times. How do you signal a plane if you are lost and one should fly by?"

"No need for condescension, uppity man." She sighed. "Total ignoramus. *C'est moi.*"

He pointed to her legs. "Your trousers will not protect you from thorns. I will order sturdy trousers from Mr. Anand. A man with a sewing machine will put in lots of pockets for gear. Plan on an emergency."

"I love to plan."

"You learn fast, Tonto."

She studied the termites. "Are you ever afraid in the desert?"

"Afraid? Sometimes. But I never panic. 'Panic makes you stupid,' my godfather says."

"Is your godfather the rule maker? I want to meet him."

"Stick with me, kid."

"I wouldn't want to be alone in the Kalahari." As she peered deeper into the broken tower, her hair fell forward. Standing behind her, he gathered her hair together, and wove it into a loose braid, surprising her.

He put his hands on her shoulders. "Lilacs. Your scent is lilacs. The first time I saw you, your hair glowed like a Renaissance painting of the Madonna. Didn't know about Sammy then. I imagined reaching through the window and touching you." He kissed her neck.

She turned around into his embrace.

He kissed her gently and pulled back.

With her left arm around his neck, she stood on tiptoes, pressed against his body, and touched her lips to his. She was starved, and he was the banquet. She wanted more. Much more.

Holding her waist, he set her away from his body. "No distractions, welcome as they may be. Predators lurk."

She picked up her pack, sighing. What had just happened? What about Eric? She could not keep loving a memory. She needed a partner and a father for Sammy. Perhaps not Jake, though.

Slinging her pack on her shoulders, she marched forward.

"Reverse course," he called out. "Wrong way."

She was headed in the wrong direction.

Naturally.

23

Jake pointed out the animal tracks to Alicia: hares, impalas, hyenas, snakes, and more giraffes.

"Kxoma's father tells me that in a traditional hunt, the Bushman uses a thin arrow with a poison tip. They sneak up proximal to the animal to make a kill. I will never be adept—you need to start training as soon as you learn to walk."

He appeared nonchalant.

She whispered to herself. "Has he forgotten about our kiss already?"

Jake went on talking. "Kxoma pointed out roots and berries, lizards and tortoises. We found tsamma melons. They are like watermelon, but tasteless. Hard to survive in the Kalahari, even for the Bushmen. If they agree, I may publish about them in an academic journal. I plan to get my doctorate."

She raised her eyebrows. He had lofty goals.

When they arrived at a kopje, he asked, "Do you remember what I told you about kopjes?"

"Uneroded rock."

"Good memory. Pick a name for this kopje."

"You could call it 'Hornbill' for the bird with the big yellow beak."

He printed the name on his map in black ink.

She ignored the increasing ache in her shoulder. "Do you think we'll discover who cut the railing on the water tower?"

"Most secrets emerge with time. Now, are you ready for your geology lecture?"

Alicia sat down in the sand beside a bush large enough to provide shade.

"Proceed, Professor Hunter. Remember Polonius. 'Brevity is the soul of wit.'"

Jake stood in front of her. "Lowly but irritating student, we will start with plate tectonics. How fast do your fingernails grow?"

She examined her fingernails. "Slowly."

"The plates under the continents are moving about as fast as your fingernails grow. The current theory is that three hundred and thirty-five million years ago, there was a supercontinent at the equator called Pangaea which was assembled from earlier continents. Africa, as I told you, is the oldest continent, formed during the Archean era. How many years ago?"

"Two point five billion years ago."

Jake kept glancing around, presumably for predators. "The land kept splitting into pieces at fingernail-growth speed. Over time, the continents shifted into the present configuration. Change continues, cyclically."

Alicia visualized the continents moving over time. "What drives these changes, Professor?"

"One theory is called 'rifting.' The East African rift system is pulling Africa into pieces. If you go north up to the Rift Valley, you will find volcanic activity and extensional faulting. Remember the supercontinent? It's still breaking up. Someday it might drift back together."

She gave him a playful grin. "Will this be on the test?"

"Ah, the mark of a student who spent way too much time in a classroom. The African rift system might end in northern Botswana. More research needed."

Another secretary bird ran by, distracting Alicia. A herd of springbok with their lyre-shaped horns appeared in the distance. The springbok could leap as much as thirteen feet in the air, running with stiff legs. "Pronking," Fey called it. Currently, the herd grazed at ease with no predators to make them race away.

"Once a great lake existed in the Kalahari," Jake said, drawing her attention back to him. "The Okavango Delta and the salt pans are the last remnants of it."

"I see no cacti, Prof. How can you call this a desert?"

"There are cacti here, but none like the saguaro in the American Southwest. The Kalahari is not a classic desert. It's an arid region or a thirstland, though it doesn't get much water. Believe it or not, aquifers of underground water could run beneath it—doctoral topic opportunity."

"What about the earthquakes?"

"Earthquakes change things for all inhabitants of a region. They can change the course of a river. They move the earth up, down, sideways, and around. The Okavango basin is changing."

Alicia closed her eyes, drowsy from the heat and not enough sleep.

Jake snapped his fingers, and she jerked back to wakefulness.

"Hey, inattentive student, eyes front." He continued his lecture. "The sediments here were pushed up to form high plateaus that were filled with basalt, molten rock. The highest places, around three thousand feet, are part of this ancient uplifting of sediments. The salt pans are the lowest part. An ephemeral river evaporates there. This brings us to the present day, with all its erosion and the remnants of plateaus called…"

"Kopjes." She perked up. "I wonder if Kukama School is rifting."

"Ripping itself apart? Maybe." He studied the kopje. "I need fresh rock samples. If I have your help, I'll get more done."

Pulling a whistle from his pack, he said, "Take this. If you sense danger, blow hard. I always carry whistles, one of my rules."

She took the whistle and blew until it shrieked. "Loud!"

"You have a loaded weapon," he said. "Get it out. Stay back from the kopje. Don't stir up any snakes. Stay near me as I move around. Keep my pack with you. Don't go all dreamy eyed on me, pretty lady."

She stood up, simultaneously ruffled by his orders and flustered by his compliment.

While watching over Jake, she studied the plethora of ants, flies, and beetles around her. A herd of antelope browsed sixty yards away. They were much bigger than the springbok, with black stripes on their faces and long, spear-like horns. When he finished his work, she pointed them out.

"Gemsbok," he said. "Magnificent, aren't they? Can go without water for months. Their heads are a favorite wall decoration of big-game hunters. They're aggressive and dangerous. Stay away from them." He touched her arm. "Please."

Alicia's face flushed. She knew why the girls at the school flocked around him. The man radiated life.

He took his pack from her. "You'll do target practice. After that, I'll show you several ways to signal a plane if you're lost."

"How did you get these weapons?" She needed to know.

Without answering, Jake busied himself setting up targets: small rocks perched on larger rocks. He only answered questions he wanted to answer.

The Colt was heavier than the pistol she owned which was packed away in storage in Seattle. She hit all the targets using her left hand. Her accuracy garnered praise from him.

"You do have good eye-hand coordination," Jake said. "I found it hard to believe when you told me you could shoot."

"You consort a lot with liars, do you?"

He gave her a wry smile. "Let's head back. No predators, yet. Police the area, make sure you leave nothing behind. Pass me your canteen again. I'll refill it."

She did as he asked and checked for debris but found none.

He hefted his pack onto his back. Pointing her in the right direction, she started walking. Earlier, she had put her sling in a pocket. The pack strained her shoulder, but she didn't want to show it. She wasn't sure why.

When they reached the Land Rover, they stowed their gear in the back. Jake drove out, creeping along, plainly worried about a puncture to the gas tank. He negotiated a rocky gully so rough she grabbed for the "Oh, Jesus!" bar.

Jake drove in silence, focused on the terrain.

After a while, he cleared his throat. "I'll answer your questions about me in the not-too-distant future."

Alicia felt uncertain. The man cherished his secrets. But at least he was honest about having them.

He stopped in the shade of a tree, set the brake, and turned to her. "Take Sammy and go back to Seattle. This place is too dangerous for a woman not born here, and you have a young child."

She did not expect this. "You want me to leave?"

"The cut railing was attempted murder—for you or Dereck. Take that as a warning, a serious one."

"Why do you get a vote, Tonto?"

He raised one eyebrow. "Aren't I Kemo Sabe?"

"Hi ho, Silver, away!" Alicia masked the anger that flashed through her. He told her what to do. Fey and the headmaster told her what to do. They could take their orders and do a backflip off the water tower. She was feeling more and more like herself. Africa fed her soul in a deep way.

How can I leave?

24

Sunday night, raucous music blared from the staff house. All the chairs were stacked on one side of the room. The teachers danced to Jerry Lee Lewis and "Great Balls of Fire." In unison, everyone shouted the refrain.

Lanterns flickered, casting shadows. Bronwyn and William slow danced in a corner, wrapped up in each other, ignoring the insistent beat of the music.

Alicia danced with Paul, her dress the color of ripe peaches. She watched for Jake, who was not yet back from a match.

Paul grabbed her waist, tossed her up, caught her, and set her down. She moved in tandem with him, responding to each nuance of his lead. She danced barefoot on the concrete floor, ignoring the ache in her shoulder. She and Paul were encircled by others, clapping and hollering.

When the song ended, they hugged each other. Paul led her toward the drinks table. Nigel put on Roy Orbison's "Pretty Woman." Jake walked in the front door, and Paul put his hand on her left shoulder.

"Hey, Science Man, I was worried about you," she said, when Jake walked toward her.

"May I have this dance?"

She turned to Paul. "Let's pick up the tempo next time, Boston Boy. You can dance faster than that."

Paul gripped her shoulder as Jake picked up a beer.

"Here, busy yourself with this," Jake said, pushing the beer into Paul's hands and pulling Alicia to him at the same time.

"Paid assassin," Paul hissed.

Alicia shook her head at the taunt. Paul headed toward the door, cursing to himself.

Jake put his arms around her, pressing his hands slowly up and down her back.

She enjoyed the solidity of his body. "You like to push the limits, don't you?"

"Is your fragrance gardenia?"

"Gardenia and sweat."

He moved her hair back and licked her neck. "Salty."

She giggled.

"I happen to need salt," he said, "being sweaty myself from a day of shepherding my illustrious team to victory." He pulled her closer. "You're the prettiest woman in the room."

"Omigosh!" She stopped dancing. "I forgot about Mpule and Glorianna. Have to run." She slipped out of his grasp and ran over to the table. Pulling out her sandals from underneath it, she hopped on one foot, then the other, slipping them on. She grabbed her torch off a shelf.

Jake walked up to her. "What happened?"

"My babysitters need to go back to the village. Call me

Cinderella. Except, instead of my carriage turning into a pumpkin, I am." She raced out the door, running toward her home without a backward glance.

☆ ☆ ☆

Alicia said goodbye to her babysitters. They walked toward the stile, a beam of light shining on the path before them.

"Ko Ko," Jake said coming up to her. "Were you running away from me?"

She looked at the sky. "The Milky Way is so thick with stars, I could dance on it. Look, there's the Southern Cross."

"Do you like to dance with Paul?"

"He doesn't lick my neck. Neanderthal."

"The Neanderthals had redeeming qualities, superb hunters, for example. Probably had good eyesight and hearing, like you. Maybe they're your ancestors."

She touched the stubble on his chin. "You have two Colt .45s and a Land Rover. Your posture is military grade. You have a shortwave radio. Who are you?" She gazed up at him.

"I'm from a military family with global contacts. Not unusual."

"Do you really do geology on weekends?"

"That's your question? You lost Eric. You worry about risk. I do, too."

"Just don't tell me you're still a soldier. I've had my fill of war."

She waited for an answer, but he was silent.

"I was crazy to come here with a young child," she said. "I don't want to be foolhardy." She turned away. "I need to go in."

He touched her back. "You can go in at any time."

She turned to him. He leaned down as she raised up on her tiptoes. Their lips met. He put his arms around her, pulling her close. They kissed, holding each other tightly. They kept kissing until she grew breathless.

She pressed her face against his shoulder, savoring the power in his body. Conflicted, she put her hands against his chest and pushed until he stepped back.

"You dance divinely, Mr. Hunter. Come back in the daylight when I'll be less tempted."

"It's a date." He grinned. "On the way, I'll stop by the charm factory. Apparently, I'm fresh out."

25

Mick Cooper sat in a bar in Bulawayo. He didn't consider himself a gunrunner, he considered himself an entrepreneur. Yesterday, he had traveled over Botswana's eastern border into Rhodesia.

He had parked his truck on a quiet street, giving three barefoot street urchins a few coins to protect it. Watching them climb onto the hood, he felt skeptical. Other men could offer them more money, and his truck would disappear. He took chances, but he hated the risk.

The bar was noisy, crowded, and hot. Mick rested his backpack on the chair beside him, never letting go of its straps. He unbuttoned his new shirt far enough to display his ample chest hair. His trousers were tight in the crotch. He recalled the leggy hooker he left in the soft bed in his hotel room. Dinner had been first-class. Prime rib. No goat meat.

He checked his watch and muttered, "Chaparadza is late again."

He jerked as the man appeared amid the swirling dancers. The gyrating lights illuminated the scarred face. Mick picked up his pack from the chair, and the guerrilla sat down. They did not shake hands.

Mick leaned in close. "My next delivery will be buried. Dynamite will defend it."

"Does the merchandise conform to our agreement?"

Mick nodded. "I expect half the payment today and half on delivery."

"You honored the earlier agreements."

"And you did not. You shorted me thousands of rand. I teach math, for Pete's sake. I can count."

A briefcase appeared in Chaparadza's hands. Mick grasped the warm handle.

"We have remedied the oversight with this payment. Extortion pays off. And the AK-47s are, as you said, reliable."

"I need a favor, Chaparadze. Eliminate Alicia Talbot, a teacher at Kukama School. She threatens my business. I'll compensate you."

"Scared of a woman? You are paranoid, Mr. Cooper. You have a temper. You damaged your own woman, such lack of restraint."

"You need me."

"That is for me to decide. There are other options. Russians, for example. Are you sure the placement of my cargo will be safer than our usual method?"

"The camouflage is perfect."

"When can we obtain our weapons?"

"Soon," Mick said. "You wanted the unusual, hand grenades, for example, and it takes negotiation with elusive people. When the time is right, we will coordinate the exact day and time using our standard means of communication."

Chaparadza bared his teeth and growled. Mick's head jerked back.

"I have failed to recruit many students from your school," the guerrilla said. "I will hijack the school and take them all, load up the weapons at the same time."

Mick opened his eyes wide. "Hijack the entire school? That's ambitious."

"I shall inspire them to fight."

Mick strained to hear the man's words over the booming music. The guerrilla leader was going rogue. How would this affect his profits?

Chaparadza laughed. "When we assume power, Ian Smith will receive the kind of treatment he and his henchmen inflicted on me." His demeanor shifted as he gestured toward the door. "We cannot meet here again."

Two White policemen stood at the doorway, staring at Mick, the only White in the crowd. The Rhodesian police were reputed to be inventive in their viciousness; there was a rumor they dabbled in poison.

Chaparadza chortled quietly. "The Whites try to hold back the flowering of Black rule, the Second Chimurenga. With more weapons and fighters, no one can withstand us."

As Mick walked from the bar toward the street urchins, backpack on his back, he hugged the briefcase to his chest. He breathed easier when his truck came into view. He felt safe, for the moment.

26

The next afternoon, Paul and Bronwyn sat together with Alicia in her courtyard. They speculated on the identity of the saboteur. They waited for Ellie to arrive so they could begin the meeting of the English teachers in the first to third forms. The scent of flowers hung in the air.

When Ellie did arrive, she looked slightly disheveled, a bit dusty.

“Mubayi hates being here. He’s the saboteur, believe me,” Ellie said. She parted her long, straight hair in the middle, an attractive woman with dark, expressive eyes.

Sammy kicked around the slightly deflated ball Jake had brought for him. The child ran on his tiptoes. Sometimes he kicked at the ball and missed. At times, he kicked the ball and it went in the opposite direction from the one he intended. His friend, Geoff, squatted in the sandbox putting sand into a cup with a tiny shovel, dumping out the sand, and starting over again. Mpule had left for the day, so Alicia and Bronwyn kept watch on the children.

"Mubayi bought old mealie-meal on the cheap, trying to save money," Alicia said. "He didn't check for worms first. That's incompetence not sabotage."

"Another bleeding cock-up," Bronwyn said, lighting a cigarette and waving away the smoke.

"At least Mubayi's not a murderer like Jake," Paul said.

"That is unkind, unwarranted, and unworthy of you," Alicia said. Paul could not abandon his prejudices.

"Why do you defend him?" Paul asked. "Soldiers are pigs."

"My late *husband* was a soldier." She lifted the papers in her lap and shook them. "We need to get some work done."

Bronwyn ran a hand through her curls. "My William aced the lottery, best number possible. Lucky me."

Alicia winced, remembering Eric's number and his draft notice. She noticed Ellie squirming in her chair. "What's wrong?"

In New York City, Ellie had worked as a model for fashion photographers. Now she was gaining weight.

Ellie scratched under her left breast. "A lump itches."

"I can fix it," Paul said without hesitation.

"Really?" The three women responded at once.

"One second flat."

"If Mick knows you touched me, he'll explode." She fluttered her hand in the direction of her hut. "Overly protective sometimes."

Alicia rarely saw a couple so entwined as Mick and Ellie, with the exception of her parents. Her father was wrapped up in his historical research and her mother was wrapped up in him. Aunt Viv, her mother's sister, had stepped in to explain the "birds and bees" to Alicia and Hannah. She bought them bras and nylons when they became teenagers. Her parents were absent but not physically or verbally abusive.

Paul pulled out a Swiss Army knife.

"Ta-da, my scalpel. I keep it razor-sharp." He opened the knife, and pulled out a match box from another pocket. Lighting a match, he ran the flame over both sides of the blade.

Ellie pulled up her long-sleeved blouse. They could see the inflamed lump.

"Yep, putzi fly," Paul said, "also called 'laundry bug.' Do you iron your under garments?"

"Mick says that's stupid," Ellie said. She sounded contemptuous, even if she was borrowing her contempt from Mick.

"If you do nothing," Paul said, "the larvae will emerge as a full-blown fly, but not until it drives you nuts with itching."

Ellie closed her eyes. "Go ahead. Cut it out."

When Paul made a tiny incision on the lump, she squeaked. He pressed out the larvae and stepped back. Ellie pulled down her blouse.

Paul wrapped the larvae in a handkerchief and put his knife away. "I'll examine the insect under a microscope. The movement of its tiny spines must cause the itching."

"The itching stopped!" Ellie sounded elated. She started to hug Paul, but stopped herself. "Don't tell Mick."

Alicia left, returning with a first aid kit that included a disinfectant. She handed it to Ellie. She also brought a large package from Hannah, which she placed beside her chair.

Paul talked at length about his ideas on the curriculum. Without warning, he stomped his feet and folded his arms. "No one is listening to me. If you want to see what's in that package, you'll have to open it in my presence. I'm not leaving."

Alicia patted his arm. "Petulant and perspicacious. More reasons to enjoy you."

"You enjoy me?" He looked hopeful.

"I'd enjoy you more if you made peace with Jake."

He looked away.

Giving up on getting more work done, Alicia sang a few lines from the "Hallelujah Chorus" as she tore off the tape on the package. She opened the crammed box, picked up the note on top, and read it out loud.

SISTER: THIS CARE PACKAGE CONTAINS THE FOLLOWING:

One glamorous, flowing, full-length, emerald gown complete with tiara and magic wand (Lara made this for our annual Winter ball.)

Sexy blouses (more cast-offs from Lara, the scamp)

Sheer, ice-blue nightgown (a brand-new gift from me)

Eyeglasses for Fey to hand out to students who need them

Lots of whistles for fun

Ms. Magazine (Yay for women's lib.)

Shirts, shorts, and sandals for my angel, Sammy

Coloring book, crayons

Cassette tapes of James Galway, Aretha Franklin, B.B. King, Johnny Cash and the Eagles (will send more of the Beatles and Rolling Stones)

Cassette deck batteries

Tiny trucks

Green wool blanket for Sammy (My first knitting project. Errors abound.)

Candies, soaps, shampoos, two new flowery perfumes

Alicia pulled out the princess gown, tiara, and magic wand and set the package down. Standing up, she fluffed out the dress.

"I modeled one like that once," Ellie said, slumping in her chair.

"Bronwyn, this color would be magnificent with your auburn curls," Alicia said. "The chiffon will swirl around you. Barely fitted. We could alter it, if need be. Try it on?"

"Should I, love? Smashing gown." Bronwyn took the dress and walked into the rondavel.

Alicia pulled out two toy trucks from the package and called to her son. "Tsena." Come.

Her son abandoned his play and ran toward her.

"Aunt Hannah sent you some gifts. Can you say, 'please?'"

"Tswee-tswee," Sammy replied.

She handed him the trucks. "Take them over to the sandbox and share them with Geoff."

Sammy ran over to his playmate and showed off his trucks. The boys argued over which one would play with the red one. Alicia watched them with concern. Last week, Sammy bit Geoff on the arm after Geoff pushed him down. Geoff decided the blue truck was exactly what he wanted, and they went back to playing.

Bronwyn pranced into the courtyard wearing the emerald dress. The others applauded.

"Splendid," Alicia said. "Take the tiara and the wand." She handed them to Bronwyn. "Twirl around for us."

Bronwyn obliged. She tapped each one with her wand. "Be happy."

Alicia smiled. "A fairy queen."

"Crikey," Bronwyn said. "William's tutoring math students, or I would show him. He's tutoring *Mick's* math students." Bronwyn gave Ellie a meaningful look before she flounced off to change.

Ellie and Paul decided to leave. Paul took the upper path, Ellie took the lower one. Bronwyn emerged from the rondavel, dressed again in her cinnamon-colored granny dress. She rested her hand on her belly. "Must crack on."

She called to Geoff. "Tsena."

"Nnyaa. Wanna play." The boy sounded determined to stay.

Bronwyn went over to the sandbox and caught Geoff by the tail of his shirt. He started howling. Sammy, unconcerned, continued to play with his new truck, making engine noises.

Alicia went back to Hannah's letter.

Enclosed please find a double-headed Buffalo nickel. Use it to hasten the marriage of Bronwyn and William. Use your wiles for a terrific cause, clever girl. A wager?

She stopped reading. A wager with a fake coin, how could that work? She went back to the letter.

Lara and I bought an enormous, ramshackle house on Queen Anne Hill with massive room for extended family. Hint. Hint. We're learning carpentry and plumbing in our spare time. As much fun as my banking job.

Meanwhile, our parents continue their travels, studying the disastrous Donner Party for Father's next book. Cannibalism! Mother orbits around him, as usual. Aunt Viv, our North Star, strides forward with vigor. She continues her campaign for the ERA. After the Senate passes it, it's off to the individual states. We do not have a constitution that guarantees equal rights for women. It's 1972, for heaven's sake.

Lara and I want to tie the knot, but we can't even hold hands in public. A kiss? Not on your life. To her family, I'm Trouble with a capital T, right here in Seaport City. I sent you TIME *magazines in a separate package, so the censors can enjoy cutting out the articles reflecting badly on the Republic of South Africa.*

Yours until the tippy-top of forever. Your adoring sister,
Hannah

P.S. *You mentioned a "Jake." Is he as groovy as Eric? If so, nab him.*

27

Alicia looked up from Hannah's letter as a herd of goats ran through her clearing. Nigel was close behind. The bells around their necks jingled. Playing in the sandbox, Sammy squealed with delight.

"Yee-haw!" Nigel yelled, twirling a rope around his head. "I'm a cowpoke. Watch me rope 'em and ride 'em."

Alicia moved to the gate of her courtyard.

Jake appeared with the stragglers. He and Nigel used a long rope to tie the goats together by their collars.

"Someone forced the goats out of the kraal," Jake said. "This has happened before, I'm told. Undermines the school."

Alicia shouted to Nigel. "I ironed today. Watch out for the coals in the fire circle."

Jake walked over to Alicia, his brow furrowed. "You built a fire to iron?"

She nodded. "Hot coals go inside the metal iron to heat it up."

Nigel called out, "You're from the Wild West, Alicia, lend me your ten-gallon hat?"

"Out of luck, pardner."

One goat escaped and jumped up on a sloping trunk heading for the upper limbs. Nigel climbed up the tree and pulled the goat down. He tied a rope around the goat's neck, but the goat slipped out and sprinted away. Nigel was running after it when he let out a screech.

"Shit, shit, shit!"

Nigel hopped around on one foot. He glanced toward Sammy. "Sorry!" When he pulled off the sandal, a smoldering coal dropped out. Sitting down, he rocked back and forth with his lips pressed together, but he didn't swear again.

Alicia went to get her first aid kit. She called to her son from the doorway. "Sammy, could you comfort Nigel?"

The boy dropped his toy and ran over to pat the top of Nigel's head. "Don't cry, my bootiful one."

After Jake secured the goats, he squatted in the sand next to Nigel, examining the burn.

Alicia brought out her kit and a pair of scissors. Sammy ran back to his sandbox.

Sitting down by Nigel, she frowned. "Don't you ever wash your feet?"

"Why wash? Dust in me carpentry shop, dust in the paths, dust in me hut. Corley does go on about 'personal hygiene.' Should I polish meself up a bit?"

"Dereck has the same attitude about his hands," Alicia said. "We long to be near you. Have pity on us."

Jake looked through the kit and pulled out a few items.

"I'll trim up your beard," Alicia said, "and your nose and ear hairs. Corley will enjoy you more if you're less feral."

"No. No. No. Not me hair. You'll cut off me virility."

"You are a terrific carpenter, but you don't know much about human anatomy. Hair has nothing to do with sexual performance. Right, Jake?"

"I'm a geologist. No clue."

Nigel threw up his hands. "Sod it all. Cut me hair. For Corley."

While Jake bandaged Nigel's foot, Alicia worked on his hair. When she was done, Nigel put his sandal back on, and Jake pulled him to standing.

"Lean on me, cowpoke," Jake said. "Alicia, I'll be back for the goats and to show you how to make sure a fire is out."

Nigel's burns were a result of her carelessness. "Forgive me, Nigel."

He stroked his newly trimmed beard, looking satisfied. "Ta, love."

As they left the clearing, Nigel began to sing.

As I walked out on the streets of Laredo, as I walked out on Laredo one day, I spied a poor cowboy, all wrapped in white linen, all wrapped in white linen and cold as the clay..."

Alicia shivered. She knew every word of the old ballad about the dashing young cowboy dead from a bullet to the breast.

28

As she walked into the staff house for dinner with Sammy, Alicia patted the Buffalo nickel in her pocket. She had a plan.

William sat next to Bronwyn at the dining table. He was not tall like Jake, but muscular in a similar way. Their dinner, prepared by Mma Sethunya, was a casserole of goat meat and vegetables, mostly cabbage.

Alicia set down her bag, which contained silverware, two plates, a canteen, and a bouquet of bougainvillea blooms.

When Sammy and Geoff saw each other, they started galloping around the room bleating like goats. Alicia added the blooms to the bouquet already on the table. She dished up her own meal. The other teachers would arrive later.

"Come feel my baby kick." Bronwyn pointed to a bulge on her belly. "Press here."

Alicia touched the spot Bronwyn indicated and felt the baby kick. "Powerful! Jake will sign her up for football in utero."

Sitting down next to Bronwyn, she had a question for William. "I'm curious. Why did you come to Kukama School? I missed that story."

He put a massive arm around Bronwyn, whipped off his granny glasses and jabbed them toward Alicia. "Rage," he said, eyes flashing.

Alicia had stepped in a nest of fire ants.

"Those damn Brits," William said, "persecuted Seretse Khama because he fell in love with a White woman. Met her when he was studying at Oxford. Khama was heir to the throne of the Bamangwato tribe. Humiliate an African prince in his own land? Hell, no."

William ruffled Bronwyn's hair. "I'm not a chief, but I'm a king, thanks to you."

"What happened next?" Alicia asked.

"The way I heard it," William said, "the Brits needed gold and uranium from South Africa, but the South Africans embraced apartheid and hated interracial marriage. Seretse's uncle, Tshekedi, the regent, wanted Seretse to marry a Black Batswana woman, not a White foreigner. The Brits exiled them from Botswana for several years."

"Churchill betrayed them," Bronwyn said. "He promised an end to their exile. He went back on it."

"The couple could not be broken," William said. "Seretse gave up his claim to the tribal throne and they returned here. This country was not much of a prize, though. Extremely poor. With the discovery of diamonds, Seretse is bringing the nation into the 20th century. I came to help."

Alicia fingered the nickel in her pocket. Showtime.

"Bronwyn and William," she said. "You have a young boy and a baby kicking its way into the world. When do you plan to marry?"

Bronwyn laughed. "Someday."

William put his glasses back on and adjusted them. "A week after we met, I got down on one knee and proposed. She accepted. Never got around to the wedding. But there's no one else for me."

William reached over to the blossoms, plucked a few petals, and scattered them over Bronwyn's hair. "Do you want to be signed, sealed, and delivered, my gorgeous Brit?"

She batted her eyelashes, looking demure. "Whenever you say, love."

Alicia suppressed her astonishment. Bronwyn was the least compliant woman she knew. After Fey.

"I have an American nickel, a Buffalo head; let's make a wager and do a coin toss. Heads, you get married in two weeks. Tails, you get married in two years. I'll flip the coin. Are you game?"

William let out a rumbling laugh. "Two weeks or two years. You would never survive in Georgia. Nothing gets done there in two weeks."

Alicia touched Bronwyn's shoulder. "William. Do you love this woman?"

"We fit together."

"Bronwyn? Do you love this man?"

She smiled at her fiancé. "Too bloody right."

Alicia pulled out the coin. "Here goes the toss. I call 'heads.'" She threw the coin in the air, caught it with her left hand, and slapped it down on her right wrist. She gave the coin a quick glance. "Heads, it is!" She shoved the nickel deep in her pocket.

"Fey gave me the name of a minister in Francistown. We'll have a party here afterwards to celebrate. Mr. Anand will help with supplies. Bronwyn, will you wear the emerald gown Hannah sent?"

Bronwyn kissed William's cheek. "Fit for a queen."

"Maybe Mr. Anand will find a suit big enough to fit me." He reached around Bronwyn to tap Alicia's shoulder. "Will you keep Geoff for us tonight? We need to write our wedding vows."

Bronwyn got up, gathered their dishes, and put them in her bag. William offered her his hand and she grasped it. Bronwyn called to Geoff, telling him to stay with Alicia.

At the door, William looked back. "You seemed pretty sure of the outcome. Fine by me. But my Mama raised me as a Southern Baptist, and I expect a high-quality hitching."

After they left, Alicia corralled the boys, who were getting a little wild. Other teachers were coming into the staff house. Mick glowered at her, more disgruntled than usual. She sat the boys down at the table.

Alicia reviewed her successes. William and Bronwyn would marry soon. Her committee had solved a few of the students' grievances, and Jake did not see signs of an impending riot.

Jake often visited her in the evenings, although he had not kissed her since the staff dance. She remembered his kindness to Sammy when they played ball. But the wedding was in two weeks, and she needed to plan the party, care for Sammy, and teach her classes.

Alicia sighed. *I have no time for romance.*

29

Before dawn on Wednesday, Alicia awoke to a gentle tap at the door. Sammy did not wake up. She turned on her torch and examined the floor, then hit her sandals together and put them on.

Last night she had pulled out her nightgown from under her pillow and a scorpion popped out, waving its stinger. She grabbed a mug and crushed it. After her breathing slowed, she cleaned up the mess.

Someone called her name. Opening the door, she peered into the darkness.

"Water is broken, Teacher."

Negotho's voice.

"Bronwyn's having her baby?" She was alarmed. It was too soon.

"Water from the river refuses to go to the water tower. Headmaster sent me."

Her heart skipped a beat. "More sabotage?"

"No classes today."

"Does the kgosi know about you and Mpule?" She suspected not.

"Nnyaa." No.

"You will be a gentleman?"

"Ee, Teacher." He backed away, being polite.

She watched him leave. If his courtship of Mpule continued, he would make her a loving husband. No wife-beating for him, not in his character.

Mpule arrived to care for Sammy. Alicia put on her jeans and a cornflower-blue blouse. She combed her hair and left for the staff house. Eric's death robbed her of much, but the grief lessened. No more sudden crying jags or sobbing for no reason.

Outside the staff house, Mma Sethunya was at work. The wood fire underneath the cooking pot crackled and popped. The smoke stung Alicia's eyes.

"Dumela, Mma." Alicia noticed the woman's waist. Definitely pregnant. The cook bent over the pot at her waist, legs stiff, stirring the mealie-meal with a stick.

"The village women wish for a pipe with water," Mma Sethunya said. "When the river flows, it is easy work to gather water. When the rains stop, it is hard work for women digging in the sand. Water is heavy to carry. For me, life is easy."

"How is that?"

"School pays me to cook. My husband makes bricks to sell. Maybe he drinks too much. My cousin left her bad husband and has a sickly girl-child. I am troubled by her new man. She lives with me and gets the water. Soon, another child for me. Healthy, I am sure."

Alicia enjoyed the woman's optimistic attitude. She reminded her of Bronwyn. "How many children do you have?"

"Seven," Mma Sethunya said. "You can be lucky like me."

Alicia blushed. Mma Sethunya could not know about her fantasy of having a baby girl someday. With Jake?

In the distance, the headmaster moved among the students, reassuring them. Dereck had shut off the water supply to the farm and the student dormitories, conserving what water was left in the water tower. Dereck would send the remaining water to the standpipes near the student kitchen and the staff house. The headmaster had ordered Jake, Dereck, and Nigel to get the water flowing, whatever it took.

With hundreds of students, the school was chronically short of water. Today it was worse. Would the students be angry enough to riot?

☆ ☆ ☆

Alicia chatted with Ellie while she ate her breakfast. William walked in holding Geoff. Bronwyn was catching up on her sleep.

Alicia questioned whether the wedding would go ahead as planned. Between Fey and Mr. Anand, she had everything ready. But Bronwyn did as she pleased, always had done. Alicia could not assume that Bronwyn would show up to her own wedding.

Through the window, Alicia spotted Fey walking between the dormitories, searching for those who needed medical care. Some students were too sick or too shy to attend her clinic.

When Ellie reached across the table for the sugar, her shirt lifted. Long, bloody scratches covered Ellie's lower back. Alicia set her bowl and spoon aside, pretending a calmness she did not feel. Mick was hurting Ellie in new ways.

Dereck rattled up in his truck. Alicia went out to say hello, grateful to leave Ellie behind. Paul and Nigel sat in the truck's bed. When it stopped with a jerk, one side of the tailgate fell down.

"Damn, Mubayi," Dereck said. He got out and wired the tailgate back in place. "Every time he borrows the lorry, he finds a new way to damage it. It'll be weeks before I have a chance to turn a new hinge pin."

Mubayi often caused a ruckus. No one at the school respected him. Was he the saboteur as Ellie suggested? After talking to a number of people, Alicia could not find anyone who saw the saboteur at work. A phantom. Without any strangers around, the culprit was someone she knew, which saddened her.

Paul and Nigel climbed out of the truck, ignoring Dereck's ill humor. Alicia gave them a cheery greeting. Nigel came over, kissed her cheek, and walked into the staff house.

"Did they find the break in the water line?" Alicia asked Paul.

He smirked. "Much as it pains me to admit this, Jake spotted the break."

Nigel came out and studied the clouds. "Crikey, rain coming." He hopped back in the truck bed.

Dereck left but returned a few minutes later, irritated. "A leaky standpipe demands my attention. Paul, drive the lorry back to where they're laying the pipe, will you?"

Paul climbed in the driver's seat and slammed the door shut. On impulse, Alicia hopped in the passenger side.

Ellie stood in the doorway. Most days her hair framed a

placid face. Not today. Ellie scowled, her mouth pulled down at the corners.

Paul drove down the hill. "Fey got me medical textbooks so I can study for my return to school. I'm going back. Face it all."

"Proud of you." She patted his shoulder. "You'll be a doctor *toute suite.*"

He whispered, "Will you reconsider my proposal of marriage?"

"No. Please don't ask again."

They fell silent. Paul brought the truck to a stop. Nigel climbed over the tailgate, jumped down and called to Alicia. "Ta, love. Cheerio. You're me girl. After Corley, natch."

Alicia patted Paul's arm before she climbed out, but he did not respond.

The headmaster was watching as Jake and his footballers dug a trench. His chin showed stubble.

"Headmaster, who was here at the school's launch?" Alicia asked after they exchanged greetings.

The headmaster reeled off the names of the academic and vocational teachers who helped build the school and open it in 1968. Some of the buildings were still being constructed. Each person he mentioned wanted to build up the school not undermine it, she was certain. Actually, not completely certain.

"I am proud of our school, so different from the others," the headmaster said. "We do not punish students, have them bend over ninety degrees to be hit with a cane over and over. We do not let male teachers interfere with young girl students. Mubayi has these tendencies which anger me, yet I cannot fire him after…" His voice trailed off.

Alicia thought she heard him say, "after what he endured." She forged ahead with her questions. "Ellie followed a boyfriend here? The boyfriend left and she stayed?"

"Mick walked in the front gate like Jake. Skills we needed." He kicked the sand. "What person would cut the water line? The loss of one day's education is a terrible waste. An invisible ghost seeks to destroy our school, but who and why?"

"Headmaster, you inspire us with your wise counsel, except, of course, with respect to Mick and—"

Suddenly, the headmaster turned and walked away, loosening his tie.

A loosened tie? Stubble on his chin? Unbelievable.

The damage to the school went beyond the lack of water. What would the saboteur damage next? Everyone wondered about it. But the teachers also pondered whether they would be attacked in their beds by their own students.

Jake peered into the shallow trench, sweat glistening on his forehead. He had attached his canteen to a carabiner on a belt loop. His shirt was not tucked in, not his usual tidy self.

The footballers sang in Setswana as they put the new pipe in place. Without warning, Lepetu threw down his shovel, climbed from the trench, and stomped off. Mmegi set the shovel aside and continued working.

"Ignore Lepetu," Jake said. "He likes to gripe. We're all hot and tired, but Lepetu still feels abused by Mubayi. Will he do something rash?"

Alicia studied him. Even splattered with mud, Jake enticed her.

"The saboteur dug down half a meter to the pipe," he said, "smashed it with a chisel and hammer, and dragged brush to cover up the area. Nary a test hole. Knew exactly where it ran."

He moved closer to her. "I've been dealing with thorny bushes. Vicious thorns." He pointed to a deep scratch on his neck. "Need your healing touch."

She longed to kiss him, but this was not the place.

"All my footballers, except for Lepetu, are automatons, focused on the water line. Want to hear my leadership spiel?"

"Short, brief, pithy?"

"First, consideration. We treat each other with respect. Second, we create structure. We set goals. We break them into manageable parts. Each footballer has a role. When we work together, we win, though we might lose a match or two."

"Pithy, indeed."

"We'll have the pipe laid in a few minutes. We'll backfill the trench. At the dorm, the team will strip and check each other for ticks."

"I had tick-bite fever once," Alicia said. "Awful. Fey cured me."

"I'm feeling feverish." His eyes glowed. "Want to come to my hut and check me over for ticks. Save a life?"

"Worst pickup line ever!"

"Ticks! Think of the thrill. Sammy is with Mpule. What could stand in your way?"

She felt light enough to levitate. Did she want to be seduced by this man? His eyes looked mischievous. Tempting.

The deluge hit. The rain fell hard, replete with thunder and lightning. She waved goodbye to Jake and ran through the downpour. Mpule was competent, but Alicia wanted to check on her son's safety. Sammy came first.

30

The skies cleared later that night with an almost full moon. Jake and William met at the staff house at midnight. The night patrols had been disbanded, but the events of the day worried the two men.

Concerned about Alicia, his footballers, and his students, Jake had cancelled the weekend work with Pierce's trainees. Pierce would be displeased. So be it.

Jake shared lengths of heavy twine with William, then they scoured the compound together. He signaled to William when he found a pile of rocks.

"Let them throw a few rocks, do some damage," William whispered, "so they can't deny their intention."

"If their target is an uninhabited building, otherwise, we intervene."

Near the rock pile, they took up a position. At precisely two o'clock in the morning, eight young males appeared. Each student loaded rocks into a gunny sack. Without a word, the students walked toward the staff house. Jake and William followed them in silence.

As a volley of rocks hit the staff house windows, glass shattered, breaking the calm of the night.

William grabbed a student from behind, shouting, "Drop or die!"

Two students froze. Several turned back toward the dormitories. Jake ducked behind a tree. He tripped one student as he ran past him. The student screamed and fell to the sand. Jake trussed his hands and his feet together. The student fought hard, but Jake left him in the sand, sobbing and helpless.

Out of nowhere, someone raced past Jake toward the teachers' rondavels, carrying a bulky sack. He recognized Lepetu, the team's fastest runner.

The student ran toward the western perimeter fence. Jake closed the gap between them, but the student hurtled over bushes while Jake wove around them. He was not as fast as he was twelve years ago, when he was Lepetu's age of eighteen. The student slowed down a bit, seemingly unfamiliar with the terrain.

A light shone in Alicia's window like a beacon.

Jake swore as Lepetu veered toward her home. Broken glass could shatter into shards as sharp as razor blades. He had seen that kind of deadly carnage.

Lepetu turned and ran down the path to Alicia's rondavel. Jake detoured, cutting through the thorny brush to head off the student. Despite his sturdy clothes, the thorns cut through, raking his skin. A rock appeared in Lepetu's hand, shining in the moonlight. The student raised the rock over his head.

From the hill above Alicia's rondavel, Jake leapt. He landed on Lepetu's back. They slammed together against a wall with a loud thud. He whipped out the twine, forced Lepetu's arms behind his back and bound them. The student shouted obscenities as Jake pulled him to standing.

Alicia rounded the corner and shone her torch on them. She put her hand to her heart as Lepetu and Jake stood there, panting and bleeding.

31

On Friday morning, Alicia arrived at assembly before the headmaster. Early, for once. The teachers and students discussed the possible punishment for the rioters. Yesterday, Alicia had visited the headmaster at his home, but he had given her only a minute to express her opinion.

Glancing toward the front gate, she noticed a blue Dodge Dart. She was sure this was the Kukama taxi, one of the few cars in the village. When the headmaster arrived, he was carrying a low folding chair made of wood with a seat made of interwoven rawhide strips. The elderly man with him sat down on the chair. With an air of solemnity, he surveyed the throng of students and teachers.

Was he the kgosi, Mpule's grandfather?

Jake showed up and touched her arm. "Ready for the big announcement?" She shrugged, unsure of what would happen.

The headmaster cleared his throat, and the assembly quieted. "Our kgosi has graced us with his presence." The elderly man raised a hand in greeting. The crowd murmured a polite response. Elders deserved respect.

"After a discussion," the headmaster said, "we have decided that those who brought violence to our school will *not* be expelled. Another punishment has been selected." Jake tensed up beside her. The audience buzzed with the news.

Jake whispered to Alicia. "He put you and Sammy in serious danger."

The headmaster went on. "The footballers have voted Lepetu off their team."

She wrinkled her brow, surprised at the news. Jake had not told her.

The headmaster continued to speak but few listened to him. Lepetu was off the team. All had reveled in the success of their celebrated striker. When the headmaster dismissed the assembly and left with the kgosi, the cacophony of voices grew louder.

"Lepetu needs real consequences for his reckless behavior," Jake said. "He's headed for more trouble."

"No other secondary school would take them with such a black mark on their permanent record," she said, relieved at the decision. "What about employers? This could follow him for years. Getting voted off the team must be a huge blow to him."

"No sympathy from me. Lepetu is obsessed with his grievances. What will it take for him to grow up?"

"You look ready to detonate, Jake. You stopped him from harming us, for which I am grateful. I know it cost you. Thank you."

His demeanor softened. "The headmaster asked us to visit his office today at one o'clock. Can you make it?"

The kgosi's appearance might mean an answer to her request for Mbengawa's surgery. Mbengawa was falling behind in class. She hoped the answer was a positive one.

32

Clang, Clang, Clang. A prefect walked between the classrooms ringing the school bell. Mubayi hovered behind the prefect, directing students to move with haste to their classrooms.

Alicia entered her First Form class. The students took time settling down. They were eager to talk about Lepetu. What did his disgrace mean for winning at football? With all the excitement, the students needed a break from their regular lessons. She set her sheaf of papers on the teacher's desk and faced the class.

"Come and talk with me, when you have any concerns. If I can, I will help."

Kxoma sat at the back. He was still in school, thanks to Jake. The desks of the two girls she suspected of pregnancies were empty. School policy.

"Today, we have a treat," Alicia said, disappointed but determined to sound optimistic. "Our own Thale will recite one of her poems for you. Are you ready, Thale?"

The student got up and walked to the front of the classroom.

Several times in private, Alicia had met with her to make suggestions about incorporating gestures into her performance. Thale glowed, looking self-confident.

"My Work Song," Thale said. She began reciting her poem.

Ee! Ee!
Pull your long staff
down upon the corn.
Crush the grain
to mealie flour.
Take turns, girls.
One, two, one, two.
Pull your long staff down
upon the corn.

She emphasized the short, steady rhythm.

Ee! Ee!
Mma will thank you
now, if you do well.
Take turns, girls, hear
the singing wood.
One more pounding.
Set milk aside to sour.
Mma will thank you
now, if you do well.

Her voice exulted in the simple clarity of the lyrics.

Ee! Ee!
Stir the iron pot
upon the fire.
Boil until the porridge
speaks and says,
'I am thick and hot.'
Stir the iron pot
upon the fire.
Mealie pap nice.

As the class cheered, Thale walked back to her seat, beaming. Alicia shushed them. Mubayi was walking around, and he would be angry at any noise, especially with the kgosi visiting the school.

With Thale's permission, Alicia had sent several of her poems to *Kutlwano,* the national magazine, as well as to several student-run anthologies in the U.S. Published poems might interest an admissions officer at a university, maybe garner a scholarship.

"Class, I mimeographed Thale's poem for you." Alicia picked up the papers from her desk and handed them to Negotho. He received them with both hands, a slight bow, and passed out the papers.

Alicia glanced at Mbengawa who eagerly accepted the mimeographed pages. Could he read the words through the white substance over his eyes? She wondered if the kgosi would have an answer about the proposed operation. Her heart beat faster.

"Class, on the handout, I included a few short poems by other African poets. We'll talk tomorrow about the techniques

Thale used in her poetry. Think about meter and metaphor. Your assignment is to write your *own* poem."

Most of the students looked skeptical. Thale and Kxoma grinned.

Alicia arrived at the headmaster's office before one o'clock, feeling apprehensive. The office was in a small rectangular building with a corrugated metal roof, much hotter than the thatched-roof huts. She found Mrs. Linchwe busy typing at her desk, ruling over her domain, dwarfed by the wooden filing cabinets around her. Dressed impeccably in a navy skirt and white blouse, the secretary peered over her eyeglasses at the intrusion. She worked unperturbed in the heat though her face and neck had a sheen of sweat.

Alicia greeted her, and they chatted for a few minutes. At a nod of approval from Mrs. Linchwe, she knocked on the door of Mr. Matlagodi's office. She heard him say, "Tsena."

She opened the door and walked in, leaving the door ajar so Mrs. Linchwe could listen. She found Mr. Matlagodi, Kgosi Monyame, and Jake seated on the three chairs in the room.

She curtsied. This was a royal audience.

Jake stood up and offered her his seat, but the headmaster coughed and signaled him to sit down. Chairs were for men. Jake sat down looking apologetic. If a man wanted the chair in which a woman sat, he would stand beside the woman until she moved down to the sand, even if she had a broken leg. Alicia did not like that custom, and she didn't like Jake at that moment, but the man was trying to adhere to a local custom.

"Mrs. Talbot," the headmaster began, "the parents of Mbengawa decline to have his eyes cut."

Her heart sank; nevertheless, she replied with politeness. "Ee, sir."

The kgosi began speaking to her in Setswana. Mr. Matlagodi translated. "Sammy must visit me often."

"I am happy to have Sammy to visit you." She addressed the kgosi, certain he understood English. "I was saddened to learn of the deaths of your son and daughter-in-law."

The elderly man spoke again in Setswana, and the headmaster translated.

"The British and their hut tax caused the death of my son, Kitsitso." Tears glistened in his eyes. "Before the tax, we feared the Boers with their big guns who stole our land. But we traded among tribes, and did not need money. Now our young men go to the gold mines in South Africa to earn cash, pay the tax. The Boers leave us alone, but our men die when the rocks fall on them."

Then he spoke in English. "Kitsitso will never take my place as kgosi."

Mr. Matlagodi shifted in his seat. "Mrs. Talbot, we have more to discuss. In private." He gestured for her to leave.

"Ke itumetse."

Alicia curtsied and backed up to the door, turned and left with all the dignity she could muster. She returned to the bright sunshine with her hopes for Mbengawa dashed. She listened to the chatter of weaver birds in the thorn trees and reviewed her other plans. Some of them might be successful, but which ones had the best chance?

33

Alicia's committee met at the staff house later that afternoon. She sat at the table with Ndona, Kgeledi, Gaeyo, Fey as well as William, who made a rare appearance. The headmaster did not attend, as usual, wanting only to be informed of their successes. He made it plain he considered the rioting a failure of the committee, which was unfair and unlike him.

"Lepetu was the ringleader," Kgeledi said. "He insisted students from his village join him. The students did not share this with me, although I am their leader." He all but hung his head. The committee agreed that nine rioters out of six hundred students did not indicate widespread discontentment. The violence of a few was troubling though.

Alicia asked the students about Mrs. Mbeki, the newly hired food supervisor for the student kitchen. Both student leaders agreed that the current food was acceptable. No worms had been found in the new mealie-meal.

Gaeyo reported that Mrs. Linchwe ordered the replacement

mattresses through Mr. Anand. They would arrive soon, a rush order done as a favor for one of his best customers. Gaeyo wore a short-sleeved blouse. From time to time, she stroked her prosthetic arm as if to assure herself it was there.

Fey reported on medical care, especially important to Gaeyo. Gaeyo said that even simple problems like repairing a pair of broken eyeglass frames required a day-long trip to Gabs, usually by hitchhiking. The train was too expensive.

"Cases such as severe diarrhea I send to the clinic in the village," Fey said. "Dereck will drive those with serious illnesses to Francistown, but I must twist his arm. Keeps an eagle eye on his budget."

"That lazy matron should be fired," Gaeyo said with a stomp of her foot. "She will not care for ill students."

"Matron is a relative of the headmaster," Kgeledi said. "Why irritate the headmaster with a request we know is certain to be denied?"

Gaeyo shrugged. "Because of this committee a good thing happened. Matron no longer warns students to stay away from Miss Oakes." She looked over at Fey who nodded in response.

Before the meeting ended, they congratulated each other. Things had improved.

As Alicia walked home, she wondered if there was enough progress to satisfy the students. Jake had promised her another trip into the wilderness. Even with all the problems, she looked forward to being with him. But he was still a mystery. Who was he, really?

☆ ☆ ☆

Alicia and Sammy stood in their doorway and waved goodbye to Mpule as she left for the village. Shutting the door, Alicia said, "Time for a nap."

"Nnyaa. Not sleepy." He jerked his head left and right, quite emphatic.

"We'll lie down for a few minutes. Will you lock the door for me?"

The boy went from belligerence to affability with blinding speed.

"Ee, Mma." On tiptoes, he tried to turn the key in the lock, but he couldn't quite make it turn.

"Not do," he said.

She finished locking the door. They laid down on a cot together, but neither could sleep. Sammy climbed out of bed and zipped over to his toy box. He pulled out a truck, and started rolling it around.

"Ko Ko?" A woman's voice outside sounded faint and hesitant.

When Alicia opened the door, Ellie stood there, dabbing her eyes with a lacy handkerchief. She blurted, "I may be…I think… I'm pregnant."

Alicia swallowed hard. Ellie was with child.

Tears ran down the woman's cheeks. "Mick might be angry when I tell him. Will you come with me? If you're there, he… he…he won't—"

"I'll put the kettle on." Alicia opened the door wide.

As Ellie walked inside, Alicia called to her son. "Can you give Ellie a little love?"

Sammy went to Ellie, patting her arm. "There, there, my sweet one."

Ellie bent down, hugged him and sobbed.

Alicia held Sammy's hand as they walked with Ellie to her home. A snake flashed onto the path before them, then disappeared into the bushes. Adrenaline flooded her body. She didn't recognize the markings, but the snake was not a harmless garter snake like the ones she knew in Seattle.

Around the school, snakes sunned themselves on the tops of low walls. A black mamba bit a villager recently. One morning, the man turned over a rock, and the snake attacked him. By that afternoon, he was dead.

A slight breeze eased the overwhelming heat of the day. The goats and cows stood under the trees, escaping the sun. The tiny bells around the necks of goats tinkled. The larger bells around the necks of cows clanked, loud and harsh.

At Bronwyn's, Sammy pounded on the door before Alicia could stop him.

"Tsena." Bronwyn sounded tired, not her usual chipper self.

"Wait a minute, Ellie." Alicia opened the door and went in with Sammy. She closed the door behind them.

Bronwyn sat in her chair, looking drained of life. Geoff was leaning against his mother. Sammy ran toward the toy box, and Geoff joined him. Within a few seconds, the two boys were jabbering to each other, deep in play.

"Knackered. No sex," Bronwyn exclaimed, sounding frustrated. She studied Alicia. "You worried, ducky? More sabotage?"

"Ellie told me she's pregnant. She wants me with her when she tells Mick. Could Sammy stay here?"

"Crikey, bad luck for her. Me? William wants a squad of squirts." She gave Alicia a weary smile. "Forget about Ellie, it's double-dodgy. Mick hates you, plain and simple. Why toss boiling oil on snow? Ka-boom."

"I promised Ellie." Where was Bronwyn's grandiose sense of optimism?

"Let William or Jake contend with Mick—someone who hits back."

Alicia gave Bronwyn a kiss on her cheek. "Gotta go."

"I'll watch from the stoop." Bronwyn got up slowly.

Alicia opened the door and stepped down on the sand. Bronwyn walked to the doorway and glared at Ellie. "I would tell you to bugger off."

Ellie flicked out her tongue, shoving her handkerchief into a pocket.

"I'll keep watch over you both," Bronwyn said, squinting in the sunlight.

Alicia squared her shoulders. "All right, Ellie, let's go."

Walking next door, Alicia saw Mick through the open door writing in a notebook. He sat at the table dressed in black shorts and a gray T-shirt, his long hair tied back with a leather thong. Under his knife-thin nose, his beard and mustache had been trimmed with care. Cigarette butts overflowed the ashtray.

"If it isn't Minnie Mouse and Daffy Duck," Mick said. "Minnie, this place is a mess. Get in here and do some work. You're not welcome here, Daffy. Do us all a favor, and go play with crocodiles in the Okavango."

Ellie whimpered as Mick fiddled with his biro. When he turned over the notebook, an orange business card fell out. He grabbed it off the floor and put it back in the notebook. He took the last cigarette from a gold-colored box and lit it. Alicia noticed it was Dereck's brand.

The smoke rose into the rafters. He squeezed the small box and tossed it toward a waste can. He missed. Geckos ran across the walls. At the windows, the curtains hung limp. The rondavel smelled of stale air.

Ellie moved behind Alicia. "I need to tell you something, Mick." Close to inaudible, she said, "I'm pregnant."

"Pregnant? Is it mine?"

Ellie gasped.

He moved to the threshold of the door, putting his notebook in his pocket. "You'll have to pay for your own abortion," he said without emotion.

Ellie cringed. "I want a child."

Mick scoffed. "Doesn't matter. My screwed-up father left me scars to remember him by. Won't pass that on."

"She's miles away from a safe abortion," Alicia said.

"*She* is miles from a safe abortion, not *me*. Being young and poor is okay, but being old and poor? Won't happen. No one gets in my way, not women and not children. That child of yours, Alicia, should be put down like a rabid dog. His chatter at dinner ruins my appetite."

Alicia felt as if she had been struck. He talked casually about hurting Sammy, a two-year-old child.

Mick pushed past the women. He went to his truck and climbed in. Why did he need such a big truck?

Mick gunned the engine and backed out. He drove toward the front gate, shouted to a student to open it, and drove out without a word of thanks. He accelerated down the dirt track, leaving a dust cloud behind him.

Ellie clung to Alicia's arm. "I'm like a puppy. He's nice to me, and I brighten up. When I irritate him, he ignores me for days until I beg for forgiveness." She started to cry. "What if he doesn't come back?"

Alicia folded her arms. "Decide what's best. The school owes you an airfare for each year of teaching. You've been here for a long time. Talk to the headmaster. Leave here, forget him. You can do better." How did Ellie endure him?

"What if the headmaster won't help me?" Ellie wailed. "Mick doesn't like me to have friends. Says he should be enough."

"You rented your rondavel. If you won't leave the school, let him find other living quarters. William and Jake have no fear of Mick." She touched Ellie's shoulder. "They will help you."

Ellie hiccuped. "I'm tied to him with an invisible thread."

"Don't let him stop you from accomplishing what you want in life."

"Is he doing that?" Ellie asked. "Sometimes, he makes me feel beautiful and smart. Cherished, even. Can you understand?"

34

Alicia watered the plants in her courtyard with water left over from washing clothes. Her clothes were drying on a rope tied between two trees. She was walking over to watch Sammy play in his sandbox when she heard the crunch of sand. Jake came into sight, his daypack on his back. His plaid shirt was red and gold.

Unsmiling, he came up to her and put his hands on her shoulders.

"In confronting Mick, you took a big risk. Why would you do that?"

She backed up until he released her. "Ellie needed help."

"You believe folks are virtuous underneath their crusty exterior. Not always." His voice was intense, his eyes fixed on her.

"I'm tolerant. True. I'm not ashamed of it." She did not need a lecture.

"I knew men in Vietnam who injured or killed their fellow soldiers. If they figured an officer would get them killed, they would throw a grenade in his tent at night. Men would snap over innocuous things, like being told to turn down a radio."

She took another step back, eyes growing wider.

"'Fragging,' it's called. I don't want you fragged. If Ellie wants help, send her to me. I'm trained to subdue violent people. Face facts. You could not repel an assault."

She shivered. Mick had spoken to her with such venom, his eyes malevolent.

"He threatened Sammy. I didn't expect that."

Jake opened his pack. "I brought your Colt as well as a flare gun. I cleaned them both and brought a cleaning kit. You've cleaned a handgun before, right?"

"Eric taught me." She remembered the scent of the cleaning oil.

"I'll put the gear on the top shelf of your closet. Sammy can't climb up there. You are well-trained in your weapon. If Mick attacks, defend yourself." He went into her home without waiting for a response.

Sammy ran to his mother and put his arms around her legs. She pulled him up, settling him on her hip. Was he responding to the urgency in Jake's voice? She kissed Sammy, soothing him in a quiet voice. Her son calmed down, and he went back to his toys.

When Jake returned, he snapped off a blossom from a honeysuckle vine and tucked it behind her ear. "You're as fragile as this blossom. As lovely, too. You do not recognize danger. Mpule told me you didn't kill a large spider hanging from a rafter. You wanted to, 'Live and let live.' Mpule banged it between two metal cups. Killed it. Rightly so."

Alicia put a hand over her eyes, inhaling the scent of the bloom.

"Mpule understands that a spider bites to defend itself," Jake said, "nothing personal, but it's dangerous. Some spider bites make your flesh rot away. With Mick, it's personal *and* dangerous."

She spoke in a rush. "I cannot find the balance between fearing real danger like snakes and ignoring real danger like Mick." She paused. "I'll consult you before I confront anyone else, but you can spare me the condescension. I'm twenty-five years old, not two."

"Your two-year-old son has more common sense than you showed today." He spoke slowly, emphasizing each word.

"Stop. Back off!" She glared at him, irritated because his words stung, and he was probably right. "You're not my father."

"If your father were here, he would be worried."

Sammy started shouting, crashing all his toys together in a toy-land apocalypse. Was he feeling the tension?

She heard someone running down the path beside her house. What was coming next?

☆ ☆ ☆

The runner, a young boy from the village, left after giving Jake a message. The kgosi invited him to visit that evening and listen to the villagers practicing for a choral competition. As a bonus, Kxoma would tell a story.

"Please come with me to hear our favorite tracker," Jake said. "Sammy, too. Okay?"

She cocked her head. "Sammy would love it."

Jake cracked his knuckles. "Don't forget we're going into the desert tomorrow. It's not a long drive, so we don't have to leave early. Short day."

“Speaking of forgetting, you won’t forget our wedding, will you?”

“Forget *our* wedding? No chance.” He smiled. “William and Bronwyn agreed to marry in what was the world’s most-crooked coin toss. William asked me to be the best man. Are you the best woman?”

“We call it Matron of Honor.”

“Mr. Anand promised to import some snazzy threads for me. Fair warning. In a suit, I’m sizzling—Fred Astaire levels of debonair. Major masculine preening. Prepare to be dazzled.”

She needed his sense of humor after the confrontation with Mick.

“Mr. Anand will pick out my tie,” Jake said. “I loathe ties, too constricting.” He put his hands around his neck and pretended to choke himself. He added more and more sound effects until she laughed. Any discomfort she held slipped away.

Sammy sat on Alicia’s lap and shrieked whenever they hit a bump on the washboard road to the village. Jake, driving, casually slung an arm over her shoulders. That was new, and she liked the feel of his body even in the heat. The small metal caps on the tops of the conical thatched roofs shone in the light of the moon. Jake parked by the kraal at the kgosi’s compound, the only vehicle around.

She got out and set Sammy down. He ran to the entrance of the kraal which was surrounded by dead tree limbs to keep the animals in and the predators out. One cow moved close enough for the boy to stroke its nose. A Batswana saying came to mind: A cow is a god with a soft nose.

Jake appeared at ease, one of his talents. He adjusted to any situation without hesitation. Alicia knew that he visited the kgosi whenever possible. Their bond sprung from their first meeting.

Above the animal and insect sounds, she heard villagers singing and clapping percussively. She recognized the national anthem, sung in multi-part harmony. The anthem was about unity, harmony, and peace, Botswana's stated values, not always lived up to, but aspirational like "life, liberty, and the pursuit of happiness."

Jake picked up Sammy and opened the gate. They went in. As they approached the bonfire, a man threw on a log and sparks flew up. Fire was considered the essence of life.

Jake introduced Alicia to the woman who approached them. The kgosi's wife, Mma Kitsitso, wore a long dress with an orange shawl around her shoulders. A cloth scarf covered her head. The woman displayed a quiet dignity. She would not tolerate any wife-beating, Alicia felt sure about that.

The kgosi sat in his special chair near the fire with an empty chair beside him. The singers, finished with their anthem, chatted with each other. Except for a few men who sat on chairs, everyone else sat on the sand.

When Sammy saw the kgosi, he struggled to get down. The boy ran to the chief who lifted him onto his lap. Their differing ages were not an obstacle. The kgosi beckoned Jake to sit on the chair beside him. Alicia assumed this was a place of honor. Mpule beckoned her to sit on the sand next to her with the other women. Alicia could watch Sammy from where she sat.

Alicia hugged her knees, fanning the smoke away from her eyes. She inhaled the scent of the burning wood. The Milky Way looked like someone had kicked over a bucket of white paint. Insects kept up their song in concert with the lowing of cattle and the occasional bleating of goats.

Kxoma stood on the periphery of the gathering, around twenty villagers. When the kgosi clapped his hands, conversation stopped, and Kxoma began to tell his story. He spoke in Setswana, not his click language. All watched him with rapt attention. Mpule whispered a translation to Alicia.

"Zebra is thirsty. He wants water. Baboon guards the water hole. He refuses to share the water."

Kxoma pantomimed the animals arguing. First, he pretended he was the greedy Baboon who strutted around. Then, he was the enraged Zebra who reared and snorted.

Kxoma, as the Zebra, pantomimed a great kick.

"Zebra kicks Baboon hard-hard," Mpule said. "Baboon lands on his bottom."

The audience cheered the zebra. The breeze shifted, and smoke floated straight up instead of into Alicia's watering eyes.

"Big kick of Zebra makes Zebra stumble."

Kxoma staggered around, almost falling into the bonfire.

"Zebra fell into the fire. Burned his fur," Mpule said.

Alicia didn't need Mpule to explain what happened next. The Baboon discovered to his horror that his rump was bare, all the fur gone. This discovery delighted the audience. Zebra, in turn, discovered black stripes in her fur from falling in the fire. The moral? Share what you have. Don't be a greedy baboon who denied water to a zebra. Zebra showed her anger in public. Wrong! Don't be an angry zebra.

The villagers applauded Kxoma, who bowed and left the

circle. The group began singing again. One woman's soprano voice soared, pure and clear.

Sammy fell asleep on the kgosi's lap. Alicia threw a pebble at Jake's boot. When he turned toward her, she pointed to Sammy and mouthed, "Time to go."

Riding home, she listened to the villagers' singing fade away. Her son snored quietly on her lap. As Jake drove, she sat close beside him. After Eric's death, she had not expected to have this feeling again. Joy.

35

The next morning, Jake drove with Alicia to an ancient grove of baobabs close to a kopje he wanted to explore. Sammy stayed with William and Bronwyn. One of Hannah's whistles hung on a string around Alicia's neck, more useful than a necklace.

At the grove, Jake examined a tall baobab with an enormous trunk. Limbs protruded from the top of the tree, with tiny twigs covered with green leaves. An oblong fruit hung from the twigs.

"What do baobabs tell us, Tenderfoot?" He was in professor mode.

"You tell me, Prof."

"Baobabs tell us bedrock lies near the surface. They only grow where they can access water and anchor their roots on rock."

"What? They access water through bedrock?"

"Water comes up along cracks in bedrock. Maybe there's a fault here. Baobabs have nutritious fruits and leaves. Remember the glacial speed at which continents move? Baobabs grow as slowly and live for hundreds or even a few thousand years, like the bristlecone pines in California."

Alicia recalled a trip with her parents and sister to the White Mountains of eastern California. The bristlecone pines grew above nine thousand feet, their gnarled trunks gray with age. She remembered touching the rough bark, astonished at their eons of life.

Jake snapped his fingers. "Want to see a magic trick?"

He pulled up his pant leg and took his knife from its sheath. He extracted a small, rectangular block from one of his pockets and held both of them up.

"Note the steel blade of my knife? Note the black block?"

Alicia watched, wondering what would come next.

"Magnesium on one side, flint on the other." He squatted down in the sand and pulled a few dry leaves from the underbrush.

"Scrape the steel blade on the magnesium side and make a mound of shavings. Next, strike the steel blade of the knife to the flint side."

A spark ignited the shavings; she drew back, surprised by the white-hot flame. She gathered dry twigs and put them on the small blaze. Jake fed the fire with a few larger sticks.

Without warning, he stomped out the fire. "Your turn."

She knelt with him beside her. The combined scent of leather, smoke, and the earth made her stomach quiver. She followed his instructions, and, after a few minutes, she, too, made fire blossom in the sand.

☆ ☆ ☆

With her handgun, Alicia shot down every target Jake set up. They stood by a fever tree with its yellow blooms. Early settlers in southern Africa thought the tree spread malaria, hence its name.

"You're a good marksman," he said. "Was Eric a hunter?"

"Growing up poor, he put venison on the family's table. Eric made his own way in life."

Jake knelt and studied some tracks. "See the outline of a lion's pad and the sharp indentations of nails?"

Alicia shuddered.

"The tracks might be old," he said. Take a gander up in that fever tree. What do you see?"

As she inspected the tree, a chill ran through her. A snake sat coiled in the crotch.

"Some snakes climb trees," he said. "With all the leaves, I can't be sure of the number of snakes in the tree." He pulled his binoculars from his pack and surveyed the tree.

"One snake. Black or green mamba, can't tell. You might have to kill a snake to identify it. Identify the snake with precision as the wrong anti-venom could kill you. I don't have an anti-venom kit yet, so we'll be ultra-cautious."

Jake picked up a long, forked stick from the ground.

"If you encounter a snake in a tree or on the ground, use a stick to move it away. In a pinch, use your knife, but estimate their strike zone. They can bite you in an instant. If you kill a venomous snake, the fangs remain deadly. Cut off the head and bury it."

Alicia backed farther away from the tree. No sense in giving the snake any ideas.

"You'll be on guard duty while I examine this kopje. I'll imagine you're Princess Diana of Themyscira—Wonder Woman. Excellent benefits come with your job."

She imagined herself in the skimpy blue, white, and red Wonder Woman costume. "Do I get an invisible plane? A lasso of truth?"

He waggled his eyebrows up and down in a Groucho Marx imitation. "Better. You get *me*."

☆ ☆ ☆

Alicia stood near the edge of a ruined termite tower as Jake explored the kopje. She unholstered her pistol, slapped in a magazine, and jacked a round into the chamber like Eric had taught her.

All around, insects hummed and birds sang. Hares hopped by as she kept watch.

She wore a broad-brimmed hat to protect her face, but the sun bore down hard. She carried Jake's pack on her back and her own in front. She moved around, following him as he took rock samples with a chisel. He examined them with a small magnifying glass and made notations in his book. Trickles of sweat ran down her back as she walked from high point to high point. The grasses grew all the way up to the giant boulders of the kopje.

A movement caught her eye. Something was moving fast, blending in with the golden browns of the grasses. She stopped breathing.

A lioness ran toward Jake.

She put her whistle in her mouth and blew, keeping her eyes fixed on the lioness. She dropped the packs and raised her pistol. She would need that "well-placed shot."

The lioness focused on Jake, her movements fluid. Alicia spread her legs apart and used both hands to hold the pistol. Her throat constricted; her hands were sweaty. She tried to lead the moving target, but the lioness went in and out of sight among the bushes then vanished.

Alicia took a breath. A moment later, the lioness emerged again, now it was headed for *her.*

No choice but to kill the magnificent creature, no room for error. The lioness was in her sights. Alicia was ready, finger on the trigger, when the lioness vanished again.

She maintained her stance. The lioness might emerge close to her, hidden by the tall grasses. A whistle shrieked, but it was not hers. Jake came up beside her and pressed her hands down so the pistol pointed to the sand.

Her heart raced. "Where is she?"

"Breathe."

She scanned the area. Were there six or seven lions, other members of a pride, surrounding them? Would they be ripped to shreds?

"Put the safety on, holster it. We leave *now.*"

When he said they must march double-time, she did not protest. As she walked in front of him, she heard him repeating his mantra. "Stay calm. Stay alert."

Reaching the Land Rover, she stowed her gear and sat down in the passenger seat. Jake climbed in the driver's seat. Hot and sweaty, she turned to him and went into his embrace.

"You're safe," he said.

Tears came to her eyes. "I didn't want to kill her, but I didn't want to die."

"The wilderness doesn't care. The lioness acted in character, and you did, too. Character is destiny."

She started to tremble. "The fear just caught up with me."

"I saved your life on the water tower. You saved mine. No more near misses. Let's call it a draw."

36

On Sunday night, Jake drove through the school gates under a full moon. He was returning from the large kopje he had identified on the flight from Francistown. He named it "Vulture Kopje" for the Cape Vultures gathered there, their wingspan over eight feet. He felt he had peered into the Late Jurassic age.

A flat tire had slowed him down.

"Murphy's Law. Anything that can go wrong will go wrong, does go wrong. Count on it."

Parking his Land Rover, he noticed a Jeep next to Fey's hut. A dim light shone from her curtained window. Pierce and Fey had become the couple Jake foresaw on their first meeting.

Loud music blasted from the staff house. Paul stumbled out the front door, bouncing off the door jamb. He lurched onto the path in front of Jake.

Jake touched Paul's arm. "Sharp teeth threaten. May I help you?"

Paul slurred his words. "She dances with other men. Can't take it anymore. Do me a favor, Soldier-Boy. Execute me." He burped. "Oh, sorry. Alicia insists I play nice with you, so *excuuuuuse* me."

The stones along the path glowed in the moonlight. When they reached Paul's home, the door stood wide open.

Jake shone his torch on the medical textbooks piled on the table. He shook out the blankets on the cot, and a scorpion fell out. He knocked it to the floor, crushed it, and kicked it away.

"Scorpion nursery," he said with disgust.

Paul collapsed on the cot. Jake pulled off the man's shoes, set them down. He was about to leave, but turned back.

"Alicia says medicine is your first love. We're desperate for another science teacher. You could start teaching science in addition to your English classes, unless you prefer your stupor."

Paul moaned. "My loves are wine, beer, vodka, and gin. Not picky." He went limp.

"You've been in the villages. Fever, glaucoma, rotten teeth, mental illness, disabilities, deformities. Cleft palates, even. You are needed."

Paul came back to life, pounding his pillow. "Don't shout at me, buddy boy. No one can call *me* a mass murderer."

Jake maintained his control. "You rail against the war in Vietnam as if it were an abstraction. I saw men die there who were desperate to live. You're alive, but you want to drink yourself to death. Face your demons. Grow up."

Jake took the key from inside the door and stepped out, preparing to lock Paul in. "I bet I can make it back to Alicia before you pass out." Maybe he could goad the man into making a change.

"Cruel, man. Cruel." Paul started cursing Jake, the war, the FBI, and all those who wronged him, including his brother and his late parents.

But before Jake closed the door, Paul yelled. "Wait! Wait! Come back. If I got sober..."

"Is this a trick? Are you going to throw your shoe at me?"

Paul tried but failed to sit up. "I will shake off the Dark Lady. I'll go cold turkey. Take all the booze from my refrigerator. Maybe Alicia will love me then."

"Kiss the booze adios, amigo." Jake opened the refrigerator, pulled out the bottles of beer and put them in the empty box sitting beside the cylinder. He added the liqueurs and hard liquor from a shelf. Cointreau, Johnny Walker Black, and two single malts with unpronounceable names, among others. Paul had assembled a full bar in the middle of nowhere.

"The staff will drink this all tonight. Sweet dreams."

No answer.

Outside, Jake locked the door and shoved the key under it. He headed toward the staff house with the booze, eager to dance with Alicia.

"Does she adore me yet? Doubtful. But as Mom says, 'If at first you don't succeed, try, try again.' And if I didn't hate needles so much, I would tattoo that on my tush."

Through a haze of cigarette smoke, Alicia saw Jake come into the staff house. She was slow dancing with Ndona and caught the flicker of anger on Ndona's face as Jake came toward them.

When Jake touched her shoulder, she moved into his arms. Ndona backed away with a snort of exasperation.

Jake pulled Alicia to him. "I learned my lesson at the last dance. I'm keeping my hands on you. You can disappear faster than a hummingbird."

Nigel was playing "Stand by Me" by Ben E. King. Jake sang along.

She looked up at him. "You said you would be here earlier. What held you up?"

He stiffened. "You're not my C.O. Don't interrogate me. I did too much kowtowing in the Army."

She stopped dancing. "Don't speak to me like that." Slipping out of his grasp, she headed for the door.

He caught up with her, touching her back. She turned and faced him. "Well?"

"I apologize. I did promise to return earlier. Flat tire. When I got back, I made a detour to help Paul get to bed."

She relented a bit. "Thanks for taking care of him. I worried about you after yesterday's brush with the lioness."

He double-tapped his forehead. "Brain transplant required. I got testy. Forgive me? Let's restart our evening, pretty please, with sugar on top?"

"Does that really work with women?"

He held out his hands, and she touched them tentatively, looking into his eyes. After a few moments, she went back into his arms. They held each other, still and silent. The melodic voices of Peter, Paul and Mary sang "The First Time Ever I Saw Your Face."

Jake brushed back her hair. "The first time I saw you, you smiled at me and waved hello. Your dress was the blue of a robin's egg. All at once, I felt excited about life again, about living. I had lost that." He covered her right hand with his, and pressed it to his chest. "I could not wait to meet you, touch you."

She reached up and stroked his cheek. The sounds of the room faded.

"We kissed for the first time in the wilderness," he said. "Remember?"

She smiled at the memory.

He pulled her closer, and they began to move to the music. "Long time coming," he said. "Long, long time coming,"

As his arms tightened around her, she felt a shift inside. Alicia heard him call to her without words. Something beautiful beckoned her. Streams of cool water flowed through all her dry and dusty places. She did not believe this was possible. Could she be falling in love in this place full of danger? She grabbed the collar of his shirt, crumpling it in her hand.

This enigmatic man was courting her. Step by step, he was becoming an essential part of her life. Was she betraying Eric, or was it the natural progression of healing, of life moving forward?

As he held her, she smelled the earth after a hard rain and slumped against him. Time lost its meaning; she was unmoored, cast adrift.

Jake murmured, "Let's leave."

He led her through the crowd. Outside, they ran hand in hand down the path to her rondavel. Sammy was asleep on his cot. Alicia sent Mpule and Glorianna home to the village with a torch.

"Shall I move Sammy to the Lizard Lounge?" Jake asked.

"He should sleep for hours." She held up a hand to stop him. "Are you prepared?"

His eyes were all smiles. "Eagle Scout."

Jake settled Sammy in the Lizard Lounge and returned to the larger room, closing the door behind him. Alicia stood at the window in the dark, gazing at the full moon. Her nude body glowed in the moonlight. The soft light flowed over her face, her breasts, her legs.

He reached her in two strides. Standing behind her, he caressed her body. As he touched her belly, she put her hands over his. He moved her hair aside with his chin and kissed the nape of her neck. He kissed every vertebra in her spine.

He took off his boots before he pulled her to a cot. She lost herself in a swirl of taste, touch, and scent.

Alicia yearned for him, which astonished her. Years ago, Eric had walked down the corridor to board the plane for Vietnam. Halfway down the ramp, he turned back. She could read his lips, but the din in the airport erased the sound. "I love you," he said. Her knees buckled, and she sank to the floor. She lay there as his parents tried to rouse her. She was pregnant but did not know it yet. How could she ever want a man other than Eric?

And yet…

She ran her fingers through Jake's hair. She had wanted to do that for some time. His hands, insistent and strong, explored her. Her breathing accelerated. Blood pounded in her ears.

The buttons on his shirt pressed into her breast. She came out of her dream. "Your clothes. Take them off."

He pulled away from her and started to get off the cot. "I cannot do this."

She gripped his arm. "Why not?"

"My war injuries left scars, ugly scars. Kath reacted with horror. I couldn't survive if you did the same."

He took a deep breath. "I have conquered fears my entire life, but I cannot conquer this one." He tried to stand up, but she tightened her grip on his arm, pulling him back.

"If you have scars, they're signs of triumph."

He shook his head. "I scream at night sometimes. Night terrors."

"You told me that you felt fear sometimes, but you never panicked. Tell me again, what does panic do?"

"Makes you stupid."

"Will your scars get in my way? I brought my two-year-old son to Africa. That's the kind of risk I'm willing to take."

He looked at her in silence.

"Your shirt. Take it off." This time, she was giving *him* an order.

With his eyes fixed on hers, he unbuttoned his shirt and pulled it off. He unbuckled his belt and took off his trousers and shorts. In the moonlight, she saw that the scars were extensive. This was what he hid with his trousers and long-sleeved shirts.

When she touched his bare shoulder, he flinched. Compassion welled up in her.

"Move my hand to your worst scar."

He brought her hand to his waist. The tissue felt stiff. She explored his skin with gentleness.

"I will see you with the eyes of love. Show me each scar."

He moved her hand from scar to scar. When he stopped, she put her palm on an area unscathed, and imagined his entire body smooth and supple. Tears stung her eyes. His external wounds had healed, but he was still wounded inside.

She felt certain he was worthy of her respect. Not a romance with a happily-ever-after story, but a real story of hurt, flawed people finding their way to each other. The cost of war on families was heavy, the damage deep and hard to heal. No one needed to tell her that.

"Whatever happens tonight, I hold someone precious."

They lay together on the cot, and she kissed him with tenderness.

After a while, he broke his silence. "If my scars don't repel you, and you still want me, that's enough. I have covered up my body long enough. From here on out, I refuse to be ashamed."

She wondered if they could help each other heal.

"I enjoy touching you," he said. "Soft. No thorns. Zippy perfume. If I cross a line, say so. Other than my scintillating personality, I am proudest of my self-discipline."

Without hesitation, he nuzzled her shoulders. The pad of his thumb touched her breast. His feather-light kisses moved to her navel, and down to her inner thighs.

"You're licking me," she said. "Again."

"Guilty in the first *and* second degree."

He reached over and pulled a foil packet from the pocket of his trousers. "I'd better suit up." He ripped open the packet.

"Glad you asked," she said, smiling.

Then lost in a dream world, delicious feelings pushed her higher and higher. The jolts of pleasure left her mind in ruins.

A quickening grew inside her. She climbed a mountain and gazed over a precipice. Something powerful pushed her off. She was in free fall, pain and pleasure mixed. Her body convulsed, and she cried out.

He shouted and collapsed on her body.

"*Te adoro, mi corazón,*" he whispered. "Magnificent flower, my bird of paradise."

From the Lizard Lounge, a voice called, "Mma? Mma?"

"Let me up. We woke Sammy."

☆ ☆ ☆

Alicia and Jake lay on the cot entwined. They talked together quietly after Sammy went back to sleep.

"I'm afraid when you leave for long weekends, afraid you might be injured."

"'Stay alive' is my first rule. I'll tell you when I plan to leave and return. But the unexpected happens. If I fail to treat you how you want, tell me in your best no-nonsense teacher voice."

"I don't want a surprise pregnancy. I'm not on the pill like the other women here, except for Bronwyn who says children should come when they're ready."

He chuckled. "After I met you, I hitchhiked to Francistown and bought the largest box of condoms Mr. Anand had in stock. I wanted to buy all the boxes, but I couldn't fit them in my pack."

She rolled her eyes, smiling.

"Playing true confessions with you is such fun," he said. "Tonight, we've revealed what takes years to share in a conventional relationship."

"Your wife abandoned you after Vietnam. How do you handle that?"

"Fey counsels me. She wants me to stop waking her up at three o'clock in the morning with my screams."

Alicia kissed him. "When we danced tonight, I tried to remember who I was before Eric died. Matthew Arnold wrote that he was "wandering between two worlds, one dead the other powerless to be born.' That's how I feel. In limbo." She closed her eyes. "What do you want of me?"

"I want *you*—every day, every night, every minute in between, starting with this one."

He covered her body with his own.

37

On Saturday afternoon a week later, Bronwyn and Williams's wedding teetered on the brink of catastrophe. The bride and groom did not appear at the chapel in Francistown at two o'clock, the appointed time.

Alicia directed the pianist to stop playing Mozart and start playing jazz standards. She had the babysitter take the children for a walk. The audience grew restless. Thirty minutes late, the bridal couple strolled in, radiant and nonchalant. Bronwyn wore the emerald gown sent by Hannah. William wore a black suit and white shirt without a tie.

The bouquet of pink lilies opened in the heat and saturated the room with its fragrance. The homily by the Reverend Adrian Sephora, a Baptist minister, was brief. Mr. Anand fulfilled each of Alicia's special requests. Best of all, Bronwyn and William became husband and wife.

After the return trip home, Alicia twirled Sammy around, singing to the Beatles' music playing on her cassette player. "The decorations you helped make will be at the party tonight."

"Dance, Mma. Dance."

"Amen!" They pranced around together.

"Me go?"

"To the party tonight? No, my darling boy. This party is for grown-ups. Mpule and Glorianna will babysit you."

Sammy began to cry, sounding heartbroken. Alicia held him, comforting him.

"Ko Ko." William stood at the open door, his southern drawl more prominent than usual. He had Geoff on his shoulders. Sammy perked up, forgetting his tears. Geoff shouted to be set down. Soon, the boys began to dance together, hopping around to the music.

Bronwyn walked in still wearing the emerald dress, now carrying the tiara and magic wand. William placed the tiara on the top of her head.

"Miss Alicia," William said over the music, "Bronwyn and I wanted to get married, but you made it happen. We are in your debt, forever."

Alicia beamed at her friends. She had changed into a sleeveless dress with a plunging neckline, a petal-soft confection the color of pearls, another of Lara's cast-offs. She did a few dance steps and swished her dress around.

"Crikey. Watch out for Jake," Bronwyn said. "He'll have you flat on your back and preggers quicker than quick."

A spike of adrenaline went through Alicia. "Too revealing?"

"You look delightful," William said. He turned to Bronwyn. "Let's go dance, Mrs. Mortensen, light of my life, mother of our children, my *wife*."

"We be dancing fools." Bronwyn walked out the door, one hand on his arm, the other on her enormous belly.

Alicia watched her leave. Bronwyn looked ready to deliver.

A few minutes later, Mpule and Glorianna slipped in the door and sat down on the chairs at the table. They both wore dresses covered with bright flowers. Alicia suspected they wore their best clothes to honor the newlyweds. No shoes, though.

Jake appeared at the door. In a suit and tie, he sizzled, as promised. Under one arm, he carried a large package.

"Welcome," Alicia said. "You look movie-star handsome."

"And you remind me of Ingrid Bergman in *Casablanca.* Luminous."

She smiled, relishing the compliment. Butter on both sides.

"What's in the package?" She was hoping for chocolate, a rare treat.

"Your new trousers," he said. "The magicians in Francistown with their treadle sewing machines put in lots of pockets. Bought you a commando knife, too. On our next trip to the deep desert, you can break them in."

Sammy ran toward Jake, who picked him up. "Shall I leave you in the rafters, big boy?"

"Nnyaa," he said, giggling. Jake set him down, and Sammy went back to playing with Geoff.

"Mr. Anand and I made secret deals," Alicia said. "Geoff needed a passport, so Mr. Anand took a photograph of him. They will need a passport for Bronwyn's baby. Mr. Anand will handle the official paperwork when I get a photo. Never know when you might have to get out of Dodge."

"A woman with a mission, that's you."

“I tell Mr. Anand what I need, and he says, ‘I will just put on my thinking cap.’ He’s far too proper for a hug. He and his wife came from India years ago, the day after they were married. ‘For the opportunity,’ he told me.” She gave Jake a flirtatious smile. “I worship him, I do.”

“Am I playing second fiddle to the owner of the Snappy Mercantile? Kiss me or I’ll go mad.”

She grabbed his hands. “You teach science and coach football, though you have done neither before. You are quite remarkable… for a man.” On tiptoes, she kissed his cheek.

“Put me in my place, will you?” He wrapped his arms around her and kissed her. He kept on kissing her until Mpule and Glorianna laughed and clapped.

When Jake released her, Alicia sat down on a cot, feeling light-headed.

“Help yourself to the refreshments,” she said to the babysitters.

The vanilla cupcakes were lopsided and soft in the center but tasty. Fey was learning how to use the Lilliputian stove her boyfriend had bought for her.

“There’s a bag of peppermint candies next to the mugs,” Alicia said. “Play all the music you want. Don’t worry about running down the batteries. Light all the candles. Celebrate!”

38

The teachers crowded into the staff house for the wedding celebration. Nigel stood by his record player spinning records, an arm around Corley. Paul held a soft drink, lounging against the wall by the front door.

Fey came in with Mr. Pierce. Alicia had met him during one of his visits to the school. He had greeted her as if he knew her. When she asked Fey about him earlier, all Fey would say was that he "worked out even better than anticipated." What did that mean?

Everyone was there except for Mick and Ellie. They did not often appear at social events. When they did, Mick resembled a black cloud preparing to spew frozen rain drops.

Mr. Matlagodi stood next to Dorcas, looking ready to bolt. He was not a man who enjoyed socializing. He was a serious man who focused on work. But everyone else was ready for fun.

Alicia signaled Fey to meet her in the small kitchen adjacent to the main room. Together they opened wine bottles and filled mugs for the wedding toast. Alicia had spent time the previous day rounding up mugs from the other teachers. Paul paid for the wine as his gift to William and Bronwyn.

Jake tapped a wine bottle with a spoon.

"Attention, revelers."

The room quieted. Fey and Alicia moved around the room handing out the mugs.

"Mrs. Linchwe, bless her," Jake said, "brought us a several telegrams for the bride and groom. Here's one from Bronwyn's mother and father in the U.K.

'We wish you the joy of years together. All love and best wishes. Mum and Dad.'"

Jake scanned the crowd. "Glasses charged?" He beckoned William and Bronwyn to come forward.

"Your deep love for each other rivals the African sunset in beauty and intensity. William, you are the most honest of men, valuing justice. Bronwyn, you are the definition of optimism. You will soon welcome the fourth member of your family. Please accept my best wishes for a zesty life together. Raise your glasses to the bride and groom."

Each person in the room raised a mug, took a sip, and cheered the couple.

Nigel put on "The Blue Danube Waltz," and the crowd moved back to give the newlyweds room. Bronwyn gripped her magic wand and gazed up at William. After a few minutes, others joined them on the dance floor.

Alicia returned to the kitchen to finish arranging the cookies and cupcakes. Paul appeared in the doorway.

"I am stone-cold sober, and I'm spending all my spare time studying for med school."

He looked expectant, so she reached over and patted his arm. "One day you'll be Dr. Winthrop, epidemiologist, eradicator of tropical diseases. The headmaster will hold you up as an example of excellence."

Paul cleared his throat. "Notice my shiny shoes and bow tie? This tuxedo is brand new. Mr. Anand scoured southern African to find everything I needed."

"Your clothes are resplendent, sublime even."

She returned to her work.

"Are you proud of me?"

"No question, Paul. Stay for the party?"

When she did not hear a reply, she glanced up. Jake stood in his place.

"Come out and play," he said.

She was miffed. Even with his size and direct manner, he made others feel comfortable around him—unless, of course, another man showed an interest in her.

He moved behind her, threading his fingers through her hair.

She shrugged him off.

"William dances with the woman of his dreams, and you're in here playing waitress. Bronwyn told William her time is near, so if we want to get in a dance, you'd better hustle your bustle."

Alicia placed the refreshments on the table in the main room along with the remaining bottles of wine and the lilies from the wedding ceremony.

Jake stroked her shoulders and kissed her neck. "I like the fragrance you're wearing."

She turned to him. "Can you tell me the name of the perfume?"

"Like a wager? Okay, but I want high stakes."

She picked up a ginger snap cookie and fed it to him. On his last bite, he captured her fingers between his teeth before letting them go.

"If I can name the fragrance," he said, "you'll agree to my favorite thing. If I'm wrong, we'll do your favorite thing, whatever it is, no matter how much it costs me."

She laughed. "Sorry. I only win with phony Buffalo head nickels."

He wiggled his eyebrows. "I'm a first-class guesser, but the correct answer could be elusive."

She tapped her foot to the music, longing to dance. "You could take me to Paris. We'll stroll down *Avenue des Champs-Élysées*, visit the Louvre, watch the mimes perform, and sit outside a café eating macarons."

He raised one eyebrow. "I won't fly you to Paris for the *boeuf bourguignon*. But I will buy you a rum and Coke in the Lioness Lounge. Bodacious generosity."

After kissing the top of her nose, he said, "Lily of the Valley. My mother wears it all the time."

The music of Crosby, Stills, Nash & Young singing "Teach Your Children" drowned out her cry of frustration. He tapped her lips with a forefinger. "Don't you dare back out of our bargain. Dire consequences if you do. Dire."

She gave her head a shake. "Why am I so gullible?"

"Must go back to being emcee," he said, "but you seem a tad anxious. I won't ask you to ride naked on a white stallion through Kukama Village. Though that idea does have merit."

He kissed her cheek and walked over to talk with Nigel, who was thumbing through his stack of albums. Corley stood close beside him. She had changed her hair from an Afro to an intricate array of woven braids. Nigel pulled out a record and put it on. African drum music filled the room.

Jake beckoned Alicia to stand beside him. He shouted to the partiers. "Dance performance time, folks. Make a circle. Corley is up first. Go, Corley!"

Corley wore a dress of bright geometric shapes. She glided onto the dance floor with rattles wrapped around her wrists and ankles. To the complicated rhythm, she moved her feet with precision. When she waved to Ndona, he danced out to join her. The sweat ran down the sides of their faces. The audience whistled and roared their approval.

When Corley and Ndona withdrew, Nigel put on Irish music and pointed to Bronwyn. She disengaged from William's embrace and began to dance. She kept her upper body rigid and her arms stiff at her sides while doing her fancy footwork. Years ago, at a summer camp in Galway, she had learned Irish dancing. After a few minutes, William joined her, moving in a circle around his bride, arms folded.

When the song ended, William kissed his wife with enthusiasm. The audience hollered, stomping their feet.

"Nigel," Jake said, over the noise, "give Alicia a chance. Put on "Sweet Caroline."" He pushed her onto the dance floor.

Alicia loved to dance but not perform alone. At their university in Wales, she and Bronwyn listened to Neil Diamond. While Alicia preferred folk music, jazz, and the blues, Neil Diamond was Bronwyn's favorite pop singer. Who told Jake that? Definitely, a conspiracy.

Alicia executed the fluid steps of a modern dance routine taught to her by Hannah. She ended with a flourish and withdrew from the dance floor to applause. She blew a kiss to Bronwyn who blew one right back.

Jake beckoned Fey, who was standing in front of Mr. Pierce. Nigel put on bagpipe music, and Fey did the Scottish Sword Dance. The audience chanted her name, urging her on.

When Fey finished her dance, Jake called to Nigel. "Ready for the grand finale?"

"Aye, aye, matey." He put on Russian folk music.

"Give Nigel some encouragement." Jake started clapping with the beat, and the others joined in.

Walking into the circle, Nigel crossed his arms and sank to his haunches. He put one leg out, and brought it back, and put the other leg out. He did this faster and faster. He kicked and leapt in astonishing ways, dancing without tiring.

Jake shouted, "Not bad for a Brit!"

As the music ended, Nigel stood up, bowed, and walked over to the table. He picked up a full bottle of wine, tipped back his head, and drank most of it. Returning to his record player, he hugged Corley, and put on "Light My Fire" by the Doors. Everyone found a partner.

"About our wager," Jake whispered to Alicia.

"What? Wasn't dancing my part of the bargain?"

"My ideas are all sexual in nature." He grinned. "But don't worry. I'll dream up a scenario that's orgasmic with only the slightest hint of kinky."

She tried to kick him in the shin, but he evaded her, pulling off his tie and stuffing it in his pocket. He took off his suit coat and dropped it on a chair. He rolled up the sleeves of his shirt, revealing the scars. How could she argue with him then?

39

Jake and Alicia left the party early, others had offered to do the clean-up. They walked close together, his arm around her waist.

"My babysitters need to go home," Alicia said. "The kgosi sits up until his granddaughters return. Muti and all the horrid stuff."

"Muti? What's that?"

"Witchcraft. Fey told me a young girl vanished from a village several years ago. They found her mutilated body later. Her sexual parts were used by a rogue witchdoctor to make muti. It's bought by men who believe it will cure their impotence or improve their business, stuff like that. Parents have sold their children."

"I'll drive the babysitters back to their village when they stay in the evening."

"Mpule told me she feels safe with Glorianna by her side. I'll ask her what she wants to do."

"Did you see those men ogling you tonight?" Jake asked.

"When you leaned forward during your dance, I wanted to cover your breasts with my hands. I want to do that a lot anyway."

Alicia sighed in exasperation. "Hector Pierce guards Fey like she's Queen Elizabeth II. William thinks Bronwyn is the only woman who exists. Dereck's taste runs to machinery. Nigel reveres Corley. Sure, there are a few unattached men, like that cute, development studies teacher."

"Simon Chiang, the stereotypical accountant? All he needs is a green visor and rimless glasses."

"Accountants can be sexy." Her tone was teasing.

"Careful! I have fault lines that could rupture. Seismic activity. Expect magnitude eight."

She looked up at the Milky Way, a white bridge across the sky. "I value loyalty, but don't try to chain me or I'll break away."

He stopped and took both of her hands in his. "Fidelity is important to me, but I may be a tad obsessive. Accept my apology? I'll overcome my flaws before the next millennium. Promise." He kissed her. "Under your tutelage, I might become a real grown-up. Watch out, world!"

☆ ☆ ☆

In Alicia's rondavel, Jake made a grab for her, but she dodged away.

"Keep your pants on."

"I do need a pit stop. Back in a flash."

He went out the front door while she went into the Lizard Lounge to check on Sammy and Geoff. They lay on their backs, side by side, asleep. She closed the door and put on her negligee, filmy, sheer, and impractical, except for one thing.

Jake walked back in. "Whoa! You deserve a wolf whistle, but I don't want to wake the boys. High cheekbones. Poise. Spunk. Just what I like."

"Nice compliment."

"Part of my nefarious seduction plan." He locked the door, shut the windows, and pulled the curtains closed. He left one lantern lit.

She sat on a cot, set her sandals under the bed and watched him. "Forget the high security. I feel safe when you're here."

He stood before her, hands on hips. "You're giving me an order? Usually, I give the orders. Maybe it's a family trait, although when my father gives my mother an order, she won't stand for it. As stubborn as he is, she goes nose to nose with him until he agrees to compromise." He sat down beside her.

"I might borrow that strategy," she said. "What a wonderful telegram William and Bronwyn received from his mother. 'Who can find a virtuous woman, for her price is far above rubies.'"

"I do appreciate your virtuousness," he said, "and your virtuosity. I enjoy being married to you." He tried to kiss her, but she leaned away and socked his arm, playfully.

"Bronwyn and William got married today. Not us."

"You walked up the aisle, and we walked out together as 'best persons.' Doesn't that count?"

"You must stand in front of a minister and make vows you plan to keep."

"'With my body, I thee worship.' Remember that line in the ceremony today? That's true for me." With a quick movement, he picked her up and laid her down on the cot. He lifted the hem of her negligee and kissed her knee. His kisses meandered up across her belly and over to her other knee.

"Sweet Lady, we may well stand in front of a minister someday, but other ideas occupy my agile mind. I have some ideas about our wager. My mother raised a gentleman, not a fool."

She giggled. "Remember Geoff is asleep in the Lizard Lounge. He wakes if a butterfly flies by."

"You want me quiet? You're the loud one. Truly inspirational."

His kisses stopped meandering. She gasped and stifled a moan.

40

Mick tracked down a weapons broker to sell him the unusual items that Chaparadza demanded. Oliver, the new broker, refused to give his surname. The man insisted on a face-to-face meeting in Jo-burg to ensure that Mick was not a wily South African policeman.

"Punctuality is paramount," Oliver said on the telephone when Mick called him from Francistown. "Be punctual or no deal."

Mick couldn't place Oliver's accent. The elusive Oliver No-Last-Name might be a trap. But Chaparadza was unpredictable and might turn on him at any time. Mick considered it a question of balancing risk.

On Sunday, Mick prepared for the long drive to Jo-burg. He wrote a note for Ellie telling her he would be back on Monday. Ellie seemed less stable these days. The woman was becoming a liability.

He reached the border in good time and stopped at the sign, "Entering the Republic of South Africa." White soldiers milled around, on alert. Each soldier kept a finger above the trigger of a machine gun.

Mick cursed when he saw another sign. It said that the crossing hours had been shortened. The border was closed. "No exceptions."

He slapped the steering wheel. "Assholes."

He was stuck, unable to cross until the next morning. He backtracked and parked off the road in the middle of nowhere. The moon revealed no village, no hostel, and no bottle store on the Botswana side of the border. He lay down on the unpadded bench seat. His back would hurt tomorrow, but it could not be helped.

The next morning, Mick sat in line for hours, ready to explode. A border guard told him revolutionaries were blowing up buildings and power plants south of the border. The government clamped down on any suspicious behavior. The swaggering guard told him that the massacres at Sharpeville and other places should have discouraged the revolutionaries, but no such luck.

Another guard scrutinized his truck, and Mick held his breath. The guard did not find the hidden compartment. It was empty, the weapons safely hidden, but the compartment would have put him under suspicion.

Mick drove across the border and headed to Jo-burg feeling like an escapee on the run. On a regular basis, Black South African prisoners fell from high buildings or "slipped" and hit their heads on sharp table corners. The policemen were not punished.

The road was crammed with slow-moving traffic, and Mick started to sweat at the delay, cursing the day he flew to Africa.

I cannot believe that seven hundred kilometers to the north, we live like cavemen. Maybe I can get Ellie a gift, that perfume she likes. Remind her of the developed world.

Alicia came to mind. Because of her, the headmaster came to him full of threats. If she died, she could not get him fired. Chaparadza could take her out. On the other hand, if her son died, she might skedaddle. That did bear thinking about, save him a few machine guns. In any case, he would get off scot-free.

He swore as a car cut in front of him.

Jake Hunter poked around, too. Worrisome.

"Let's get rid of him."

Oliver had told Mick to meet him at one o'clock on the steps in front of the Great Hall at the University of Witwatersrand. This was Mick's first visit to the university, and he couldn't find a legal parking spot big enough for his truck. Having it impounded would be dangerous, and the police were ubiquitous as flies.

The minutes slipped away, ticking like a time bomb. At last, he found a parking space.

The Great Hall loomed at one end of a gigantic quadrangle. Eight tall Corinthian columns decorated the front of the massive building overlooking a pond and a fountain. In the Republic of South Africa, the Whites built the trappings of a sophisticated culture, even if it was a veneer.

He rushed up the steps, checking his watch. "Quarter past one. Late, but not very late."

No one gave him a second glance. Being White made him invisible in a Whites-only crowd.

As he stood next to an immense column, he glanced down at his feet and saw something orange. There, on the steps, lay his business card, torn into four quarters. Oliver had been here and left.

Mick wanted to throw a tantrum, jump up and down, but he could not draw attention to himself. The police watched for any sign of troublemakers. He smelled his sweat. His mouth tasted of ashes.

The substantial deposit paid to Oliver was gone along with his anticipated profit. His dream of buying his island paradise receded a bit. He dismissed the idea of buying a gift for Ellie.

He needed to get back and figure out an alternative plan to satisfy Chaparadza. It might take some time. He headed to his truck and the drive back to the school. He could make the crossing before it shut for the night, unless they changed the hours again.

I am not going to let dumb luck outsmart me twice.

41

On Friday, Alicia carried a stack of papers as she walked into her First Form English class. The students quieted down.

"Class, today we'll work on poetry. We'll talk about the Batswana tradition of praise poems that exalt heroes such as a kgosi. You know about this tradition?"

Most students said, "Ee." Yes.

Thale raised her hand. "Shall we write a praise poem about you, Teacher?" A few students giggled.

Alicia felt her face grow warm. "Please write a poem about your kgosi or another person who is important in your life. I have an example of a praise poem, one for Tshekedi Khama, an uncle to Seretse Khama and his regent."

She handed out mimeographed copies. The purple ink smeared in places, but was legible. "Negotho, will you read the poem, please?" Last week, he joined her committee to address students' concerns. She wanted to bring him to the headmaster's attention. With some luck, his intelligence, hard work, and steady nature would bring success. He needed to distinguish himself in a way that resulted in a scholarship to higher education. His family could not afford either university or medical school.

Negotho walked to the front of the classroom. He accepted the paper from her. Holding it in both hands, he turned to his classmates.

Alicia watched the class as he read. They seemed enthralled. He emphasized the last line.

O Duiker, our chief, we thirst. Bring us rain.

"Outstanding, Negotho."

But the student did not sit down. "Teacher, I can tell a story about the duiker."

She gestured for him to proceed.

"Khama the Great, Tshekei's father, fights many Matabele warriors. He retreats behind a fallen tree. Matabele warriors come, and the duiker runs from them to the same fallen tree. The Matabele think no man could hide where the duiker rests. They depart. The duiker saves our chief, protects Khama the Great."

"Thank you. I hear the duiker is a totem of the Bamangwato tribe."

"My tribe." The student walked back to his desk, and with his usual poise sat down next to Mbengawa.

When she arrived months ago, many of her students were too shy to speak English in class. They were coming along just fine, and they would go further.

"Class, let's talk about the elements of a praise poem."

Thale raised her hand. "Is metaphor one of the elements?"

Before Alicia could answer, the door to the classroom opened. Mpule stood framed in the doorway. She rushed to

Alicia's side and struggled to get out the words. "Mma Sammy, your son is not found."

Alicia steadied herself. She remembered Jake's rule, "Panic makes you stupid."

Facing the class, she said, "Negotho, please supervise silent reading until the bell rings. Students, take out your library books."

Mpule turned around, and they walked through the open door. Outside, Alicia closed the door behind them.

"What happened?" She needed facts.

"I lock door," Mpule said, her voice high and strained. "We have nap. I wake. He is gone. I cannot find."

"Go to Rra Jake," Alicia said. "He's in the science lab near the Fifth Form classrooms. Tell him to meet me at my home. Go next to the headmaster and ask him to search the school."

The girl stood there, frozen in place.

"Sammy may have gone to visit Dereck."

Mpule started walking up the hill, moving like she carried a great burden.

Alicia shouted, "Run!"

The nanny glanced back, her face a mask of despair. She began to run.

Alicia leaned against the warm bricks of the wall and willed the world to stop whirling. A stabbing pain in her belly made her double over. Where was Sammy?

When she straightened up, nothing moved except a herd of goats in the distance. The sun, the sky, the sand, the thorn trees looked normal. But nothing was normal.

She recalled a Bible passage her Aunt Viv often quoted.

"Fear not… When thou walkest through the fire, thou shalt not be burned; neither shall the flame kindle upon thee."

Now she knew what to do. She opened the door to the classroom. Negotho watched over the class, exuding calmness. She spotted Kxoma in the back row.

"Kxoma? Please come."

The student closed his book and walked outside. His bare feet meant he was in touch with the warm sand, the earth.

"My young son has wandered from my rondavel. Wandered off…" She was stammering. "I need you to find him. Follow his tracks. Bring him home." Her mouth felt dry, her throat tight.

"He cannot escape my eyes."

Kxoma took off, running toward her hut. She followed hm.

They found Jake already there, studying the sand. He stood up and put his arms around her. Her rapid breathing slowed. She opened the door expecting her son to run toward her, but the room held a terrible stillness.

"Rra Jake." Kxoma pointed to the ground.

Jake went over to Kxoma, examined the ground, and turned back to Alicia.

"He found Sammy's sandal print headed toward the stile over the northern fence. Ask Mpule to stay here in case he returns. Kxoma and I will follow his tracks. You walk the path to the village. Bring water and Sammy's hat. We will find him." Jake and Kxoma headed toward the stile.

Could Sammy unlock the door now? Where was he going? The Tip Top Shoppe? Did he go to the village to visit the kgosi?

Did a wild animal snatch him? Was he kidnapped to make muti, the gruesome talisman made by rogue medicine men?

Mick threatened Sammy. Could Mick kill a child?

☆ ☆ ☆

Alicia walked the dusty path toward the village with her day-pack. The white heat of the day grew more intense. Kxoma and Jake would find Sammy, she needed to believe that.

She asked a man on the path if a little boy had passed him. He had not seen a boy. She felt faint but caught herself before she fell. The thorny bushes and tufts of grass did not provide any shade. Taking out the canteen from her pack, she took a long drink.

Near the village, she passed two girls standing on either side of a large, wooden mortar using long staves to pound maize. They took turns bringing the staves down on the corn. This was the scene Thale described in her poem. Their dresses were unzipped in back, their skin glistened. Close by, a woman winnowed grain.

Alicia spoke to the girls. "Nnyaa," they said. They had not seen Sammy.

Something made a noise on the path behind her. As she turned, Nigel pulled her into a hug. She felt his soft beard on her cheek and his sturdy body, but she was not comforted.

"My son is lost," she said, fighting back tears.

"No fear, love. Sammy will turn up in a trice. Not steered you wrong yet, have I?"

She blinked away her tears.

As they went on toward the village, Nigel sang "You'll Never Walk Alone" several times. Nigel made music wherever he was, no matter the situation.

They reached the tall tree at the kgotla. The kgosi sat in his special chair with the elders beside him. Sitting on the sand under the tree were a dozen men waiting to present their cases for adjudication. They focused on what their chief said. She felt a keen disappointment. She wanted Sammy to be at the kgotla, but he was not.

In the far distance, a movement caught her eye. She recognized the slight stature of Kxoma. Jake ran toward Kxoma and stopped in front of him, blocking her view. What was happening? Did he have Sammy? Nigel put his arm around her, steadied her. For once, he was silent.

Jake walked towards her, carrying something. Her heart jumped. He held her son. Sammy waved to her.

She took off, racing toward them. Soon, she held Sammy, hugging him, kissing him.

Sammy wiggled, complaining. "Me get down."

After setting him down, she opened her pack and pulled out her canteen and Sammy's hat. After helping him take a drink, she tied on his hat.

He was dressed in his red and white striped shirt, brown shorts and sandals. His skin looked pink, but not burned. She rejoiced, grateful for what she felt was a miracle.

"He went to visit the kgosi," Jake said. "Missed a turn on the path and ended up in a dense copse. He fell asleep under a mopane tree. Kxoma is the one who followed the sandal tracks through a jumble of human and animal tracks."

She was close to fainting.

"You're white as a sheet. Alicia, take a breath."

Sammy pointed to the kgosi in the distance. This was the

person he wanted to visit. He started toward him, calling out, "Dumela Rra." He ran straight to the kgosi, and the elderly man welcomed him. Alicia and Jake followed the boy, stopping at the edge of the gathering.

She went over to Kxoma. "Thank you for finding my son, for saving him." Kxoma looked down at his feet. "Ee, Teacher." He rubbed his peppercorn hair with both hands.

Sammy sat on the kgosi's lap. When he saw his mother, he waved and called to her. The kgosi motioned to Alicia to come forward.

Kxoma went first. Alicia took Jake's arm, and Nigel walked behind them. She curtsied. A murmur of approval rippled through the gathering. Jake spoke in halting Setswana.

The chief responded, and Kxoma translated his words. "Sammy is a fine son. A man must take care of his mother. This is our way."

Sammy pointed at the chickens pecking in the sand. He slipped off the kgosi's lap and headed for them, but Jake intercepted him, picking him up.

"Let's go," Jake said softly. They backed away from the chief.

As they left the kgotla, the kgosi raised his walking stick in farewell. Alicia studied the azure sky, the unrelenting sun, and gave thanks.

"The flames did not consume us."

42

At home, Sammy fidgeted on his mother's lap. Fey stood next to them, satchel in hand. Before Jake and Nigel left them, they promised to spread the good news that Sammy was safe. A relieved Mpule returned to the village.

"You gave me such a scare, Sammy," Alicia said. "Please do not leave by yourself again. Were you angry at me when I didn't take you to William and Bronwyn's party?"

He nodded. "Ee, Mma."

She wanted to hold his sweaty body forever, but her son wanted down. She let him go, and he went to Fey.

"Up. Up. Pick me."

Fey set down her satchel and picked him up. Her laser eyes bored into Alicia. "Death wishes. You want to fly off the water tower. You and Jake go into the central Kalahari and attract a lioness. Bronwyn ignores my stellar advice on her pregnancy. Sammy decides to visit the kgosi on his own."

Fey sat down on a cot with Sammy beside her. "My lustrous

black hair will turn snow-white. Our guardian angels are incompetent. Have we worn them out? We need the 'A' team, the first string, the alpha angels. The next question is whether or not Mpule is too immature for the job."

"Mpule stays as nanny," Alicia said. "No one knew Sammy could unlock the door."

"Mpule may have forgotten to lock it," Fey said. "Maybe she was off with Negotho. Why are you so trusting? Try to be more skeptical, like me." Fey opened her satchel, pulled out a salve, and proceeded to slather Sammy with it. He did not complain.

Fey pulled out a screw-top jar full of liquid. "How's your injured shoulder?"

"I have twinges."

"Drink this," Fey said, handing over the jar. "I'm learning more about the unique herbs grown here. Dr. Lekota mentors me."

Alicia rubbed her aching shoulder. She had not yet met Dr. Lekota.

At a knock on the door, Fey got up and opened it. She stepped out, talked with someone, and returned.

"Next crisis. Mick hit Ellie in her abdomen. Sounds like a miscarriage." Fey picked up her satchel, kissed Sammy, and walked out the door, her mouth set in a hard line.

Later that evening, Jake arrived at Alicia's doorway with a plate of food.

"Ko Ko."

She wore a short-sleeved top, a light aqua, over her black capris. Sammy was studying one of his books. She laid down her biro, put a bookmark in her journal, and set it on the table.

Sammy climbed down from his chair and ran to Jake. "Rra. Rra." The boy tugged at his trouser leg. Jake bent down, scooped Sammy up with one hand and set the plate on the table.

"Couldn't face dinner," she said. "What did you bring us?"

"For you, porterhouse steak and rice pilaf with toasted almonds, asparagus with béarnaise sauce, and black forest cake with vanilla ice cream. For me, quesadillas, black beans and rice, like my godmother made for me."

"Our cook's a wizard, but there may be no béarnaise sauce within hundreds of miles. What is it?"

"Shepherd's pie made with goat meat and woody carrots. I want Mexican food. Hot, tonsil-burning chiles. Yum."

"We're guests here," she said with a smile.

Jake carried Sammy around examining the prints of Impressionist paintings on the walls. She lit another lantern.

Nasturtiums bloomed in two of her flowerpots. The flowers hung down from the windowsill and matched the red and yellow curtains. Tiny red tomatoes hung on the tomato plant.

Sammy gripped Jake's shirt. "Rra?"

Jake sat down, and held the boy on his lap, holding him so they were face-to-face. "What's up, Young Sarge?"

"My daddy loves me."

Tears came to Alicia's eyes.

"Yes. Your daddy loves you," Jake said.

The night had cooled. Alicia placed the blanket from Hannah around her son's shoulders. The lanterns flickered, throwing shadows on the walls. Outside, the cicadas sang in full voice.

"My daddy's gone," Sammy said. He patted Jake's ear. "Pictures."

"Your mother showed you pictures of your daddy? Are you sad?"

The boy nodded. Sammy rubbed his face on the front of Jake's shirt.

"See this blanket? Your auntie knit love into every strand. When you're sad, touch it and remember all the people who love you. Your mother, Aunt Hannah, Auntie Fey, Bronwyn, William, Geoff, and me."

Alicia turned on the cassette deck sitting on a shelf, and James Galway played a flute solo. She divided the food on two plates, adding cherry tomatoes and nasturtium blooms, and sat down next to them. His tenderness toward Sammy soothed her anxiety.

"Smell the aroma," Jake said. "The Ritz. Where's the wine list?"

Alicia put Sammy to bed. He fell asleep on top of his blanket, clutching Pinkie. She walked back into the main room and closed the door behind her. She trimmed the wicks on the lanterns and sat down.

Jake caressed her cheek. "Are you tormenting yourself?"

"I'm supposed to protect my son." She felt a tightness in her chest.

The light from the lanterns made the room glow. "Isn't Sammy too young to talk about death?"

"When he points to the tin box, I open it and we talk about what's inside. He likes to touch Eric's medal. I wish I had the one Dinizulu took." She took Jake's hand and kissed it. "My fracture lines are all visible. If I were tapped in the right place, I would fall to pieces like a cracked vase."

He massaged her neck and shoulders. He pushed her hair behind her ears. "Who did you send for when Sammy went missing?"

"An able scientist learning to track animals."

He touched her chin. "You trust me, inside, where it counts. When Sammy went missing, my response told me how much I care for you both. In case you're worried, I would never be violent with you or your son."

He tossed back the sheet on her cot. After taking off his shirt, he hung it on the back of a chair and sat down. He undid the laces of his boots and pulled them off, setting them on the floor.

Glancing at the window, she saw only darkness; it was the new moon.

"Hey, I'm doing a striptease."

She turned to him. "I like the beard you're growing. What a hairy man! I want to touch you all over."

"Easily arranged." He stood up, took off the rest of his clothes, and lay down on the cot.

His scars seemed normal to her. She blew out the lanterns and sat beside him. She kissed him, then studied his face.

"Don't stop the kissing thing," he said.

She inhaled the tang of his sweat. He began to take off her clothes, fumbling with her top, pushing her hands away when she tried to help.

"Just a glimpse of you excites me," he said. "It's that damn testosterone. Out of my control." He pulled her into his arms, whispering his love words.

A flush of heat swept through her. A feeling, delicate and fragile, grew inside her. Her eyelids flickered. A tide turned in her body. Warmth flooded over her, with exquisite pleasure.

When she awakened in the morning, he was gone. She looked over at the table. Her journal was in a different position. When she opened it at the bookmark, she found his note.

"Never doubt me."

He had signed his full name: Jacob MacLaren Hunter.

43

On Monday, Fey told Alicia that Ellie had miscarried. Alicia felt sick all day. That night, waking in the dark, a surge of adrenaline passed through her. Someone was crying, but it was not Sammy. She reached over to the cot beside her and tugged on Jake's T-shirt.

"Someone's outside."

He rolled off the cot, grabbed his trousers from the chair, pulled them on, and went to the door.

"What?" His voice sounded thick with sleep.

"Mma Sammy?"

Alicia knew that voice.

"It's Lepula, Ketumile's nanny." She shook out her sandals and put them on.

He unlocked the door, bringing the girl inside.

"What do you need?" Alicia was concerned. "You're safe here."

The girl spoke through her sobs. "Rra Nigel. Snake bite." She caught her breath. "I help with sick Ketumile, leave for home late-late. Rra Nigel calls as I pass. He says, 'Hold torch.' He has stick. The snake moves. He screams. I come to you. You are kind."

"Did you drop the torch?" Alicia asked.

The girl's head bobbed up and down.

Alicia grabbed a torch from the table, turned it on, and put it in Lepula's hands. "Take this. Go home to your parents. Ke itumetse." The girl took the torch and rushed out the door.

"I'll alert Fey and the headmaster," Jake said. "You take Sammy to the Mortensen's. Get William. Meet me at Nigel's."

While he pulled on a sweatshirt over his T-shirt and put on his boots, she struck a match and lit a lantern. Fear rose in her body, but she tamped it down.

Jake strapped his knife sheath on his ankle, and retrieved the Colt from the closet's top shelf, tucking something in his pocket. He touched her face, and the warmth of his fingers remained on her skin as he left with one of the lanterns.

After checking the fuel level in the remaining lantern, she left it burning. False alarm, she hoped. They would be back soon. She turned on her spare torch and put it in a pocket.

In the Lizard Lounge, she picked up her son, wrapping him in his blanket. His body was limp. She could carry him but with difficulty.

After William opened the door and she explained the emergency, she laid Sammy next to Geoff. Geoff woke up, but, at a reassuring word from his father, went back to sleep. Arm in arm, she walked with William to Nigel's home.

☆ ☆ ☆

Nigel lay on a blanket outside his hut; Jake sat beside him. The geometric pattern of Nigel's blanket was familiar, no doubt woven at the textiles shop. Several teachers stood nearby, holding their lanterns, creating a large pool of light.

Corley ran into the circle calling Nigel's name. He did not respond, his breathing labored.

"I was in the village with friends," Corley said, close to tears.

"Snake bite," Jake said. "Affects breathing."

Corley threw herself on Nigel as if she could give him her own breath.

Jake stood up, backed away and put his arm around Alicia.

Fey emerged out of the darkness with her satchel. "Where did it bite him?"

"Right ankle, several times," Jake said.

Fey knelt beside Nigel. "What kind of snake?"

"Have to kill it for an accurate identification." He turned to Alicia. "Help me?"

Her voice quavered. "Anything.

"Everyone, move back, except Corley and Fey," Jake said. "We need space." The other teachers did as he asked, talking among themselves.

Alicia borrowed a lantern from another teacher. Jake opened the door to Nigel's hut, and she followed him inside. Nigel was not a tidy housekeeper. Clothes and books lay scattered on the floor. His records stood upright on a shelf with an ostrich egg in a large woven basket on one end.

Jake signaled for her to raise the lantern high. When she did, he jerked back the cot.

A gray snake, coiled in the far corner, opened its inky-black mouth. The snake's forebody rose, raising a slender hood on its head, ready to strike.

"Black mamba, maybe," Jake said. "Too dangerous to let live. Matlagodi might confiscate the pistol. Have to take that chance."

He pulled out the Colt, staying back from the strike zone. Aiming, he fired one bullet into its head. The snake collapsed. The noise resounded in the small room, the odor of gunpowder pungent.

Jake prodded the snake with his boot. No movement. He put on the safety, and tucked the pistol into the back of his waistband.

He squatted down and examined the snake. "The black mamba's venom attacks the nervous system. The snake bit Nigel far from his heart, but Nigel said he jumped around when the snake kept biting him."

He took out his knife and cut off the head, what was left of it.

"We need the snakebite kit this minute. The delay's bad. Goddammit, where's the headmaster?"

He picked up a shirt from Nigel's floor and wrapped the snake's head in it. He put the shirt in the open space between the mud-brick wall and the thatched roof. He handed her the rest of the snake. She followed him out the door and set the snake under a bush.

Nigel groaned as Jake lifted him up and carried him inside. He laid him on the cot, and Corley lay down beside him.

Nigel spoke with effort, licking his lips. "Blimey, Jake. A six-shooter, a real cowboy. Have a secret life?"

"We'll talk later, cowpoke."

William built a fire outside the hut. The moonless night grew cold, and the teachers pulled their blankets tighter around their shoulders.

Mr. Matlagodi walked into the light. He carried a stack of boxes. Matron, much shorter, was behind him, running to keep up.

Fey reached out. "Give them to me."

The headmaster handed her one, and Fey opened a box. Empty.

Alicia could not believe it. No vials. Fey opened box after box, all were empty. There would be no shot of anti-venom for Nigel.

She remembered Nigel singing the ballad about the cowboy dying on the streets of Laredo and cried.

44

The headmaster held out his hand to Jake, palm up.

"No weapons here, Mr. Hunter. School policy. Give it to me, and I will say not one word more."

Jake took the pistol from his waistband, checked the safety, and handed it to the headmaster. The headmaster put it in his pocket; the pocket sagged.

Nigel beckoned his friends with a trembling hand. Alicia went in and touched his shoulder.

"Crikey," Nigel said, "my sole regret is leaving my girl, Corley."

Corley kissed him. "You'll do your Russian dance again."

"Jake, take my ostrich egg," Nigel said. "Fill it with water. Put it in the deep desert for the thirsty."

"Count on me."

"Ndona, my boots, you covet them, old chap. Should fit you."

Ndona ducked his head. He had just walked in. The bush telegraph reached Ndona at the farm in the middle of the night. Alicia was grateful for his calming presence.

"You will wear out many boots," Ndona said.

"William, my carpentry tools are yours," Nigel said. "You're a fair man, let others use them." He turned to Corley. "You're me wife. Enjoy me records. I'll sing you love songs forever."

Alicia studied Nigel's face as he struggled to breathe. She memorized his bushy eyebrows and beard. The cicadas sang with such clarity, she believed she could identify each one. The thatched roof smelled of dry grass. The Milky Way shone above the hut, vast and impersonal. Every detail while Nigel lived became dear to her. Could she bear another loss?

"William?" Nigel asked.

"Whatever you need."

"You're me mate." Nigel's voice was thin, gossamer. "Give me a good send-off. A hymn?"

William began to sing in his powerful voice.

Guide me, O thou Great Jehovah, pilgrim in this barren land. I am weak but thou art mighty; hold me with your powerful hand…

Alicia joined him, her soprano harmonizing with William's bass. The desert's song was the accompaniment for each word. The last line pierced her to the core of her being.

Land me safe on Canaan's side, bid my anxious fears, bid my anxious fears, goodbye.

Jake, Alicia, and William stood with Fey by the fire outside Nigel's hut. Corley closed the door to be alone with Nigel. The others drifted off.

"Nigel would die before we could reach the hospital in Francistown," Jake said. "He wants to spend what time he has with Corley. Fey, go home. I'll stand watch."

Fey frowned.

Jake sighed. "I should have checked Matron's anti-venom kits. 'Beware the fatal assumption.'"

"Keeping up with the kits was Mubayi's job as Matron's supervisor." Fey said. "The saboteur knows how to hurt us. I should have anticipated this."

William put his arm around Fey and kissed her cheek. "Strong as you are, you can't control everything." He murmured, "Sala sentle," and headed back to Bronwyn.

"I'll handle whatever comes next," Fey said. "Life or death. I have a flask of brandy in my satchel, courtesy of my boyfriend."

Jake started to object, but Fey raised a hand. "If you say it's a man's job, I will—"

"I'm trained."

"Be gone, my dear ones." Fey was resolute.

Jake pulled a whistle out of his pocket and handed it to Fey. "Blow this if you need me. I'll be back in four minutes tops." He pulled off his sweatshirt and put it around her shoulders.

Sadness weighed down Alicia. When Sammy went missing, Nigel ran after her in the heat, stabilizing her. At William and Bronwyn's wedding party, Nigel danced the Russian folk dance with amazing stamina. But Nigel was running out of breath. How could such a vital man die?

Alicia and Jake walked down the path to her home. Lightning had struck with a vengeance. She patted the goosebumps on his bare arm. Jake was so alive, but his life might be threatened.

At the rondavel, he lay down on a cot fully clothed and pulled Alicia to him.

"I'm an ordinary man with a lot of rules for survival. I wish I were omnipotent, but I'm not."

They held each other as they lay awake, listening to the night's song. Too soon, they heard the wail of a woman whose lover had died in her arms.

Corley's cry filled up the world. She was every woman who had lost her man.

Alicia clung to Jake, pressing hard against his body. They held onto each other as if they could stop death from entering their lives, stop the earth from turning.

45

The next night, Alicia stood beside the bonfire Jake built in her clearing. Teachers and villagers streamed in. When the clearing was full, some climbed up the trunks of the thorn trees and sat among the branches.

The headmaster had asked Alicia to lead the memorial service. She felt inadequate to the task, but she wanted to honor Nigel. She would do the best she could.

The dry wood in the fire crackled, smoke hovered over the clearing. Fey sat on a chair holding Sammy. Hector Pierce stood erect behind her. Jake positioned himself on the far side of the fire from Mr. Pierce. Alicia knew they had met. Did they dislike each other? If so, why? But she didn't have time to worry about that.

When Corley came and stood beside her, Alicia raised her hand for silence. The crowd grew quiet.

"We gather around the fire under the Milky Way to honor the memory of Nigel Lennox, a teacher, a carpenter, and our friend. The book of Ecclesiastes says there is 'a time to be born and a time to die.' A hard lesson. You cannot pick and choose which bits you want. Life is unpredictable. I believed his youth and joy would protect him, but they did not."

Her voice broke. Regaining her composure, she continued. "The earth has gathered Nigel to herself. We hear his music, and, in our mind's eye, we see him dance through life. Nigel runs with his hair streaming behind him, chasing goats. He shows his students how to understand wood and create beauty. He teaches his students to work with numbers. He made our lives better by being himself. We will miss him."

She struggled to keep the tears at bay. Paul sobbed openly along with several of Nigel's students.

"Nigel was a part of our community," Alicia said. "In his honor, please share your memories of him. Pick up a piece of wood from the woodpile, say what is on your heart, and throw the wood into the fire."

No one moved until William stepped forward holding Geoff and picked up a piece of kindling.

"Once I walked by the open door of Nigel's hut. He lay on his cot with a mouse on his chest, nose to nose. They gazed at each other. Animals didn't fear him. They knew he was gentle."

William threw the wood onto the fire. Geoff watched wide-eyed as the fire blazed up. William went back to stand beside Bronwyn who sat on a chair, hand on her belly.

Fey held Sammy and walked to the fire. Alicia gave her son a sliver of wood.

"Nigel," Fey said, "I am heartsick for your parents. Only thirty-five years old. You helped build this school, then taught carpentry. You showed your students decency, as any true mentor. The future work of your students is your legacy." Fey helped Sammy toss the wood into the fire.

Others shared their memories of Nigel.

Corley picked up a piece of wood. "I am proud to say that Nigel and I loved each other. We began by talking about music, and we fell in love. We had lots and lots of plans." She wiped away a tear. "We kept our romance a secret at first. I didn't want my friends to know I loved a White guy. Foolish. He would not want me to mourn, but I do. We have a favorite song by Graham Nash that I want to sing for him. It's called 'Our House.' Nigel made life easy."

Corley began to sing in a halting voice, but stopped, unable to go on. She clutched a piece of wood to her breast, then thrust it into the fire.

Bronwyn went to Corley and put her arms around her.

Jake stepped forward. "Nigel, I came to value you highly in the short time we had together. When I needed the correct species of grasshopper for dissection by my students, you ran after the grasshoppers until they were tired and stopped flying. Nigel talked the grasshoppers into giving up their lives for the students." He turned to Corley. "His death leaves a hole in our lives. I will keep Nigel in my heart of hearts all my days."

After each person had a chance to speak, Alicia stepped nearer to the fire. "Listen to the words of the poet."

How clear, how lovely bright,
How beautiful to sight
Those beams of morning play;
How heaven laughs out with glee
Where, like a bird set free,
Up from the eastern sea
Soars the delightful day.

"Nigel, you are like a bird set free. Thank you for blessing us with your presence. We will carry your memory with us wherever we go. You have been to us a teacher who exemplified devotion. Tsamaya sentle. Go well, our friend. May the Creator gather you into eternal peace and give you rest. So be it."

She walked among the crowd, whispering to the distraught students. She glimpsed Ellie and Mick hovering at the back of the crowd, but they did not speak.

Bronwyn led Corley back toward Nigel's place. The women teachers, African, American, British, and Canadian, followed them. All the differences between them were forgotten. Alicia hoped the male teachers would call a truce, too. How would Nigel's death affect the students?

She knew Fey would take the shaken Corley under her wing. Nigel liked to sing a Beatles song about getting by with a little help from his friends. Maybe over time, Corley would recover with that kind of help.

The clearing emptied bit by bit. All evening, Mr. Pierce stood behind Fey, his hand on her shoulder. When they left, Alicia sat down in Fey's chair with Sammy on her lap. Jake knocked apart the fire with a shovel, covered the embers with sand, and poured a bucket of water over it.

He walked over to Alicia. "Shall I put Sammy to bed?"

"Let's both do it."

In the Lizard Lounge, she shook out the bedding and pillow, and Jake laid him down.

"Mma?" Sammy said, sounding sleepy. "Ke batla Nigel."

She fought back her tears. "Nigel has gone away. We can no longer see him, but he is with us in spirit."

They sang Sammy a lullaby. After her son fell asleep, she walked outside with Jake. He patted the sand in the fire pit, making sure the fire was out. After that, he stood beside her, regarding the Milky Way.

"I put on a brave front," she said, "but inside I'm vanquished."

"Nigel told me that for months he would meet Corley at midnight," Jake said. "During the day, they pretended to be just friends. You and I don't have to wait. Let's enjoy every minute."

She held him with a fierceness she did not know she possessed.

46

When Mpule knocked the next morning, Alicia staggered over to open the door. "Please get Sammy dressed. Go to Fey, tell her I cannot teach today." Mpule went into the Lizard Lounge, and Alicia climbed back into bed. She closed her eyes.

The death of Nigel brought her grief for Eric crashing back down on her. If the world did not include Eric and Nigel, how could she go on? She drifted into a haze, not hearing the door open.

"Get up."

Alicia groaned. She knew that voice. Death was preferable to more orders from Fey.

"Get the hell up. Water's broken."

Alicia refused to budge. "You can mend the water line quicker than any man."

"Bronwyn's water broke. The headmaster will deal with our classes."

An image of a very pregnant Bronwyn sneaked into Alicia's brain.

Fey harrumphed. "She's not due for another month. Not a normal birth. A breech birth. Has she listened to my advice? No."

Alicia became more alert. "Breech?"

"The baby is *not* in cephalic presentation, head down. Bronwyn figured the baby would get 'sorted' and be 'jolly good.' Neurological trauma or cerebral palsy threaten the child."

Bronwyn had been positive the birth would be easy, although her sister, Catrin, had died in childbirth along with her baby. At their university, Bronwyn had told Alicia that rather than die of grief, she had taken a "vow of perpetual optimism."

"She should be in Francistown with Dr. Lekota," Fey said, pinching one of Alicia's legs.

"Knock it off."

"Too late to send Bronwyn bouncing over the washboard roads. The midwife at the village clinic attends another dangerous birth."

Alicia rolled over.

For once, strands of Fey's dark hair escaped her sleek French roll. She wore a canvas apron over her dress, the color of ripe tangerines.

"Jake will contact Dr. Lekota," Fey said, "and arrange transportation for her. I told him to move heaven and earth. He said he knew how. Smarty pants."

Alicia got off the cot slowly, took her black cords and a seersucker blouse from the closet and sat down to dress.

"Leave Sammy with Mpule," Fey ordered. "Geoff is at the headmasters to play with Ketumile. William is with Bronwyn. Bring anything absorbent. Do not dawdle. I forbid you to faint at the sight of blood. Tomorrow, you can grieve for Nigel. Today, you do scut work."

Fey glowered at Alicia. "Get cracking, woman."

☆ ☆ ☆

At Bronwyn's home, blood stained the sheets and floor red. Alicia willed herself to stay upright. William staggered out the door and did not return.

Bronwyn lay on a cot, groaning.

"Keep up your breathing" Fey said, "the way we talked about the last few months. Dr. Lekota will arrive with pain meds. She trained at the same university as the headmaster. Her bedside manner is arrogant. Considers herself an *artiste.* Never you mind. I respect her."

Alicia prayed for Dr. Lekota's speedy arrival.

"Dr. Lekota will do an episiotomy," Fey said, "give the baby more room to emerge. Alicia will take over your classes until you are able to teach again. Right?"

Alicia already taught one of Bronwyn's classes in addition to her own, and she wanted to object. Just then, Bronwyn screamed. Fey looked distraught.

Fey, who was *never* at a loss, was at a loss.

Alicia whispered words of encouragement to Bronwyn, hands on her shoulders.

Without any warning, the door flew open, crashing against the wall. A short, wide woman carrying a satchel stood before them. Alicia saw Jake in the doorway for less than a second, then he disappeared.

"I am here," the woman said, "to prevent a debacle. Stand aside. Let the master work."

Fey's soulmate, Dr. Lekota, had arrived. Alicia did a mental victory dance.

After the episiotomy, Dr. Lekota birthed the baby and cut the umbilical cord. Alicia wiped Bronwyn's face and neck. Fey held the newborn, wrapped in the last clean towel.

Dr. Lekota sewed up the episiotomy, talking non-stop. "The baby's head is distorted. Some. Not much. All fingers and toes in the correct places. No extra digits to cut off. I am sewing with my usual superb skill. What needs to be antiseptic is antiseptic. You will heal, Mrs. William. No infection will enter you. I have spoken."

The doctor stopped sewing. She looked around as if seeing Fey and Alicia for the first time. She gazed on Bronwyn with kind eyes.

"Your tears are present, Mrs. William. I see them, as I see all. I will give you another shot for pain. Effectual soon. Slight damage, yes. May need surgery later, maybe not. You have fine daughter. Cause for joy. Do not be pigheaded next time about coming to my hospital. I may not be available to save you. I am busy. Important. Do as I tell you. All will be fine."

Alicia's feet hurt from standing all day, but she felt revitalized as Fey placed the newborn in Bronwyn's arms. Mother and daughter were safe. She remembered the poem of Kalidasa, the Sanskrit poet, and his admonition to live each day well. In honor of this baby and Nigel's life, she renewed her resolve to do just that.

In her chair, Bronwyn held her newborn; the baby wailed, flailing her hands and feet.

"Do you hear that lung power?" Fey exalted. "This girl will be a forceful talker like her mother." Fey's confidence had returned, full throttle.

Without ceremony, Dr. Lekota packed up her satchel and left so quickly that Alicia did not have a chance to thank her.

"Ko Ko." William entered the room and headed straight to Bronwyn. He patted his daughter's head, dwarfing her tiny body with his hand.

Bronwyn stroked the baby's cheek. Her daughter turned to her, mouth open wide.

"Lovey wants to feed," Bronwyn said, sounding awed.

"She's rooting," Alicia said. Sammy had done that as a newborn.

Nestled in Bronwyn's arms, the baby started to nurse. Fey walked around the room stuffing bloody towels into a sack. She washed her hands in a bucket and threw the water out a window.

Alicia kissed Bronwyn's forehead as the baby took its first meal. "What will you name her?"

Bronwyn pushed back her hair. "Emelina Alicia Mortensen. Dark eyes, creamy brown skin, black hair. A princess. Geoff's got me dad's name. Fair's fair. She's 'Emelina' after William's mother and 'Alicia' after me best mate."

Stunned by this news, Alicia stammered her thanks.

Bronwyn gave her a weak smile. "Emmie, meet your groovy godmother and your bossy auntie."

"Emelina is the grandest name and suits her," Fey said, sidestepping the jest. "If we were Batswana, we would shave off Emmie's abundant hair. The two of you would quarantine for a while so you could recover from childbirth and bond with your infant. Lots of sense there."

William and Bronwyn focused on their daughter.

"Let's leave these folks alone," Fey said. "Alicia, take me to your place and make me a cup of tea. Got any vodka?"

"No booze. Sorry." They went out the door and headed toward her home.

"This birth would have been educational for Jake," Fey said as they walked together. "Sammy needs a sibling. Was his birth easy?"

Sammy's birth was easy, but Eric's absence had been painful. Eric had been killed three days before the birth. He didn't know that he had a son. Now he would miss all the years of his son's growing up.

Fey interrupted Alicia's thoughts. "I want more honorary nieces and nephews. You and Jake need to get busy."

"Get busy yourself."

"I would be a geriatric mother at age forty. Might be too old to conceive. I started late on sex." Fey was matter-of-fact.

Alicia did a double-take. "What?"

"You don't speak English? Timothy and I chose to wait until our wedding night for sexual relations. Some traditions still believe in that."

Alicia stopped walking. "Who is *Timothy*?" Fey had never spoken of him.

"Timothy was from Georgia like William. A physicist. A genius, probably. He died the day before our wedding, killed by a drunk driver. I was your age, twenty-five. Today is the fifteenth anniversary of his death."

Alicia stared at Fey. The desert sounds receded. "Wait, wait, back up. You had a fiancé? He was killed?" She touched Fey's arm.

"When Timothy died, I devoted myself to serving others. Would he have wanted me to hide in dark corners longing for his touch? Hell, no. He would say, 'Carpe diem. Dance. Sing. Carry on, Sweet Praline.'"

"Timothy called you his 'Sweet Praline?' Oh, Fey."

47

The next day, Jake was late for football practice. Kgeledi, following Jake's rules, started the drills without him. The footballers practiced passing the ball up and down the pitch.

Jake stayed in his rondavel to listen to Pierce's clerk on the short-wave radio. The clerk reported in code that they had background information on each teacher at the school. That was the good news.

The bad news was that guerrillas had attacked a farm in Rhodesia, murdered a White family—parents and young children—and slipped back into Botswana's borderlands. The Rhodesian military followed in hot pursuit. A gun battle ensued, and a PMU was caught in the crossfire. A Motswana was killed, one of the men Jake was training.

When Jake arrived at the pitch, his heart ached. He was sick of death. He set up an obstacle course and pushed them hard. The students moved through the drill, zig-zagging at top speed. They were panting when Jake called out, "Stop."

The footballers sat in a circle under a shade tree waiting for Jake to begin. They would often visit him at his hut. Most students were boarders, far from home, and homesick. Only Mmegi stayed aloof. Kgeledi was a frequent visitor, and they had mapped out his education and career. Botswana did not have a university yet, so Kgeledi was applying to universities in the U.K. Jake had written a letter of recommendation to send with the applications.

The team recited their motto. After that, they could bring up any topic for discussion.

"Rra Jake," Kgeledi said, "some Batswana students want to join the guerrillas. Many young Rhodesians come to Francistown wanting to join them. The police take their weapons and send them to refugee camps. The police might deport them to a third country like Zambia where they train as guerrillas.

Mmegi leapt up, startling his teammates. "I will join the Second Chimurenga. Be a hero."

Jake grimaced. "You think war is heroic?"

"We must free Black Africans from oppression," Mmegi shouted.

"Are you a military recruiter? You sound like one. What do *you* believe?"

"Ian Smith must die. All Whites in Rhodesia deserve death. They are not human."

"That kind of thinking is common in war," Jake said. "A famous soldier, General William Tecumseh Sherman in the U.S. Civil War, said, 'War is *hell.*' The truth is that war is destruction, pain, terror."

Mmegi made an obscene gesture.

Jake ignored it. "At times, we need to defend our homeland, which is why I trained as a soldier. But Botswana became independent through diplomacy and international pressure not war. Rhodesians need to figure out another way, maintain their humanity."

"You cannot talk Ian Smith into allowing Black rule," Mmegi said. "A bullet will convince him."

"Do you know anything about war?" Jake said.

"I will learn!" the student yelled.

Jake stood up. "I fought in Vietnam. Here is what I learned." He pulled his sweatshirt over his head, exposing the scars on his chest and arms.

The footballers stared at him, mesmerized.

He took off his sweatpants, leaving him only in his shorts. "This is what can happen to you. If you live, that is."

The team members jumped up, gathering close around him. Tamisha, their goalkeeper, whispered. "He fell into the fire." A few touched his waist, running their fingers over the ridges of the scars. Only Mmegi hung back.

Kgeledi picked up the sweat clothes from the ground. "Sir. I beg you to put these on."

Jake took his clothes, but he wasn't finished.

"I spent two years learning to walk without a limp. Is that what you want? The pain will drive you out of your mind. You cry, though you don't realize it. Men have lost their balls. Understand? I wanted to die rather than endure another operation. How many of you want to join a war that is not yours fight?"

He inspected their faces. All seemed awestruck except for Mmegi.

"Why should you be maimed or die? Forget about being a guerrilla. Build your own young nation. Study and learn. *That's* your job."

Mmegi spat on the ground and walked away without a backward glance.

Tamisha lingered after the others left. He told Jake he had heard something strange after a recent match. The Rhodesian guerrillas would not just recruit students at the schools but force students to join them—kidnap them and make them fight.

Cannon fodder.

"Incoming! Incoming! Danger close!" Jake's screams woke Alicia that night.

Sammy slept through most noise, and she hoped he would do so now. She tugged at Jake's arm until, with a moan, he woke up.

A mosquito whined. The mosquito coil had turned into a pile of ash. Forgetting her sandals, she stood up in her bare feet. She took a fresh coil out of the box and lit it. The tip glowed red, filling the room with the scent of incense. That done, she sat down on his cot, touching his arm.

"Have you grieved for your friends? You came to love those who fought beside you, didn't you? Most don't lose as many people as you did, at least, not all at once."

"A few of my buddies couldn't take the flashbacks. Killed themselves. I will not do that. I promise you."

She stroked his face. "Let me hold you as you grieve. Bring the faces of your friends to mind, say their names. Say goodbye. Imagine that the men who died are safe in their Creator's arms."

"Can you take it?"

She smiled. "You think me unfamiliar with grief?"

"Let's make love instead." He reached for her, but she deflected his hands.

"That won't take the pain away for long."

She lay down beside him and put her arms around him. Gradually, he relaxed. After a while, he whispered a name, but she couldn't make it out.

He said the name louder. "Scottie."

Then, he sobbed. After a while, he called out another name, then another. Hours went by.

At last, he slept. The night cooled. She found her sandals and checked on her son. When she returned to Jake, she pulled a sheet over his back. He didn't stir. She unlocked the door, and stepped down to the clearing and the scant moonlight. She paced on the sand, needing to free herself from his sorrow. He had his story. She had her own.

She looked up to the Milky Way, the white river that flowed above her.

"Let Jake come home from war."

☆ ☆ ☆

Jake woke in the predawn, reeking of sweat. He threw back the sheet and glanced over at the other cot. Alicia slept on her side facing away from him.

He pulled on his trousers, socks, and boots, opened the front door, and went outside, bare-chested. He relieved himself standing near the bushes, and found his favorite constellations, Pegasus and Andromeda.

"I feel lighter," he told the cicadas. "Why was I saved by our chaplain? Why did I live while my buddies died? I'll never know why. I have to accept that."

He identified more constellations. "What did Fey say? 'You can't stop life. Accept what is and go on.' This is a start, a very good start."

Back inside, Jake wiped down his body with a wet cloth. He brushed his teeth with baking soda. Rinsing his mouth, he swallowed the water. Waste not, want not.

He eyed Alicia, asleep on her cot. "Now for the grand finale to a memorable night."

Alicia woke up when Jake rolled her over and lay down behind her.

She growled. "Go away, mister. Best dream ever. Dessert smorgasbord: root beer floats, chocolate sundaes with maraschino cherries on top, boysenberry pie."

"You're my dessert." He kissed her shoulder, breathing a damp heat through her nightgown.

She pulled away from him. "Need sleep."

He pulled her back. "I've been mewling like a baby. I need to remind myself that I'm a *man*."

She wanted sleep, but something in his voice compelled her to listen.

"The guilt just faded away," he said. "Like mist."

His voice sounded altered, deeper.

She put aside her weariness and turned toward him.

He pulled her nightgown up and off, then nipped at her

neck. He kissed her breasts. Though tired, she responded. As he caressed her, electric sparks zipped through her.

He rested a hand on her hip and smoothed over the skin.

"I watch you as you walk," he whispered, "wanting you. Being a young male is a full-time job. Fun, though."

She writhed under his touch.

"Soft," he said. He kissed, licked, and probed her with his mouth: lips, teeth, and tongue. He seemed to be everywhere at once, whispering to her.

She did not tell him to stop. She did not want him to stop. He was freed from what bound him, and she would let him celebrate that freedom on her body.

Full of glorious sensations, she shattered into an exhausted mindlessness. She didn't hear him cry out or feel him on her spent body. She was a balloon floating up, glowing, sure they could light up the world with their love.

48

Friday evening, Jake stood with Pierce on his veranda watching as bee-eaters swooped around catching wasps. Jake was weary from both the previous night and the day of instruction in hand-to-hand combat.

"Congratulations on your engagement to Fey. Fast work, Pierce."

"Why waste time?" He gave Jake one of his rare smiles. "Let's recap the intelligence you brought. The guerrillas shift from *persuading* students to join their war in Rhodesia to *forcing* them to join."

The goats bleating outside the walls did not distract Jake. He had adapted to the African bush. "One of my footballers heard this at a match in Mahalapye, nowhere near the border with Rhodesia. Could be speculation."

"A similar report came in from a source in Bulawayo. It's a sign of weakness in the guerrillas. The Rhodesian government is also weak. A quarter million Whites cannot rule over five million Blacks forever."

"Our headmaster won't be happy with this news," Jake said. "We headed off a student riot, but the saboteur eludes us."

Pierce changed the subject. "How did your PMU training go?"

"By the end of our session," Jake said, "they knew each one bled the same shade of red. If they want to be in an elite corps, they must be up to the physical standards and work together. No backstabbing."

"The translator is working out?"

"The patient Mr. Rebaone has taught me more useful phrases. I still sound like a two-year-old in Setswana."

"Your additions to the map on the northeastern border are accurate."

"You checked my work?"

"No disrespect meant."

Jake let it go. "I don't want the men tested beyond their abilities. Losing Mompati hurt morale. No more violent deaths."

"Impossible goal. Rhodesian military killed two Batswana herders yesterday. Not even close to the amorphous border. Both sides, Rhodesian military and guerrillas, traumatize women and girls. I'm told that many rapes are not even reported."

"Reprehensible."

Pierce opened the door, gesturing for Jake to go inside.

"I teach my trainees your rules," Jake said. "Protect your buddy's back. Each one is only as strong as the squad. No man left behind."

Pierce picked up a pile of papers from the table next to the couch and looked through it. "Here's the background information I received on the staff at your school." He sat down on the couch, and Jake joined him.

"No sign Dereck wants to help the guerrillas," Pierce said.

"Dereck keeps the school's infrastructure running," Jake said. "He's a straight arrow."

Pierce shuffled the papers. "Mubayi fled here from Rhodesia where he headed a prestigious school. The Rhodesian government jailed him for sedition, tortured him. He escaped with his life, left a family behind."

"Might explain his anger."

"Mick Cooper is a pseudonym. He is, in fact, Michael Gregory Cromwell."

"I distrusted him the moment I met him," Jake grumbled.

"Mick held a variety of positions that kept him from carrying a rifle in Vietnam. He's fluent in Chinese and knows some Russian. The military sent him to school at a major university in Illinois. Later, he was in weapons procurement. Vanished after committing financial fraud."

"Not surprised."

"Moved his mother to a luxurious nursing home and set up a trust fund to pay for it."

"Mick cares about his mother? That does surprise me."

"Mick came here two years ago, before the Rhodesian bush war turned serious."

"With his background in languages and contacts from his defense work, he might be a gunrunner. We need proof. What about Paul Winthrop? He wants my blood."

"The feds want him for bomb-making. Numerous citations for arrests at protests against the war. Your girlfriend is squeaky clean, other than a sole citation for jaywalking."

"You checked her out?"

"SOP. Fey insisted I check out each teacher. You pass muster."

Jake glared at him.

"Joke. I would never sic the spooks on you."

Jake shrugged. "By the way, I'm training Balakile to be my replacement."

"You just got here!"

"'Localization' is the key word, training Batswana to do jobs done by expats."

Pierce stood up and paced. "My long-term goal, too," he said, at last. "Fey warned me. She told me to be civil when you brought it up."

Jake stood to leave. The sun was setting. A powerful generator kicked on, and massive floodlights lit the compound.

When Jake climbed into his Land Rover, he started to turn the key but stopped. He studied a Batswana guard he had not seen before. A thin white scar ran in a zig-zag from the outside corner of his right eye to his chin. This must be the man who stole the medal awarded to Alicia's late soldier-husband.

Jake casually climbed out of his Land Rover and went back inside on an urgent matter.

☆ ☆ ☆

Mpule came as arranged on Saturday to care for Sammy, and Alicia headed out to check on the downed tree for a second time. With the sabotage, Nigel's death, and the rioting, she was worried. Jake did not follow up on her concern about the downed tree. He said he wanted to help, but he was too busy. The tree was important in some way, she knew it.

She walked past the football pitch and the farm, scaring up birds, insects, and hares. She carried her mopane wood walking stick but doubted she would encounter a predator this close to the school.

At the end of her hike, she found the dead tree lying on the sand, its root cavity packed with sand. Sand was piled up higher than normal around neighboring trees. A ripple of fear went through her. Something had been buried. Weapons?

The school had several vehicles, and a few teachers had vehicles, too. She could not examine the tire tread as something had been pulled behind a vehicle to erase the tracks.

In a landscape of muted greens, grays, and browns, a flash of yellow caught her attention. Leaning closer, she saw that it was a half-buried cigarette box, the same brand Mick and Dereck smoked. The paper looked harmless, but Jake's rule was, "Beware the fatal assumption."

Someone invisible tugged on her arm, insisting that she leave.

"I will not assume anything," she said, backing away. She left the gold box undisturbed.

"Jake will know what to do."

49

Monday evening, the teachers crowded into the staff house. Sammy sat on Alicia's lap looking at a Dr. Seuss book. Jake sat beside her with his arm around her shoulders, tight-lipped, agitated. Alicia did not know what was going on. He had returned late Sunday night after having been gone since early Friday morning. They had not had a chance to talk.

When the headmaster called the meeting to order, Jake raised his hand. Mr. Matlagodi called on him. He stood up and walked to the lectern. The headmaster stepped back, and all eyes were on Jake.

"The civil war in Rhodesia intensifies," Jake said, looking around the room. "The guerrillas want majority rule. I've learned that to swell their ranks, guerrillas plan to kidnap many students and train them to fight."

The teachers started to murmur.

"Hijacking schools in Botswana is unlikely, but we must consider the possibility. We're a stone's throw from the border, and schools on the Rhodesian side of our shared border are vulnerable. My recommendation is to close Kukama School to keep our students safe. Rhodesian guerrillas now have AK-47s which they use to intimidate, kill."

The murmur grew into a roar. The teachers shouted questions, but didn't wait for answers. Jake gave up trying to speak and sat down. The voices grew louder. The headmaster asked for order, but the teachers ignored him.

Alicia sat there flabbergasted, hugging Sammy. Jake was talking about guerrillas taking students at gunpoint. He should have warned her. Did he not consider her opinion worthwhile?

"Silence," Mr. Matlagodi said, over and over. At last, he got their attention, and the teachers quieted down. "We do not accept Mr. Hunter's suggestion. We fixed the break in the water line. We replaced the broken windows from the riot. We replaced the anti-venom kits. Our students must prepare for the important examinations to come. I hereby adjourn this meeting."

Jake stood up. "Why abort the meeting? Face the problem head on."

The headmaster made his way out of the room. The noise level rose even higher, and the meeting dissolved.

Jake leaned over and picked up Sammy from Alicia's lap.

"Tell me what you're thinking, Jake."

"If we close the school, we keep everyone safe. Don't you agree?"

Alicia's mouth went dry. "We're one of a handful of secondary schools in all of Botswana. Our students would lose an entire year of education. I want them to be both safe *and* educated. Is that combination possible?" She hated conflict, but she needed to be honest.

"I should have talked with you beforehand. Just used to going it alone. How can I keep you, Sammy, and the students safe if we don't close the school?"

"You would interrupt the education of hundreds of students. What about their examinations? Their future?" She felt her body tense. Showing emotion was frowned upon, but she was losing her temper and couldn't hide it. She wasn't sure she wanted to.

Alicia took Sammy back from Jake, set him down, took his hand, walked out the front door.

Jake followed her. "Don't turn your back on me," he said. "Please!"

She waved him away. "Stay in your own place tonight."

The next afternoon, Alicia sat cross-legged on the cot in the Lizard Lounge. She needed to go over the account for the Scarlet Pimpernel Fund. With students, there was always a health emergency of one kind or another. The tiny village clinic with one nurse could not begin to handle the need. The school was under-funded, so Paul's money was essential to the students' health care.

Even as she went about her task, Jake was on her mind. After the night apart, she felt his absence keenly. He *should* have talked with her before recommending that the school close. They were a couple. Couples shared. At least, she and Eric had shared everything. Well, to be honest, not everything.

She gave Mpule a few coins to take Sammy to the Tip Top Shoppe to buy "fat cakes," the deep-fried morsels of dough rolled in powdered sugar.

These days Sammy was staying close to his mother, Mpule, or Fey. Alicia hoped he would not decide to take more walks on his own. She could not handle any more crises.

The curtains at her open window moved in a slight breeze. The fabric for the curtains she had bought months ago at the textiles building. When she saw the tie-dyed fabric hanging on a clothes line to dry, she went in and bought it even though her budget was tight. The electric colors of the curtains often lightened her mood. Not today. She pulled at her blouse where it stuck to her damp skin.

She heard Jake's gait on the upper path. He had not attended assembly that morning. Her heart beat faster.

She shoved the financial documents under a pile of essays. She wanted to tell Jake about the Fund, but she needed to clear it with Paul, whose aversion to Jake's military background seemed to grow instead of diminish.

Jake walked inside carrying a bag that looked familiar.

"I'm hungry," he said, "but Bronwyn is out of the eggs she sells for Ndona. I want to make an omelet on my new one-burner stove. Have any eggs to share?"

She thumbed through the essays, averting her eyes. "The eggs are in the woven basket between the can of plums and the tin of powdered milk."

He went into the main room and returned with the basket. He sat down on the cot beside her, putting his bag on the floor.

"It's over 120 degrees outside, but it's forty below zero in here." He put three eggs in his palm and turned to her. "I may be wrong to recommend closing the school, but we need to talk."

She tossed her essays aside and stood up, pencil in hand.

"What's worse, fear or ignorance?" She stared at him. "That's not rhetorical. I'm asking. I'm hit from all sides. The war in Rhodesia, the sabotage, the drop-dead exams…." She let out a cry of exasperation.

He stroked the flecked eggs. "Wonder if these eggs are fertilized? More real to break open ones with bits of blood in them. A shame to steal a hen's potential chicks, but there you are. We make choices."

She wanted him to hold her. Instead, she sat down and picked up an egg from his hand. "I admired the eggs today, too. The shells are bumpy and rough. I never expect that. They're used, I suppose, in a way. Want them?"

"I'll tell you what I don't want. I don't want you to shut me out when you disagree with me. That's not good for *us*."

She put the egg back in his palm and rubbed her temple. "You're giving me an ultimatum?"

"Some things I will not tolerate."

"You're right. Immature of me. I took out my uncertainty on you. Forgive me?"

He kissed her cheek. "I'll accept it, if you convince me you can't live without me." As he pulled her onto his lap, she dropped the pencil.

"Hold on," she said. "I need to talk to you, too." She stayed on his lap and snuggled against him.

"Make it snippy-snappy," he said. "I'm fantasizing about some heavy French kissing. My new research project is on the physiology of orgasm. I'll give up the field of geology for anatomy."

"I would stick with geology, if I were you." She smiled. "By the way, I went back to the place I told you about. In the prohibited area, remember? I found a gold cigarette box sticking out, maybe marking the spot for a weapons cache."

"You could not wait, eager beaver. Risky. You ignore danger. But I will check it out…later."

She gave him a quick kiss. "I needed to see if there were any changes. Weapons are a threat. Right?"

"Forget weapons. Let's get back to the important business at hand. Kissing."

She pulled back. "Rather than closing the school, let's sketch out a plan for the school's defense."

"You already have an idea?" Jake lifted her off his lap and set her beside him. "Before we go further, I need to replace the pistol Matlagodi confiscated." He picked up his bag and went into the main room.

The welcome bag she gave him on his first day at the school now contained a weapon. She heard the closet door click. A Colt .45 was back in her closet, along with the flare gun. She had her own private arsenal.

When he returned, he pulled her close and nibbled her earlobe. "Let's have a blissful time of kiss and make up. Much, much later, we'll devise a plan to defend the school. Since it's leap year, and leap day is coming up. You could ask me to marry you."

The marriage suggestion seemed premature. But Sammy and Mpule would not be back for at least an hour, and Jake was a champion kisser.

50

After dinner that evening, Jake organized his rock samples on the bookcase Nigel had made for him. He taped a map of Botswana on a wall and wrote the name of each footballer by their home village.

On his floor was a kaiross, a rug made of springbok hides sewn together with dried entrails. A man in a loin cloth had emerged from the brush on one of his trips offering it for sale. He paid what the man asked, no haggling.

Dereck called to him through the open door, sounding distressed. "My lorry. The tires!"

Jake came to the door. "Sabotage?"

"Slashed. Can't patch them. I parked it by my door this afternoon. Mubayi, the bastard, snuck past. He never apologizes for bashing up the lorry. Other than that, just the usual suspects." Dereck rubbed his greasy hands together. "Bloody hell. I've got a pain in my gut, getting ulcers."

Jake took a deep breath. "Impossible to predict where the saboteur will strike next. Random."

Dereck took two pieces of paper out of his pocket and handed them to Jake. "Here's the specs for the tires plus a map to the tire store. Put the bill on the school's account. They're expensive. I'll have Mrs. Linchwe tell them you'll come tomorrow afternoon." He paused. "You're a good bloke."

Jake stood outside his door, watching Dereck head home.

"Dereck calls me a 'good bloke.' Pierce might call me an SOB. If I don't tell Alicia about my double life, I'll be DOA. After years of a fractured life, I've found her. Lucky, lucky me."

Stepping outside, he picked up a stone. He threw it at the perimeter fence, startling several weaver birds who flew up, complaining.

"Hey, buddies. I'm Humpty Dumpty reassembled. Tell your friends. Major miracle."

☆ ☆ ☆

Jake visited Pierce briefly the next afternoon before getting the tires. He told Pierce he needed to tell Alicia about his mission. Pierce agreed without an argument. Jake took that as a good sign and departed, whistling "Penny Lane."

"I'll tell her I'm working undercover. Then, I'll get down on one knee and propose. Great wife, wonderful life. Verifiable proof that even I can learn from experience."

He swerved around a slow truck, and checked Dereck's map. He located the tire store on a dusty back street in Francistown. He pulled his Land Rover in front, rolled down his window, and honked the horn. The store looked deserted.

Jake sensed movement in his peripheral vision just before someone yanked open the driver's side door. Jake grabbed the

Oh, Jesus! bar, lifted both feet and hit the man in his chest, shoving him back.

At the same time, the passenger door opened, and someone came at him. Pain flared in his side.

In one seamless motion, Jake pulled his knife from his ankle sheath and jabbed at the eyes of his attacker. Blood spattered the windshield. The man shrieked, hands to his face.

On the driver's side, he sensed another man. Knife in hand, he turned toward him. In a split-second, he recognized Dinizulu. A medal gleamed on his shirtfront. Jake slashed across the man's throat with his right hand. With his left hand, he ripped off the medal. Dinizulu staggered backward, falling into the sand. He struggled to his feet and ran away, holding his bleeding neck.

Jake threw the Land Rover into reverse and roared back onto the road. After he turned, he gunned the engine and sped forward, leaving a cloud of dust. He checked his rearview mirror. No one followed him.

Blood trickled down his side and leg. He pressed the wound with his fingers to stem the bleeding. As he headed toward the school, he kept watch for another ambush. He would not trust a visit to the hospital. The enemy might be lying in wait. The men meant to kill him.

The thorn trees flowed by him in a blur.

"I need Fey and that damn satchel of hers, preferably, before I pass out."

Jake drove through the main gate at the school. For once, the gate stood wide open. He refused to worry about the goats getting out. No time. He drove up, parked, and walked to Fey's, keeping his hand pressed to his side. No one was close enough to notice the growing red stain on his shirt and trousers. Somehow Pierce had made it to the school before him; his Jeep was beside Fey's rondavel.

Jake knocked on the door and turned the doorknob. Locked.

He kept his voice low. "Fey?"

After a minute, Fey opened the door dressed in a vermillion robe. Pierce was tucking in his shirt.

"Attacked," Jake said, walking in and sitting in a chair. "Fey. Sew me up."

"Who did it?" Pierce asked.

"Dinizulu and two of his cronies. They're out of commission."

Pierce slapped his hands together.

Fey poured water from a jug into a basin and washed her hands. She lifted Jake's shirt and probed the wound with her fingers.

"It's significant, but no organ involvement," she said. "The scar tissue on your waist may have saved your life."

She lit a lantern and took her sewing kit from a shelf. "Take off your shirt and lie down on the table. I don't want blood on my new sheets, a gift from Hector." She shot a smoldering glance at her fiancé.

No one called the colonel by his first name except Fey.

"We were giving the sheets a test drive," she said, "when we were rudely interrupted." She handed Jake a jar. "Drink this. It won't kill the pain, but it will help."

He drank all the liquid and began to unbutton his shirt. They would see his scars, but he no longer cared. He stretched out on the table, his legs hanging over the edge. He closed his eyes, took a deep breath, and relaxed his body systematically.

Fey cleaned the wound. She pulled out a spool of surgical thread and threaded her needle. "I'm competent at sewing, but not as fast as Dr. Lekota."

Pierce went outside and closed the door behind him. He walked back a few minutes later, shutting the door hard. "Spill it."

"Dereck set me up, by accident, in all likelihood."

"Your cover is blown. The Rhodesian guerrillas know we strengthen the border with your training. This threatens their ability to attack sites in Rhodesia and hightail it back to the border lands."

Pierce put his hand on Jake's bare shoulder. "You grow calmer in a crisis. You never panic. Admirable."

Someone knocked at the door.

"Ko Ko."

Jake groaned. Now he was close to panic. Alicia was at the door.

51

Alicia pushed open the door to Fey's and stopped, shocked by the tableau. Jake lay on the table, eyes closed, his abdomen streaked with red. Fey sewed on his flesh. Mr. Pierce touched Jake's bare shoulder. Behind them, green herbs crowded the windowsills, a touch of normalcy.

Jake lay with his hands open beside him, his palms mottled with blood. Alicia could not even say his name. Mr. Pierce stepped back.

Alicia fought her nausea. "What happened?" She needed answers.

Fey kept on pulling a needle through his skin. "This wound is the least of his worries."

"Who did this?" Alicia took a breath and touched his cheek. His eyes opened.

"Let me explain," he said in a flat voice.

"Is Mr. Pierce military? Does that mean you are, too?"

No one spoke.

She glared at Pierce, then Jake. "You said you resigned from the military. Do you go mapping on the weekends, or is it something else?"

Jake held up a bloody hand. "I promised Pierce confidentiality. I have known him all my life. He's Colonel Pierce, my godfather."

"The man with all the rules?" Alicia wondered if she should laugh, cry, or walk out the door. "After you were injured in Vietnam, he brought you to Botswana next to a war zone?"

Jake spoke with effort. "I train Batswana to defend their nation. I gather intelligence. You want to know who I am, that's who I am."

"Go on." Alicia contained her confusion and hurt.

"Several hours ago, three men jumped me. One of the men was Dinizulu."

This was not making sense. "Dinizulu attacked you? He's Batswana not Rhodesian."

He evaded her question. "After I train a Motswana to take my place, I'll be done."

Fey finished her stitching, cut the thread, and put away her equipment. She poured a liquid over the stitches. Jake stiffened.

"Change the dressing twice a day," Fey said. "Drink plenty of water. Rest. I'm duty-bound to give you these instructions, whether you follow them or not is up to you."

Jake sat up. "No time to rest. I hope to take Alicia and Sammy to the Tsodilo Hills and the Okavango Delta on the school break. We'll eat tilapia. When did you eat fish last, Alicia?"

"Someone tried to kill you, and you want to talk about fish?" She struggled to make sense of the situation. "Shortwave radio, pistols, flare guns, Land Rover. I wanted to believe you were no longer a soldier. What kind of a fool, am I?"

Fey handed Jake his shirt. He got off the table and put it on. He reached out to Alicia, but she backed away.

"I turn policemen into Rangers. That's important, isn't it?" Jake's eyes pleaded. "Not enough? I want to be with you for the rest of my life."

She turned and walked to the door.

"Wait," Jake said. "Talk to me."

She turned to him. "Has anything you've said been real, or am I part of your job?"

"Our bodies never lie."

"You lied by omission. Did you bring us more danger? The guerrillas don't want you here. I'm sure about that."

Alicia opened the door and stepped down onto the sand, blistering hot in the afternoon sun. She walked toward her home; Jake caught up with her.

"I will not lose another man to war," she said. "I chose to trust you. Was I wrong?"

"Listen to me."

In a daze, she kept walking.

"Stop! I have what you lost," he said.

She turned to him. He held an object in his palm. "Dinizulu wore this on his shirt."

She picked up the medal, streaked with blood. A Vietnam Service Medal. Static filled her mind.

"Eric died two years ago in Vietnam, yet here he is." She

brought the medal to her lips and kissed it, tasting the salt and iron of Jake's blood. Then she ran, holding the medal to her heart, tears blurring her vision. She was running, but she did not know where.

52

Saturday morning at dawn, Jake picked up his footballers at the front gate. The footballers squeezed together in the school van. Badisa, a Fifth Former recommended by Kgeledi, replaced the disgraced Lepetu.

Jake bumped through potholes on the dirt track as he drove southwest toward a match in Serowe. The bumps jolted his wound, but he ignored the pain.

Piet's bottle store was on the road to the match. Jake would buy the team soft drinks. As he drove, he avoided a collision with an erratic driver and swerved to miss a kudu. His football team sang and laughed the entire time, oblivious to danger. He kept his window wide open. The sweaty teenage bodies smelled acrid, but living in a land with scant water, they were used to it.

Before he and Alicia split up, she and her committee had developed a plan to defend the school against a possible hijacking. An essential member of that committee was Kgeledi, sitting next to him. Jake asked for silence, and Kgeledi began to outline the plan to his teammates.

When Kgeledi finished, Jake said, "Consider this an opportunity for leadership. Each of you is important to the *secret* plan to thwart a hijacking. We cannot do it without you. If the school is attacked, you must do your part without hesitation. What's the goal? No one kidnapped or hurt. The school must survive. Understand?"

The footballers shouted their assent, proud to be enlisted. They sang the national anthem with enthusiasm.

Kgeledi spoke to Jake in an earnest voice. "I will not lose one student you entrust to me."

☆ ☆ ☆

That evening, Mick sent a note to Chaparadza using the usual channel. A messenger on a motorbike would deliver the note to the guerrilla's camp hidden in a thick stand of trees by the Ramokgwebana River on the Botswana side of the border.

The note was terse.

> *Your promised weapons will be ready soon. You can kidnap the students and obtain the weapons at the same time. My next message will give you date and time. When you get rid of Alicia Talbot, four extra AK-47s are yours. Jake Hunter continues to be a threat to us both. Try again to kill him. If you succeed, I will reward you well.*

Mick scowled as he signed his fake name on the note. "Waiting feels like a line of putzi flies under my skin. I made

Chaparadza wait, but I still need one more item. He is an erratic man, not a patient one."

Jake rose before sunrise Sunday morning. He headed into the wilderness to the north of the school. He would check on the downed tree that concerned Alicia. He wanted her to listen to him, but he had not listened to her. He had let her request slide by him, lost under other responsibilities.

"Mistake number four trillion and seventy-three. Sounds low. Might be higher."

After a frustrating search, he found the downed tree and the gold box sticking out of the sand. A gunrunner operated out of the school. He was now convinced of it.

Jake drove as fast as possible to Francistown, straight to Pierce's compound. Much as he hated to postpone it, visiting Alicia would have to wait.

Standing before Pierce, Jake argued with him. "We need an explosives expert *today!*"

"No expert can make it here for a week," Pierce said. "My clerk checked with the South Africans after you radioed."

"What about the rest of the known universe? If you cannot get an expert, arrest Mick and Mubayi, my top suspects."

Pierce shook his head. "You want an expert to examine disturbed sand which may or may not be a weapons cache. Or you want me to convince the local police to arrest expats without any evidence of wrongdoing. Though come to think of it, Mick Cooper is wanted on fraud in the U.S. Although, I could get the authorities to arrest him, I'm not inclined to do so."

"What about keeping the students safe?" Jake stayed calm. "What about keeping the weapons out of guerrilla hands?"

"Hold on. Unfortunately, I have news. About Balakile, your trainee."

Jake refocused. "What about him?"

"Guerrillas beat up his wife, traumatized his kids, and kidnapped him from his home."

"You're telling me this *now*?"

"You will *not* go to his rescue. It could be a trap, and I don't want to lose you. Let me worry about liberating Balakile."

They stood close together, facing each other.

"Stand down, Major Hunter. You're not a one-man army. Dinizulu's pal was able to slice you open, which should tell you something about your current readiness. You've gone civilian. What would Alicia want?"

Jake strode to the front door, and turned to Pierce. "I'm resigning from your mission. I no longer take orders from you. *You* get an explosives expert. *I'll* rescue Balakile." He put his hand on the doorknob. "The guerrillas will torture Balakile. I cannot allow that. I will not lose another man." He walked out of the room.

Pierce shouted after him. "Don't be an ass!"

Jake headed to the storeroom for gear.

I need my cabinet of magic powers.

53

"Down-he-go," Alicia said as Sammy fell down on the sand. They were kicking a ball back and forth in her clearing, but his foot rolled over the top, and he lost his balance.

"Up-he-come," she said. Sammy stood back up and they went back to kicking the ball around. Fall down. Get back up. Sammy could be demanding, but she always admired his resilience.

Saturday morning, she had found a note from Jake slipped under her door. He said he would visit her soon. But on Sunday afternoon, there was still no sign of him. She had not seen him since he had been wounded. He avoided morning assembly and dinners.

Fey knew about his undercover work all along, but kept it a secret from her. This hurt. It felt like a further betrayal.

Alicia went through the motions of life. She missed Jake. And part of that was practical. If the school were attacked, she would need his expertise.

Her committee held an emergency meeting and revised their plan. Each chose a task, some more dangerous than others. William said he would collaborate with Jake, if he could find him. If not, he would go it alone.

Alicia's task relied on her superb hearing. She needed to hear the guerrillas' trucks long before they arrived. The stakes were high.

Anger rose within her. "Am I supposed to be awake night and day? Why didn't I leave with Sammy when Jake urged me to go?"

Sammy stopped kicking the ball, sat down, and started to cry. As she patted his back, she realized that she had spoken out loud. He hiccuped; tears ran down his cheeks. Sammy reacted to her moods. When she worried, he became teary-eyed, unlike his usual cheery self.

She dried his eyes, wiped his runny nose, and tied on his hat. She picked up her daypack and put in all the gear she had gathered. With a resolute air, she took her son for a walk. Their first visit was with William and Bronwyn. She gave William almost everything in her pack.

Bronwyn did not worry about a hijacking. All would be "splendid, brilliant even." Bronwyn chose to believe that life would work out somehow, without much planning. Alicia was sure a plan could improve the odds of success.

When Alicia departed, William followed her outside. "An attack on the school is an attack on my family. I am ready with my blade." His dark-brown eyes flashed with conviction. Who would dare cross William?

At the boys' dormitory, she talked for a few minutes with Negotho, explaining her special request. After that, she sought out Kgeledi.

"We are ready, Mrs. Jake," Kgeledi said. "We refuse to join with the guerrillas. We must earn our education and lead a literate nation into a prosperous future."

She flushed. He called her "Mrs. Jake." She doubted she would ever be Jake's wife.

Sammy tugged at her pant leg. "Walk, Mma." He could be insistent.

She held his hand as they went into the girls' dormitory to find Gaeyo. When they found her, the student said she and her prefects would do their part.

Alicia gave Sammy a drink of water before they climbed over the stile on the way to the farm. There she talked with Ndona. He reaffirmed his vow to defend the school no matter the cost.

Returning from the farm, Alicia knocked on the headmaster's door. When he opened it, he wasted no time in expressing his skepticism.

"Mrs. Talbot, you create trouble where none exists. No attack will come. I must go to Gabs to defend the school. The bureaucrats in the Department of Education are the real threat. They have received a complaint from a parent and want to end our independence." He closed the door with more firmness than necessary.

The headmaster did not believe an attack was possible; this was Botswana, not Rhodesia. He was right, she hoped. If he was wrong, her committee would execute their plan. It was not a surefire plan, in fact, it was a half-assed plan, but it was all they had.

54

On Tuesday, there was no sign of Jake. Fey taught his classes. Alicia was still miffed at her. Alicia had left Sammy with Bronwyn so he could play for an hour with Geoff. Needing to collect her son, she opened her door. Ellie stood there. The woman's eyes were puffy, her skin flushed. Alicia remembered her promise not to confront Mick, and she would not.

Ellie's face crumpled. "Dorcas told me that Onyana, my house girl, stole her fancy dress from her clothesline."

"What do you need?" Alicia could not get involved.

"Dorcas asked if Onyana has stolen from me. I checked. My silk scarf, bracelet, and slip are gone. Worst of all, I discovered the black notebook of Mick's is missing, too. He told me not to touch it. Ever. He will be back later today."

Mick was often absent from the school. Alicia wondered where he went, not for the first time.

Ellie became more distraught, wringing her hands. "He usually takes the notebook with him. Maybe he's testing me.

Dorcas said I must visit Onyana's hut in the village, and bring back her dress."

Alicia put her hands on her hips. "She is Motswana and speaks Setswana. Have her go."

"Dorcas says her mother is sick and needs her."

"You can refuse Dorcas. She has other options besides you."

Ellie wailed. "I have to find the notebook. Come with me." She sank to her knees. "I beg you."

Two days ago, Alicia made the long walk to talk with the kgosi about the committee's plan to defend the school. Jake and his Land Rover were absent, so a speedy visit was not possible. She did not want to take the walk again, but Ellie looked frightened.

Alicia sighed. "When do you want to go?"

"Now."

"Dumela Rra. Dumela Mma."

Alicia greeted each person they passed. Ellie ignored everyone.

Alicia wore an ankle-length dress with a high neck and full-length sleeves. She carried a daypack and a hankie in her pocket. Modesty was expected of all traditional Batswana women. The sexy creations by Lara would not be appreciated. Ellie wore a long-sleeved shirt and a skirt that fell below her knees. Both women wore hats, protection from the sun.

Before she left, Alicia went to Bronwyn's and asked her to keep Sammy longer, until she returned from the village.

"What a bloody great fool ye be," Bronwyn said and closed the door in her face.

Bronwyn was grouchy these days, overwhelmed by the needs of her family, especially Emmie.

After a mile of walking in total silence, Ellie spoke. "Dorcas said the police will come and take a statement about the thefts. I have to go to the kgotla to accuse Onyana. Will you go with me?"

Alicia frowned. "A man must go with you to the kgotla. Women can't go solo. That's not done, Mpule says."

Ellie sneered. "What does she know?"

"Mpule gives me clues about Batswana life swirling under our noses. According to her, the kgosi determines the placement of individual huts in the village. He will decide who Mpule marries. The husband's family will give a gift to her grandfather, the kgosi, in cattle."

They lapsed into silence. At the village, Ellie pointed. "Over there. That's Onyana's. She showed me once when we went to the orchards by the river to buy grapefruit."

The village was clean and tidy. Small boys ran around with toy cars they made from wire and tin cans. Within each compound, the dirt was hard-packed. In one, a woman bent double, sweeping the dirt with a short broom. Dead branches surrounded Onyana's place, encircling three small huts.

"We're not the police," Alicia said. "We don't have permission to search their property."

"We can, at least, ask." Ellie sounded determined.

Standing by the gate, Alicia called out to the woman she saw in the compound.

"Ko Ko, Mma Onyana?"

The older woman, barefoot and skeletal, left her dishes in a pan of brown water. She came to the gate wearing a head scarf. Gray hair poked through the holes in the cloth. Over her long dress, she wore a tattered shawl. She opened the gate and gestured for them to enter.

Alicia pointed to herself. "Mma Sammy. Ke batla Onyana." I want Onyana.

Mma Onyana gestured toward the river. She pointed to the stools by the cooking fire. A three-legged caldron stood over the coals of a fire. Steam rose from the boiling water.

"Ke itumetse." Alicia walked to a stool and sat down. Ellie sat down beside her.

Mma Onyana walked inside. A few minutes later, she brought out three cracked ceramic cups and a tin of Five Roses tea all arranged on a piece of cardboard. Proper hospitality was central to Batswana culture. Alicia wondered if Mma Onyana could afford the tea.

In the distance, Onyana walked toward them, a pail of water on her head. When she arrived, Onyana set the pail on the dirt by the fire, and they exchanged greetings. The girl stood erect, her hair short, her dress a froth of flowers.

"That's my dress," Ellie blurted out.

"You forget, Mrs. Mick," Onyana said, "you give this to me."

Ellie stuttered. "Can't be possible, can it? I bought that dress in New York to celebrate the end of a photoshoot."

"Which hut is yours?" Alicia asked Onyana.

Onyana pointed to the one farthest away in the compound.

"Please ask your mother if we may go inside."

Onyana seemed defiant, and Alicia assumed she would refuse. Onyana spoke with her mother. Her mother replied in rapid Setswana, shook her head, and waved for them to go inside.

The door was made of bits of wood nailed together in a haphazard fashion. Alicia opened the door and walked onto the dirt floor. Strips of cardboard had been pushed into the gaps in the thatch.

A mattress leaned against one wall. A basket of seeds for stringing into necklaces hung in the glass-less window hole. In one corner sat two battered boxes full of clothing. A rope was strung between the walls. A few dresses and a slip hung over the line.

"Here's my slip." Ellie took it off the clothesline. "I can tell by the blue ribbon around the hem." She held it up. "Filthy. Don't want it back." She laid it back over the clothesline.

Ellie rolled up her sleeves and began to sort through the boxes. Alicia noticed cuts on her forearms in varying degrees of healing.

"Here's Mick's favorite hat," Ellie said. "I got a good sock in the arm when he couldn't find it. No sign of Dorcas's dress or my other things."

An object in the corner caught Alicia's attention. "Is this Mick's?" She picked up a leather notebook. Ellie grabbed it from her.

Opening it, Ellie cried out, "It's empty!" Her hands shook.

Alicia took back the notebook and went outside. She called to Onyana, holding up the notebook. "Where are the papers that were inside this?"

Onyana pointed to the firepit. Alicia walked over, squatted down, and picked up bits of scorched paper. She slipped a few scraps into the pocket of her dress. Some of the words were legible. Mick was up to something.

"Ellie, are these Mick's?"

Ellie walked toward her, stumbling on the uneven ground in her haste. She picked up a page. "Yes, this is from his notebook, but what use are these pages? I need the book whole, so he won't know it was ever gone."

Villagers began to gather at the gate, talking among themselves.

"We'd better leave," Alicia said. "If the kgosi finds out about Onyana's thievery, he may punish the mother."

She said goodbye to Mma Onyana and her daughter. Looking forlorn, Ellie carried the empty notebook and Mick's hat. They walked back toward the school.

"If you want to get away from Mick, maybe I could help," Alicia said.

Perhaps the Scarlet Pimpernel Fund could come to Ellie's rescue. The money was for the students, but it was Paul's money. He might agree to it.

"The notebook isn't as important to him as I am," Ellie said with confidence.

Alicia studied her. The woman was deluded.

"I'll tell him the truth," Ellie said. "Onyana took it, used the pages to light a fire."

"Mick won't care. We both know what he's like."

Ellie glared at her. "Did Fey tell you lies about us? She's an incompetent gossip."

The venom in her voice startled Alicia. "This has nothing to do with Fey. You were terrified of what Mick would do if he found out the notebook was missing. I could borrow a school vehicle and take you to the hotel in Francistown. We could get you out before he gets back."

"Can you keep me safe?" Ellie spoke in a childlike voice.

Alicia realized she might have overestimated her abilities. "I can try."

"If I ran away and he found me, my life would be hell." Ellie's tone changed. "No, I cannot leave." She began to whimper.

Alicia knew the cause of Jake's scars, but what about the wounds she saw on Ellie? She remembered seeing the bloody scratches on Ellie's bare back when the water line was cut.

Alicia's mind raced. She started to walk again, faster this time, thinking about the acts of sabotage. Was Ellie responsible for it all? She arrived before the school opened, and when it did open, she taught students English. Could she undermine the school after all of her labor? If so, she put people in danger, including Nigel and herself. Was it to please Mick? Mick owned a truck. To carry weapons? Maybe the guerrillas were coming for weapons and students. She walked even faster.

Ellie shouted at her. "Slow down. It's hot."

Alicia glanced back at Ellie. "I need to get to Sammy."

"You seem weird," Ellie said. "Did you read Mick's notes? What did you see?" Her demeanor changed. She shrieked, "What did you see?"

Alicia was startled by the transformation in the woman.

Ellie shook her fist at her. "You self-righteous bitch. You prissy, Pollyanna do-gooder. You give gifts to students, get them to love you." Spittle shot from her mouth. "You have everything I want. You have Sammy. I wanted you to fall from the water tower. I want your son!"

Alicia walked a few more steps then began to run. She ignored the blistering heat. She ran as fast as she could. Heatstroke be damned.

Bronwyn, you are right. I am a bloody great fool.

55

Alicia picked up Sammy, shouting a goodbye to Bronwyn. She ran to Fey's, struggling with his weight. She needed to tell Fey her revelation.

Breathing hard, she pushed Fey's door open. Fey didn't seem surprised to see her. Alicia pulled out the charred scraps of paper from her pocket and set them on the table.

"Ellie is the saboteur. Does she do it for Mick? Her house girl stole his notebook. Are these pages a record of weapons sales?"

"Sit down." Fey reached for Sammy, but Alicia shifted Sammy to her other hip.

"Sit," Fey said, with more force.

Alicia stayed standing. "Where is Jake? He wrote me he would be back last Saturday."

Fey said, "I contacted Hector's clerk using Jake's shortwave—"

"The headmaster is in Gabs." Alicia talked fast, trying to get it all out. "Mrs. Linchwe will help me call the local police.

How about the U.S. Embassy? Where's William? He wasn't at his home." She turned to leave.

"Give me Sammy." Fey reached for the boy and took him from his mother. "Hector will be here tomorrow afternoon with a munition's expert who's flying in from Pretoria. He'll check out the possible weapons cache you found."

"Listen!" Alicia tuned Fey out, hearing sounds in the distance. "Mick's truck is coming in the front gate. Ellie fears he will hurt her when he discovers the damage to his notebook. She called me names, but I don't care, we need to get her to safety."

"Missy."

The note in Fey's voice caught her attention. "Yes?"

"Guerrillas kidnapped Balakile, a young policeman Jake trained. Jake went to rescue him from the borderlands."

"He wrote me he was finished with the military."

"Jake went into no-man's land. Hector has little hope he survived. The guerrillas kill with impunity."

Alicia tried to grasp the meaning of Fey's words.

"Hector said the guerrillas don't keep prisoners," Fey said. "They extract information. After that, they kill them."

The meaning began to sink in.

"When my Timothy died," Fey said, "I was in shock for—"

Alicia held up her hand. "Jake's first rule is to stay alive. Have some faith."

She took Sammy from Fey, and walked outside. At the same moment, Mick's truck smashed through the front gate. The sound reverberated through the compound. The truck headed toward the main road. Ellie was in the front seat, hunched over.

Mick had destroyed Ellie's pregnancy with a single, vicious blow. What would happen to her?

Alicia set Sammy down and held his hand as they walked past the twisted remains of the metal gate. Holding Sammy, she fixed her eyes on the eastern horizon.

"Listen to me, Mr. W. B. Yeats. The falcon *can* hear the falconer. We will *not* fall apart. The center *will* hold. 'Mere anarchy' be damned. Got it?"

56

Alicia rose into consciousness like a bubble reaching the surface of a pond. What had awakened her?

"Come back to me, Jake," she whispered.

The previous evening, she fed Mpule and Sammy, but was too worried to eat herself. The kgosi allowed Mpule to stay overnight with her for a few days. Like the headmaster, he didn't believe there would be a hijacking.

Sammy and Mpule slept on the cots in the main room. Alicia lay on the cot in the Lizard Lounge. She concentrated on an unusual sound in the distance.

Trucks. She was sure she heard trucks. But how many?

With a sinking sensation, she strained to hear. "Four, maybe five trucks."

They moved toward the school from the east. No roads existed there. Wilderness. The guerrillas drove across the roadless desert toward the school. They came inexorably.

The police convoy had roared into the school in January.

Now, a few months later, another more dangerous convoy moved toward them. Jake had told her that guerrillas had killed children at a mission station much younger than Sammy. The memory electrified her.

She went into the main room. She would not panic. The headmaster was in Gabs, but she and her committee were ready with their plan.

She touched Mpule, asleep on the cot beside Sammy's. "Wake up."

With her left shoulder, she pushed the freestanding closet out to reveal the fireplace.

Mpule sat up, dazed.

"You must hide in the fireplace with Sammy. Bad men may come."

Alicia took a sweater from a shelf and went to her sleeping son. She tugged the sweater down over his pajamas. Wrapping him in his blanket, she picked him up. He didn't awaken. His closed eyelids shone in the moonlight through the window.

"Mpule, get into the fireplace."

"Nnyaa, Mma." She looked alarmed.

"Listen to me. Dereck sealed it up. I put in blankets, a torch, water, and extra clothing. Nothing will hurt you in there."

"Nnyaa, Mma. Please."

"You must get into the fireplace and hide with Sammy."

Mpule sat unmoving. She gazed toward the opening into the fireplace. Babies knew not to put their hands in places they could not see. Scorpions and snakes hid in dark places. Death hid in dark places. But this was important, and she must win.

"Move," she told the frightened girl. "Move *now*."

Mpule got up and walked to the fireplace. She backed into the dark hole with evident reluctance. In the dim light, the rows of braids across her head disappeared last. Her hands emerged from the darkness. Alicia handed Sammy to her. That done, Alicia pushed the closet back into place and smoothed down the bedding.

Pulling off her nightgown, Alicia buckled on her ankle sheath, slipped in the knife, and pulled on her heavy trousers. She buttoned up her flannel shirt, put on her socks and boots, and tucked her trousers into her boots. She double-tied the laces.

The trucks sounded closer to the school, but she pushed the panic away. She would think only of the next step.

Pulling a chair next to the closet, she stepped up on it. On the top shelf, she touched the bag that contained the flare gun, the Colt, ammunition, and a holster. Grabbing the bag, she stepped down.

She loaded the flare gun the way Jake showed her. She went to the front door, unlocked it, and went outside. She set down the Colt and its ammunition in the open doorway.

Standing with legs apart in the sand, she held the flare gun with both hands. She aimed it upward at a slight angle to the east. She needed to alert William as well as the student leaders in the dormitories and Ndona at the farm. She pulled the trigger.

Nothing happened.

She broke into a sweat; her hands grew slick. Their plan depended on the flare gun. She repeated Jake's mantra. "Stay calm. Stay alert."

If the flare gun did not fire, there was no quick way to communicate. She broke the gun open, popped the flare out, and reinserted it. Her hands shook.

She raised the flare gun and pulled the trigger. With a jolt, a red comet zipped over the school.

Relieved, she reloaded and aimed the flare gun upward, to the west this time, toward the village. She wanted the kgosi and the villagers to come. At least, that was her hope.

She pulled the trigger, and a comet soared. She hid the flare gun in her courtyard. Picking up the Colt, she loaded it and put on the safety. Cocked and locked, as Jake would say.

After closing the door, she ran to the nearest stile, she put her concern for Sammy and Mpule at the back of her mind.

As she climbed over the stile, a school bell clanged. William rang it. He was handing out whistles and torches to Gaeyo and Kgeledi. Hannah had sent the whistles. The torches were from the mercantile.

Alicia heard whistling in a variety of patterns. Gaeyo and her prefects would lead the girls out of their dormitory; Kgeledi and the footballers would lead the boys out of theirs.

Ndona would place water and blankets at various spots at the farm. He would direct each group to their hiding place. With a full moon and the torches, they could walk in safety.

The trucks were slowly negotiating the trees and bushes in their way, coming closer. Alicia headed toward what she figured was a weapons cache. If she were correct, a truck would stop there.

Fey's task was to contact Pierce with the shortwave radio. The local police were unarmed and immobile. The colonel, his soldiers, and the PMU could not reach the school in time to prevent a hijacking, but they could intercept the guerrillas later—hopefully. In the meantime, the school was on its own.

When she reached the gold box in the wilderness, she turned off her torch. Nearby, she stretched out flat on the sand, took off the safety, ready for whatever came next.

"Attention scorpions and snakes," she whispered, "please view me with disinterest and stay underground in your comfy holes."

The sound of whistles tapered off and ceased. Those who wanted to hide would have done so. The few students who chose to go with the guerrillas were no doubt by the staff house. Letting them go was the best way to avoid betrayal. The normal night sounds of insects, predators, and prey returned. The Milky Way comforted her with its familiarity.

Alicia hummed a melody from the *Messiah*. Rounding up goats, Nigel liked to sing, "All we like sheep have gone astray." As the trucks drew closer to the school, the memory of both Eric and Nigel gave her courage.

Bronwyn called William her "Man of the Night." In black clothing, she said he was invisible. Now he would execute his task. Alicia did not envy him. He would defend his family and the school with his life.

She heard an unexpected sound. Singing.

Amazing grace, how sweet the sound that saved a wretch like me,
I once was lost but now am found, was blind but now I see...

William's voice rang out across the desert, strong and clear. He was an Old Testament kind-of-guy, an eye for an eye. But like Nigel, he knew his hymns.

57

An extended blast of machine gun fire announced the guerillas' arrival. Alicia heard four trucks arrive at the fence near the staff house.

"They must plan to kidnap a lot of students," she whispered.

A fifth truck came toward her. The headlights on the truck lit up the thorn trees. When it stopped, men with shovels climbed out. Mick's truck pulled up beside the larger truck. Only Mick got out. No Ellie.

Mick shone his torch back and forth over the sand. He was looking for the gold box, she was sure of it.

She crawled closer to the trucks, her heart almost thumping out of her chest. Holding the Colt in both hands, she aimed for a front tire and pulled the trigger. The truck slumped to one side. Men shouted. She shot out the other tire. The truck lurched again.

She shot out a tire on Mick's truck and began to back away when a machine gun fired.

"Stop! Detonators. Dynamite!" Mick screamed a warning.

Too late. Fireworks boomed in the desert, even though it was not the Fourth of July, it was not America, and Alicia wasn't a child twirling a sparkler in her parents' backyard.

An immense force hit her. She thought no more.

Alicia could not move her wrists. When she opened her eyes, she looked around and recognized the back of Dereck's truck. She was leaning against the damaged tailgate. Her hands were tied in front. She blinked several times to clear her vision. By the staff house, a dozen strangers milled around with weapons. Twenty or so students stood with them, none of them her students. Of the four trucks outside the perimeter fence, two slumped at odd angles.

A short, heavyset man with a scarred face marched up to her. The man beside him held a lantern in one hand and a machine gun in the other. The scarred man grabbed Alicia's bad shoulder. She ignored the pain, refusing to show weakness.

"You are Mrs. Talbot!" he shouted. He waved his hands skyward. "Where are the students?"

The man's British accent surprised her.

The man was livid. "What ghost cut the tires?"

She almost smiled. William was at work with his righteous blade.

Another man came into the lantern light. "Diplo," the scarred man asked, "did you get the money?"

"A woman is refusing to open the safe."

Another guerrilla ran into the light shouting, "Chaparadza!" Alicia did not understand his language, but she understood the dismay in his voice.

The guerrilla commander screamed. "Dead? You found their bodies? Pono, Tinashe, and Kenosi?" He grabbed the machine gun from his aide. "Debacle." He spat on the ground and turned back to her. "You will pay."

Dereck shouted from behind her. "Leave her, and I'll drive a truck for you."

"Kenosi is dead. You will drive his truck, or you will die. Diplo will drive yours."

Chaparadza put his face close to Alicia's. "I strangled Major Hunter."

Her body went cold.

He leered at her. "I will enjoy your body."

Someone called her name, and she turned to the voice. In the moonlight, Paul ran toward her, full tilt. Two men were close on his heels. One shrieked and fell back, vanishing. Perhaps William grabbed him.

Paul shouted, "Take me. I'm rich! Take me for ransom."

She shouted. "No, Paul. No. Run. Run away!" Their eyes met. Their love for each other flashed between them.

Chaparadza's machine gun rattled, and red blossomed on the front of Paul's white shirt, an exotic flower in the desert.

Paul fell to the sand, unmoving.

Alicia gasped, stunned by the sight.

At a cry behind her, she turned. Lepetu and Mmegi stood beside the truck with their eyes wide, their mouths open.

Alicia heard shouts from the west. The villagers were coming. They faced automatic weapons with their machetes, hoes, and antique Tower muskets. They came to defend the future of their children. Only fearless warriors did that.

"We leave now," Chaparadza said. "Get the students in the trucks. Leave the dead. Those who pillage will find us later."

Chaparadza snapped his fingers. Darkness overwhelmed her.

58

When Alicia regained consciousness, her head throbbed. Something trickled down her neck; she tasted iron in her mouth, like biting a rusty nail.

She faced the tailgate, lying on her side. She tried to loosen the knots in the rope that bound her wrists, but the knots were too tight. With effort, she rolled over. Mubayi, Mmegi, Lepetu and two strangers, who held machine guns, leaned forward over the cab of the truck.

"Mubayi has joined the guerrillas," she whispered, astonished.

Mubayi and Lepetu were now brothers-in-arms after their mutual hatred.

In the moonlight, Lepetu peered back at her, then with a jerk, he turned away. He had closed his heart to her. No help would come from him.

The truck hit something and went airborne, landing hard. A single pair of headlights glimmered in the night, only one engine roared. The truck must have separated from the others.

She inventoried her injuries: cut head, painful shoulder, bad bruises. But she could move her fingers and toes. No broken bones.

Jake had told her that soldiers, if taken prisoner, had a duty to escape. Chaparadza had alluded to her fate. Being in the desert alone was dangerous, but staying in the truck was certain death.

Her wrists were tied, but her feet were not. She had her knife in its sheath, no one had searched her. With the truck lurching around, she did not dare try to cut the rope. With her hands tied, she could not climb over the tailgate and jump.

She studied the tailgate. After Mubayi damaged it, Dereck secured it by pushing a sturdy wire through a hole in the tailgate and a hole in the rear bumper, making a loop. The two ends of the wire were twisted together on the inside of the tailgate.

If the tailgate dropped, she would fall out, maybe knocked unconscious. They could turn the truck around and run over her, but she would take that chance.

After a series of spectacular bumps, someone shouted in the cab, and the truck slowed down. The men in the truck bed still faced away from her.

She got on her knees. Bracing a shoulder on the tailgate, she touched the twisted wires. Bit by bit, she unwound them. The ends of the wires were sharp and cut her fingers. With a fierce tug, she pulled out the wire. Suddenly, her end of the tailgate dropped.

She fell.

Alicia hit the sand on her injured shoulder. Arrows of pain shot through her body, but there was no time to weep. Someone was pounding on metal, and the truck came to a halt. She crawled through tall grasses until she reached a tree. She curled up behind it.

Men screamed at each other. Something hit the sand with a light thump. A machine gun chattered. Bullets thudded into her tree. Voices argued. The machine gun fired again. She heard another object hit the sand, this time with a heavy thump.

After more shouts, the truck moved on.

As she crouched in the sand, her shoulder burned. Her vision blurred. The rope around her wrists cut off the circulation. With numb fingertips, she pulled up her trouser leg, touched the ankle sheath and pulled out the knife.

In the light of the moon, she got on her knees and turned to face the tree. Her fingers were bleeding, making her hands slick and the knife slippery. She wiped her fingers on her trousers. With her wrists bound, each movement proved difficult.

Holding the knife handle in her fingertips, she used the blade to dig a narrow hole in the sand. She turned the knife upside down and forced the handle into the hole, the blade perpendicular against the tree. She moved her wrists up and down in small movements, pressing the rope to the blade while holding the blade steady.

She was making progress when she heard an eerie laughter. Fear threatened to overwhelm her. A cackle of hyenas moved toward her. She refused to panic; she must climb a tree to get away from them, but the knife was sharp. If she hurried, she could cut her wrists, and Fey was not there to sew her up.

Each time a strand of rope broke, she cheered herself in silence. Strand by strand, the rope disintegrated. The hyenas were closer. With one last movement, the final strand fell. Her wrists were unbound. She was free, but she had no time to rejoice.

She massaged her wrists and flexed her fingers. She stood up, putting the knife back in its ankle sheath. Reaching into a pocket, she pulled out her penlight.

She shone the light into one thorn tree after the other, finding a snake in each one. She found one without a snake. The sound of hyenas grew louder, but the crotch of the tree was high.

"There has to be a handhold."

Adrenaline overrode her pain. She backed up, ran toward the tree, and scrambled up. In the crotch, she pulled her feet up under her. Less than a second later, hyenas encircled the tree with their bobbing gait. They snapped at the air in a frenzy.

A faint sound came from the upper branches. She used her penlight to scan the limbs. She had been wrong. A snake was in the tree.

The snake moved toward her, mouth open wide, its body thick and muscular. Her heart lurched. The mouth was inky black. Black mamba. Nigel's killer.

She kept her penlight on the snake, and with her other hand retrieved her knife. The snake moved toward her. She stood up in the crotch and raised her knife. One chance.

With a swift motion, she slashed at the snake's head. She connected with the heavy weight which threw her off balance. She grabbed a limb. When she recovered her balance, the snake was gone.

She sheathed her knife, then wiped the sweat off her forehead with the back of her hand. She listened for the hyenas. They had left her tree and were yards away, ripping something apart.

She crouched in the tree. A protrusion poked her in the back.

"I must not sleep, another snake might come."

The Southern Cross shone above her. She pulled up the collar on her shirt and tucked her hands in her armpits. Her head throbbed, and the double vision came and went. She would concentrate on living through the night.

59

In the pre-dawn light, Alicia, chilled, watched from her perch in the tree. A vast landscape of thorn trees became visible. She turned to see the sun rise and gasped. A massive kopje loomed behind her. Was this the enormous "Vulture Kopje" Jake had told her about?

"I could climb the kopje and look for a village, but I can't risk a snake bite or a fall."

Her voice sounded odd.

"Blown up, bashed in. Call me muddle-headed. Concussion, for sure. At least the cut on my head stopped bleeding." Dried blood streaked her hands. "On the bright side, I didn't faint at the sight of blood."

She gazed around to get her bearings. The shrikes made their one-note calls, the boubous whistled. She called to denizens of the desert, "Rise and shine. It's a beautiful day in Botswana."

Tears came to her eyes. She had often said those words to Sammy. She was determined to say them to him again. The sun rose higher. Soon, it would be oven-hot.

Would a secretary bird race by? She would keep her nerve.

She saw a cluster of termite towers. She could forage for termite larvae. She could search out the moths and beetles Jake said were nutritious.

A patch of grass was black from what must have been a lightning strike. "I need signal fires." She rummaged in her pockets. "What do I have?"

She climbed down from the tree, hesitated, somewhat afraid to move. But the hyenas must be gone, otherwise, they would have come when she started to speak. She sat down on the sand, pulled out the items in her pockets, and placed them in front of her.

"With the compass, I could walk toward the school. Without water, though, the heat would kill me. In Camp Fire Girls, they told us to stay put if we were lost."

She turned over the small black block with magnesium on one side and flint on the other. Her salt tablets would help replace the salt she lost in sweat. She cradled the sugar packet and her penlight. She touched the knife in her ankle sheath.

With her pack, she would have had more resources: maps, water, food, extra clothing, a hat, and a first aid kit. Jake insisted she prepare for emergencies, but she did not have her pack or Jake.

She searched for a whistle but found none. She had given them all to William.

"No chance of one gallon of water per day."

Nigel had told Jake to bury his ostrich egg full of water in the desert. Where was it?

Jake said that most people could survive three days without water and three weeks without food. But the heat changed the equation and not in her favor.

She took the sugar packet, tore off the top, and poured the sugar on her tongue, letting it melt. She brought to mind the desserts of her childhood. Jelly-filled doughnuts with chocolate sprinkles. Banana splits with three kinds of ice cream topped with nuts, cherries, whipping cream, and chocolate syrup. She remembered the taste of a strawberry milkshake.

She licked up each granule of sweetness from the packet. After that, she tucked away the paper to use as tinder.

Whap, whap, whap.

Startled by the noise of a helicopter, she leapt up, dumping her gear on the ground. She picked up the penlight from the sand. No time to light a signal fire.

With sweaty hands, she turned on the penlight. She flashed the Morse code for SOS in the chopper's direction. Three short flashes, three long flashes, three short flashes.

"Sammy, I'm coming!" she yelled.

The sounds faded.

"You miserable excuse for a search and rescue party," she screamed. "Come farther east and find me!" In a softer voice, she said, "At least, I hope you want to find me." A helicopter was a rarity in Botswana. "Does anyone know I'm out here?"

She turned off the penlight and stuffed her gear back in her pockets.

Maybe a mirror would have worked better than a penlight. She felt around in her pockets. No mirror.

Jake said that dew collected in the crotches of trees overnight. Alicia pulled out her knife. From a clump of sturdy grasses, she cut a stalk and trimmed it until it resembled a straw. She went from tree to tree sucking up the moisture she found, but it was not enough to quench her growing thirst.

A few giraffes browsed in the distance. A herd of springbok drifted toward her.

"With my Colt, I could shoot an antelope, drink its blood, and cook the meat. I have a knife, but no pistol. No bow and arrow with a poisoned tip."

A kettle of gigantic black vultures flew toward her. Their scrawny necks and large beaks made her skin crawl. The vultures landed about twenty yards away and gathered in a huddle where the hyenas had been last night. What were they feeding on?

As she walked toward them, she saw something gleam in the grasses. She leaned down, parting the stalks.

Am I hallucinating?

When her eyes came into focus, she saw a man-made object. She touched it. A canteen.

Her heart leapt. Did it hold water?

She picked it up. Water sloshed around. The screw-top cap was loose, beetles clustered around it. She wanted to wail. It was only a quarter full. Every living being wanted water.

Two thumps, one light and one heavy. Was this the light thump?

"In a crisis, eat anything edible. Jake's rule."

She sat down in the sand and extracted the beetles. She pinched off their heads and put their bodies in a pile. Closing her eyes, she put them all in her mouth, crunched them with her back teeth, and swallowed. Lifting the canteen to her lips, she drank, relishing the water. No dessert ever compared with the magnificence of water.

She stopped before she drank it all. She needed to save water to wash down the termites, but it was hard to stop. She screwed the lid on, walked back to her tree, and set the canteen by the trunk.

The sky turned a deeper blue. As the sun rose higher, she would soon need the shade of her tree. She picked up a long, sturdy stick and walked closer to the circle of vultures. One vulture opened its massive wings and rushed another bird. The warned-off bird decamped, and returned later. More of the huge birds flew in.

The vultures eyed her with suspicion. One vulture raised its wings and rushed her. She batted it away with her stick. She pulled out her knife and held it in one hand and the stick in the other. She moved the knife and stick back and forth. The vultures parted.

For a moment, she could not comprehend what lay before her. Once it had been a man. The khaki clothes were shredded. Bones showed through the torn clothing, eye sockets empty. One ear was smaller than the other. Light reflected off a silver belt buckle.

"Mubayi," she whispered.

Mubayi had worn his belt buckle with pride at morning assembly, keeping it buffed to a high sheen.

The vultures menaced her. With her knife and stick, she kept them at bay. They backed up, squawking. She laid down the stick, knelt beside the corpse and tugged at the buckle. It came off in her hand. One end was a dagger, just like Bronwyn described. She put it in a pocket. Without delay, she waved her stick and knife at the vultures and escaped from their circle.

To her horror, the vultures went back to their meal. She walked back to her tree, blinded by tears.

"Mubayi, even if I could keep the vultures away, I have no shovel to dig a hole and bury you. I am sorry."

Did Mubayi throw her the canteen? The heavy thump must have been Mubayi as he fell to the sand. Had he objected to the guerrillas shooting at her?

He was no longer the "Cruel Beast." She started to cry.

"Stop! Conserve your moisture," a voice said.

With eagerness, she turned to greet the speaker, but no one was there. In confusion, she looked around, but saw only thorn trees. She swallowed hard. She was alone, lost in the vast Kalahari.

60

Alicia studied Mubayi's belt buckle. The buckle reflected back her image, a face streaked with blood. Mirror. She held a signaling mirror.

"A sunny day, a mirror, and a helicopter. Two out of three elements for a rescue. Such a lucky girl."

The desert heat became stupefying. Giving up on a helicopter, she searched for the Tsamma melons Jake had mentioned, but found none. Her hunger grew.

I need to eat a termite.

She picked up her canteen and walked over to the termite towers. The mounds stood at least nine feet tall. The exteriors were hard as concrete. All were intact but one. The canteen still contained a little water.

Years ago, she had picked huckleberries on the wooded flanks of Mt. Rainier. She would pick an entire palmful of the tiny blue-black berries, toss them in her mouth, and savor the sweet crunchiness. Better than beetles.

She noticed a red-headed lark perched on a thorn tree nearby. Each time it sang, it lifted a few head feathers and flapped its wings. She listened hard and was able to discern four separate notes in its trilling song.

With a jolt, she slapped her thigh. "If I had listened as closely to Jake, we would still be together."

Her anger at Jake was pointless. He worked undercover in the service of Botswana, no different from her teaching job. He should have told her sooner, but what did it matter? She shut him out twice without giving him a chance to share his perspective. Eric had complained that she did not listen to him, either.

"I can change," she said. "I will change." If she got the chance.

She decided to wait on the termites and build her signal fires. She broke off branches from trees and gathered sticks. She cut dry grass. The work was slow as both her right shoulder and her head hurt.

She created three separate piles of sticks and grasses in a line, separated by several yards each. She paused to put a salt tablet in her mouth.

As she carried a bundle of grass, she heard the dim sound of a chopper in the distance.

"Wait!"

No time to get out the magnesium and flint and light the fires. She was not ready.

"Keep your lamps trimmed and burning." A song from Sunday school years ago came to mind.

Alicia recalled Jake's method to signal an airplane with a mirror, but there had been no airplane in the sky with which to practice.

She took Mubayi's belt buckle and rubbed it on her pantleg to remove the dirt and blood. With her right hand, she held the silver buckle toward the sun, then tilted it so the reflected light shone onto the trunk of a nearby tree. She extended her left hand so the light shone between her thumb and forefinger. As a unit, she turned her body and the buckle until she aimed the reflected light toward the chopper. The chopper was a smudge on the horizon. She wobbled the buckle, making it more likely she would hit the right angle.

Light and movement attracted attention. Jake's rule.

She wiggled the buckle, but the sound faded away. The birds and the insects were her only companions. Using all of her strength, she climbed up to the crotch of her tree. Lighting the signal fires would have to wait, she was out of energy.

Already her clothes were dirty. Her trousers had ripped at the knees when she fell from the truck. She didn't care. She wanted Sammy, Jake, water, and food. She scratched one of the mosquito bites on her neck until it bled.

"Fey will take care of Sammy until my sister flies into Botswana." She brushed away a tear.

"I am a two-time loser with the helicopter, but I will refuse to assume anything. The third time will be successful. I will light the signal fires. I will be prepared."

She shook her head in disbelief. "I am alone in the thirstland talking out loud to myself." She gazed out over the desert. "And now I wish I had not said the word 'thirst.' My mouth is dry and my tongue is swelling. Soon I won't be able to talk to myself. Now *that* would be a real catastrophe."

61

"Lean on the horn," Jake said to the driver, a glum Cedric Selkirk. Jake was impatient to get through the gate to Pierce's compound. Balakile lay in the back, his eyes shut, repeating the word, "Gorata," his wife's name.

Jake had rescued the badly injured Balakile when the guerrillas abandoned their camp by a river. He carried the man on his back to where he had hidden his Land Rover, but the vehicle had been stolen.

For hours, Jake continued to walk carrying Balakile. Finally, he stumbled across the remote farm of an English couple, Cedric and Nell Selkirk. Cedric wanted to turn away the strange men who appeared at his door before dawn. He hated the guerrillas, the PMUs, and the Rhodesian Security Forces equally. The two men looked suspicious to him. But Nell insisted on helping them, her duty as a Christian. She bandaged Balakile's wounds with care, and insisted Cedric drive them to Francistown.

The gate opened wide. A guard motioned them in, and the gate closed behind them.

Cedric parked his vehicle. He got out, reached in, and picked up Balakile. He carried him into Pierce's residence with Jake close behind him.

Standing next to Pierce, Fey spluttered. "God have mercy. His nose and ears are gone."

After Cedric had placed Balakile on a bed, Jake walked him out. Remembering Nell's kindness, he took out his wallet and pulled out all his cash. Cedric was in the driver's seat when Jake reached through the open window. He tucked the bills into Cedric's breast pocket.

"Tell Nell I will always remember her. Thanks for your help, too. I was close to exhaustion."

"Maybe you're not such a bad sort." Without another word, Cedric backed up and drove out.

Jake went to Pierce's living room and collapsed on a chair.

"The guerrillas left late yesterday evening headed west. I found Balakile half-dead on their garbage heap. Did the guerrillas attack the school? Are Alicia and Sammy safe?"

Pierce stood in silence looking at him. Jake jumped up from the chair, his clothes grimy and torn. "Answer me."

Fey walked back into the room and sat down on the couch. "I gave Balakile a sedative. He's asleep. I called Dr. Lekota. She and Balakile's wife will come soon. I told them not to bring the children. Too shocking. Jake, I need to check your stitches."

Jake ignored her request. "Alicia? Sammy?" He stood toe to toe with his godfather. "Tell me."

"They're missing," Pierce said, at last. "The guerrillas did attack the school. The students who followed the student leaders are safe. Alicia was kidnapped."

Jake kicked the chair over. "Goddammit!" He wanted to kick it to smithereens. Instead, he took a breath, righted the chair and sat down.

"To be clear," Pierce said, "Alicia and Sammy are *both* missing but not together."

"That makes no sense. The guerrillas want students to turn into fighters for their war, not a woman and a child. Ransom?"

"No ransom demands. At least, not yet," Fey said. "A guerrilla detonated the dynamite accidentally at the weapons cache. Mick and three guerrillas died. The buried weapons were destroyed."

"Go on." Jake's mind raced. "What about Sammy?"

"I'll get to Sammy," Fey said. "William slashed the tires on two of the trucks. He cut the throats of three guerrillas who attacked teachers in their homes. The deaths of his men sent the guerrilla commander over the edge. He murdered Paul."

Jake shook his head.

"With the villagers coming, three trucks left, including the school truck which has Alicia."

Jake's shoulders tightened. "What have you done to locate her?"

"I hired the best search and rescue helicopter pilots in South Africa," Pierce said, "Aussies. They flew here from Jo-burg before dawn. They refueled and took off from the Francistown airport."

Jake paced in the room. "Go on. I want to hear it all."

"The helicopter pilots spotted the school truck headed overland. One of the PMUs intercepted it, a battle ensued. Four guerrillas died. The two students with them were retrieved. We'll find the other two trucks. One might be headed to Kasane in northeastern Botswana, going into Zambia. I alerted the police at the border crossing."

"Names of the students rescued?"

Nervously, Pierce tapped his foot. "Lepetu and Mmegi. They're being cagey."

"My footballers. Both were ripe for recruitment. Bring Lepetu to me."

Pierce went to the door of his office, gave an order to his clerk, and returned to the living room.

"Mrs. Linchwe refused to give the guerrillas the school's money," Fey said. "They beat her to death. She died in my arms, faithful to the headmaster to the end. No greater love, eh? A formidable woman."

Jake nodded. "Where's William? We need to—"

"The Mortensens and their children are on a flight to Seattle," Pierce said. "Flew out an hour ago. Bronwyn insisted they fly to Seattle not Atlanta, William's hometown. Fey sent a telegram to Hannah to meet their plane. If they stayed, reprisals from the guerrillas would have been nasty. Bronwyn wanted to be thousands of miles away from the school. Lucky for them their passports had just been updated."

"What about Sammy and the others?" Jake feared what he would hear.

"After the guerrillas left," Fey said, "Ndona, Kgeledi, and Gaeyo led the students back to their dormitories. William and Corley contacted the authorities in Gabs. I went to Alicia's home and found the place ransacked. No Sammy."

"Is he with the kgosi?"

"I sent a soldier to talk with him," Pierce said. "The chief refused to cooperate. The man trusts you. Go talk with him."

Jake nodded.

"The only positive outcome," Pierce said, "is that the Rhodesian guerrillas will not try to abduct another student in Botswana. They lost trucks, men, and weapons. My hunch is they'll stick to kidnapping Rhodesian students in undefended schools. Cowards."

Jake stood up. "Nine dead at the school, and I abandoned my post to save one man. I could not live with myself if—"

"You're not omniscient. We make choices based on the information we have. Accept your humanity." Pierce opened his arms, and Jake went into them, leaning against his godfather. Pierce embraced him.

"You haven't leaned on me since you were a young boy in the Sonoran Desert. You had been scared by a rattler who struck at you and missed. You have good reason to be angry with me. I cheated on Maria Elena." He glanced over at Fey. "I will never make that mistake again. Please forgive me, Son."

Jake stepped back. "You want me to stop being an arrogant, judgmental knucklehead? Deal. Do you forgive *me*?"

They shook hands.

"Pierce," Jake said in an unsteady voice. "Help me find my family."

62

Jake viewed the topo maps spread out on a table in Pierce's office. He waited for a soldier to bring in Lepetu.

Pierce studied the maps over Jake's shoulder. "The Kalahari is gigantic, spreading over multiple countries with few landmarks. How will we find her?"

Jake pointed to a mark on the map. "This shows where your men intercepted the truck. Do you have radio communication with the pilots?"

"Intermittent."

A soldier brought Lepetu into the room. When the student saw Jake, he tried to escape, but Pierce grabbed his arm.

"Rra Jake hates me," Lepetu said.

Pierce forced Lepetu into a chair and kept a hand on his shoulder.

"Was Mrs. Talbot in your truck?" Jake needed answers.

"I refuse to speak." Lepetu turned his face away. "You do not want to end White rule in Rhodesia."

Jake and Pierce watched the student. Soon Lepetu became agitated, tugging at his clothes.

Without warning, Lepetu cried out. "They killed Rra Paul! They killed Mr. Mubayi! They will kill me!" He rocked back and forth in his chair.

Jake and Pierce exchanged glances.

Tears flowed down Lepetu's face. He pulled at his shirt. But after a few minutes, he grew still. Using his shirttail, he cleaned away the tears, sweat, and mucus. He sat up straight, hands in his lap. "Mrs. Talbot has blood on her head."

"Did you help her?" Pierce asked.

"Nnyaa." Lepetu jerked his head from side to side.

"Injured, but you did not help her?" Jake stayed calm. Giving Lepetu the brunt of his anger would not help Alicia.

"She fell out." Lepetu's voice was a whisper. "Machine gun fire."

"Was she killed?"

Lepetu lifted his shoulders and let them fall.

"How many hours were you in the truck until she fell out?"

After a pause, Lepetu said, "Maybe four hours."

"Do you remember any distinctive features, big rock piles, hills, or tall trees?"

Lepetu rubbed his eyes. "Rocks so high the moon could not light the darkness. Bad place."

"A big pile of boulders? Was the pile of boulders taller than the kgotla tree in Kukama Village?"

"Taller." Lepetu stretched his hands toward the ceiling.

Jake returned to study his maps. "Distance, time, terrain. The remnant of the pre-Cambrian basement that large in this area is Vulture Kopje."

Lepetu slumped in the chair. "Mrs. Talbot tells the headmaster he must keep me in school. I attacked her rondavel, but I am not expelled."

Jake's face was expressionless. "She spoke in your favor?"

"She said to expel me hurts our nation, wastes our education." Lepetu squirmed. "You showed me your scars, but I want to be a hero. I told my father to complain to the Education Department about the sabotage at the school." He started to hit his chest. "Mrs. Talbot helps me, but I refuse to help her. I think I am brave. *I am not!*" He shrieked the last three words.

Pierce patted the student's shoulder. As the student sobbed, Jake studied his maps. He wrote several numbers on a scrap of paper and handed it to Pierce.

"Radio the pilots to head to these coordinates. Posthaste. While they're searching, I'll go to Kukama Village."

"Take my Jeep. It has a transmitter. I'll figure out how to send a message to Lepetu and Mmegi's parents. Headmaster Matlagodi must be back at the school by now."

The sun approached the horizon. Floodlights illuminated the front gate as it swung open. A civilian vehicle drove in with Dr. Lekota and Balakile's wife. Jake did not envy them the sight they would witness.

Jake headed toward Kukama Village. He gripped the steering wheel and shouted to the setting sun. "Time is running out, Alicia. Come back to me."

63

The strength in Alicia's right shoulder drained away; she had not followed Fey's advice about caring for her injury. She had not listened to her body nor to Jake's request to return to Seattle.

She heard the hyena pack heading toward her. As the sun set, she opened her heart to the beauty of her arid world.

"Sammy, I wanted to fulfill your father's dream of teaching in Africa. Did I fall in love, with Africa and with Jake, and fail to listen to the warning signs? Forgive me."

She stood more erect. "Jake called me Wonder Woman. Since I can't jet away, I'll be Davy Crockett at the Alamo and face danger head on."

She tried to climb back into her tree, but with her weak arm, she could not. It was too late to look elsewhere.

She could not gather enough firewood to keep the fires alive. The flames burned down to embers. The sky glowed lavender and gold.

Hyenas yipped. She tried once again to climb up. No luck. She stood with her back to the tree. Soon, six spotted hyenas loomed before her, chattering.

Hyenas were afraid of fire, but apparently not of embers. Their powerful jaws and sharp teeth would bring her down in seconds, tear her apart. Where was Khama the Great's duiker to distract them, fool them?

As they edged closer, she reached down and grabbed a handful of sand. She threw the sand in their eyes with a sweeping gesture. They backed off, snarling. With her left hand, she pulled the knife from her ankle sheath. In her weak right hand, she held Mubayi's dagger.

The hyenas focused on her. Their teeth glistened. She smelled their stink.

She launched herself at them, screaming her son's name, slashing with her strong left hand. Her knife connected with living flesh.

She was full of life, now at the moment of her death, enraged that she should die when she wanted to live so much.

She would fight for Sammy. She would fight to the end. She would never surrender.

A loud noise filled the air, and the desert turned as bright as noon.

64

Under the full moon, Jake talked with the kgosi. The man murmured to a boy who stood near him. The boy disappeared, and, in a few minutes, Negotho appeared carrying Sammy. They were flanked by Mpule and Kxoma. Villagers gathered to watch.

When Sammy saw Jake, he shouted, "Rra! Rra!" Jake took Sammy from Negotho, thanking the student for his help.

"Ke batla Mma," Sammy said. He started to cry.

Jake spoke to the child in a soft voice. When Sammy quieted, Jake got in the Jeep and settled him on his lap. The young boy snuggled against him.

When they reached the compound in Francistown, he brought Sammy inside. The little boy reached out to Fey. He pressed his face to her neck. "Mma?"

Fey walked around the room, singing to him. Jake left Sammy with reluctance, but he needed to talk to Pierce.

In the office, the clerk who monitored the shortwave radio told Jake that the choppers were not yet back at the airport.

"We reached the pilots," Pierce said. "They did find Alicia, but the situation is unclear. The pilot used the word 'corpse.'"

Jake cleared his throat and clasped his hands together.

"The police caught Chaparadza," Pierce said, "at the border town of Kasane before they crossed the river into Zambia. He'll stand trial for the murder of Paul Winthrop. Dereck fled when they stopped to steal petrol. He's in hiding, but I'm sure he'll resurface. No word on the other truck, but we'll find it."

Jake rubbed the back of his neck.

Pierce went on. "The students retrieved at Kasane are at the police station waiting for their parents. They can decide later if they still want to join the guerrillas. Some will, no doubt."

Jake and Pierce returned to the living room where Fey listened to Sammy talk about his time with the kgosi, the goats, and the chickens.

Jake picked up Sammy. "Fey, the kgosi said to tell you that Mbengawa may have his surgery. He said that the parents changed their minds. What's that about?"

"The Scarlet Pimpernel Fund," she said with a broad smile.

"What's a pimpernel?" He handed Sammy to his godfather. "Forget it. Tell me later."

Jake climbed in the Jeep and started the engine. He signaled for the guard to open the gate. Pierce held Sammy on his lap.

Jake drove fast on the dark road toward the airport, turning the corners on two wheels. They reached the airport as the chopper landed.

Sammy pointed to the helicopter. "Mma flying." He clapped his hands.

As Jake brought the vehicle to a halt at the edge of the airfield, Pierce touched his arm. "I'll keep Sammy here until we know, one way or the other."

Jake jumped out, running toward the chopper. The copilot climbed out, unlatched a side door and opened it. A light shone inside. Jake saw a body bag. Tears came to his eyes.

The pilot came around and helped the copilot move the zipped-up bag to the ground. As Jake neared the chopper, the pilot stepped in front of him.

"The woman kept saying, 'Sammy.' Are you Sammy?"

"She's alive?"

"She set signal fires. When I saw her, I zeroed in. Paddy shot the hyenas attacking her. Not a second—"

Jake dodged around the pilot and climbed into the cargo hold. Alicia lay unmoving, her eyes shut. He put a finger on her carotid artery and found a pulse. Dried blood streaked her face. Her arms were wrapped with bandages, stained red. With his thumb, he rubbed away a smudge of black on her cheekbone.

"*Mi corazón.*" He kissed her forehead.

Jake pulled away and signaled Pierce to come closer. Pierce parked beside the helicopter and got out holding Sammy.

"Hand me Sammy," Jake said.

Pierce moved closer. "Let's get Alicia to Dr. Lekota."

"Do as I ask."

Pierce held up the boy, and Jake took him into the cargo hold.

Jake set Sammy down beside her, and the boy patted her face.

"Your mother is sleeping." What could Jake say?

Sammy kissed her blistered lips. "Here's your big boy. Wakey, wakey, my sweet one."

When she did not respond, Sammy raised his voice. "Rise and shine. Bootiful day Botswana." He put his face next to hers and fluttered his eyelashes on her cheek. "Butterfly kisses, Mma. Kisses."

65

Alicia was lost in a dream. The teeth of the hyenas glowed in a strange light. A great weariness overcame her. She pulled inside herself. She did not want to feel the rip of her flesh in their strong jaws. She knew the vultures would peck out her eyes.

Her longing for Sammy ached in her chest. She heard him calling her. He was her own blood, her own bone.

She remembered the touch of her son, his kisses, feather-light, on her cheek. She imagined holding him.

Eric was dead. Nigel was dead. Were Paul and Jake dead? She would embrace her own death, if Sammy, too, were dead.

In a dim light, she walked on a downward, sloping path. After a while, it slanted upward to a door. Light seeped out from underneath. A soft voice encouraged her to open the door, but she refused. Too much loss.

She turned and began walking away.

The voice said, "Fear not."

Alicia took a deep breath. With resolution, she turned back to the door. She pushed it open. Light! Death had been so easy!

But she felt breath on her neck and tiny hands on her face. She opened her eyes.

Sammy.

His lips moved, but she could not hear him.

More illusions.

She closed her eyes, preparing to retreat.

The voice said, "Trust me."

She opened her eyes again. Pain engulfed her, yet she heard Sammy singing. He was singing their night-night song.

She looked at Jake who sat beside them, watching her.

He whispered. "You and Sammy are safe. The students are safe."

Relief flooded her body. The center *had* held.

Jake touched her hand. "I promise to change, be less secretive, less overbearing."

She spoke with difficulty, her mouth dry. "I promise to listen."

He lay down, encircling Alicia and Sammy in his arms.

66

Alicia lay on her back in a large bed with Sammy asleep beside her. Fey had bathed her, bandaged her wounds, and dressed her in a nightgown. Jake sat in a chair next to the bed. Several times during the night, Alicia was aware that he was changing the bag on the IV that snaked down to her left hand.

She remembered little of her rescue and nothing of the helicopter ride. She did remember the moment Sammy's hands touched her face.

She tried to piece the bits of information together. Negotho had taken Sammy and Mpule from her hut to the village as she had asked him to do. The kgosi had cared for Sammy in her absence as the chief had promised. Her son seemed to adjust to her reappearance, yet she was worried.

Fey told her that all the students had been sent home for the break between terms. Headmaster Matlagodi would soon welcome new Peace Corps teachers. In November, the students would take their all-important examinations as planned. A few, such as Kgeledi, would go on to university after graduation.

As she feared in January, the Rhodesian bush war had slammed into the school. Her committee's plan to stave off a mass kidnapping was successful, but the price had been high.

She drifted back to sleep. When she awoke, Jake slept on one side of her, and on the other side was her still-sleeping son. She listened to their rhythmic breathing. Fey sat in the chair beside Alicia, concentrating on her knitting. When did Fey learn how to knit? And why was she knitting booties?

Baby booties.

Alicia smiled.

That evening, Jake and Alicia sat side by side on the veranda, his arm around her. Her right arm was in a sling, both arms bandaged. The Milky Way shone above them, a white banner that welcomed her home. The desert sang in full voice. She could hear Fey and Pierce through the screen door telling Sammy the story of Jack and the Beanstalk.

Alicia leaned against Jake, savoring his presence. Chaparadza had lied. Jake was alive, solid, and comforting.

She turned toward him, gazing into his hazel eyes. "You sent the pilots to find me in just the right place at just the right moment in the immense Kalahari Desert. How did you do that?"

"Lepetu helped."

"He did?" She remembered Lepetu in the truck. "He has bravado, and he's learning about bravery. He'll become a good man."

The shriek of a hunting hawk made her shiver. "You rescued Balakile. I'm glad. Fey says he'll cope with his wounds, like you did."

"You help me heal." He kissed her forehead, and moved down to kneel in front of her, grasping her hands.

"You captivated my heart from the get-go." He took a deep breath. "Would you do me the honor of becoming my wife?"

She tugged on his hands, pulling him up to sit beside her.

"I told you I would listen to you, not turn away. Please listen to *me.*" She took a moment to collect herself. "You knew an attack on the school was coming. But when you learned Balakile was kidnapped, you chose to rescue him instead of defending the school, Sammy, and me. I'm not sure what to think about that."

His eyes welled with tears. "I'm sorry. Tunnel vision tripped me up. I will not abandon you again."

Without warning, her own tears came as a torrent. He held her close as her body shook with sobs. She sobbed for those who had died and for all the shattered dreams.

Alicia cried until Jake's shirtfront was wet with her tears. He offered her a handkerchief, and she took it. When she was able, she patted her eyes and blew her nose. "Sweetheart, your rules helped me survive."

Jake's eyes lit up. "You just called me 'Sweetheart.' You *do* love me."

"I must have known you were still a soldier, yet I fell in love with you anyway. But I put Sammy's life in danger by coming here. I need to take him back to Seattle, to Hannah—home." She squeezed his hands. "Do you need to stay, help defend the border?"

"My home is with you."

"But doesn't Pierce want your help training policemen?"

"He's making other plans. I vow to be an invincibly devoted husband and a super-deluxe dad to Sammy."

"See that you do!"

"Is that a yes?" He smiled. "We can be together always?"

She nodded and lifted her lips to his.

After a while, she leaned back. "Jacob Hunter, you're such a decent man. Let's make a magnificent future for ourselves, shall we?"

"*Te adoro.*" He kissed her again.

Sammy burst through the screen door, shouting, "Mma! Mma!"

Jake pulled him onto his lap and pointed upward. "Look! I trotted out my lucky stars tonight. I knew I would need them."

Sammy piped up. "Bootiful!"

Alicia touched Sammy's cheek. "Beautiful, indeed."

Together, they listened to the timeless song of the desert. The "cradle of lightning" shone above them like a pathway from one world to the next, to a world eager to be born.

The End

Historical Note

On September 30, 1966, after eighty years of dependence on Britain, the Bechuanaland Protectorate in southern Africa became the Republic of Botswana. Seretse Khama who had renounced his position as the hereditary chieftain of the Bamangwato tribe became the first president of the new nation. Khama's vision was of a nonracial, democratic nation with multiple political parties and universal suffrage. His farsighted statesmanship was crucial to the survival of the nation.

At independence, Botswana was impoverished with a literacy rate of twenty-five percent—few schools, no university, and poor infrastructure. The nation was landlocked and heavily dependent on its neighbor to the south, the troubled Republic of South Africa, for imports, exports, infrastructure, and access to the sea and international markets. Botswana was also economically dependent on its neighbor to the east, Rhodesia (now Zimbabwe), a South African ally. Neighbors to the west and north, South West Africa and Angola were also in turmoil.

Significantly, diamonds were discovered in 1967 at Orapa, Botswana; mining began in 1971.

In the 1970s, both South Africa and Rhodesia had minority White governments with nationalistic movements waging guerrilla war against them. President Khama told the Organization of African Unity that Botswana would remain neutral and nonaligned and that no one would be allowed to use his nation as a base for terrorist activity. Without a military, though, he could not enforce this policy. Moreover, the Batswana people were sympathetic to the cause of the guerrillas. But the Batswana who lived on the borders were caught in the crossfire.

The Rhodesian Bush War, 1964 to 1979, was called the Second Chimurenga as well as the Zimbabwean War of Liberation. The Soviet Union supported the larger guerrilla faction, ZANU/ZANLA led by Robert Mugabe, Shona tribe. China supported the smaller one, ZAPU/ZIPRA, led by Joshua Nkomo, Matabele people. The Rhodesian ruling party of Ian Smith, the Rhodesian Front, framed its opposition as anti-Communist and was supported by Western allies. Both Rhodesian and South African underground movements used Botswana for cross-border raids and weapons caches. The history of this era is replete with stories of spies, sabotage, bombings, murders, gunrunning, rape, asylum seekers, and refugee camps.

President Khama put revenue from diamond extraction into infrastructure, not a military, but something was needed. In 1967, he created Police Mobile Units. In 1968, in a bilateral agreement, Britain began to provide army instructors for the Batswana police. In 1977, the Rhodesian border incursions became so frequent and bloody that Botswana's Parliament created the Botswana Defense

Force, a fledging army. Later, the United States and Botswana developed a strong military-to-military relationship. Most Batswana military officers train in the International Military Education and Training program, funded by the U.S. Congress.

In the early 1970s, the Rhodesian guerrillas began a campaign of kidnapping students to train as guerrillas and bolster their forces. They hijacked entire schools including those along the 523-mile border between Rhodesia and Botswana. Kidnapped students were sometimes marched across the border into Botswana and then sent to training/indoctrination camps in Zambia and other countries such as the Soviet Union, North Korea, Tanzania, Ethiopia, and Libya.

Over time, guerrillas abducted an estimated twenty thousand Rhodesian pupils from private and government schools, maybe more. The guerrillas contended they were recruiting willing would-be insurgents, others contended it was recruitment at gunpoint. Guerrillas murdered teachers, such as those killed at Elim Mission by ZANLA guerrillas in the Vumba mountains of Rhodesia. Students also died. The theft of school funds during hijackings was common.

The actions of the Rhodesian Security Force were also egregious. A woman drawing water from the Ramokgwebana River was shot by Rhodesian Security Forces. In 1978, two boys riding with a Police Mobile Unit were killed by the Rhodesian Security Force along with fifteen Botswana Defense Force members at Lesoma, in northeastern Botswana. This incident was a national trauma for Botswana. The death toll of the Rhodesian Bush War included guerrillas, Rhodesian Security Forces, Rhodesian and Batswana civilians, expatriates, and members of the Botswana Defense Force.

In 1979, the United States, along with several other countries, brokered a plan to hold new Rhodesian elections and form a government. In 1980, Rhodesia became Zimbabwe with majority Black rule, and Robert Mugabe of ZANLA became its first president. South Africa emerged from armed struggle in 1994 when Nelson Mandela became president.

Botswana has faced many challenges since its independence in 1966, including severe droughts, corruption, the HIV/AIDS crisis, student riots, and the perennial dearth of arable land. On a positive note, the University of Botswana was established in 1982, and by 2007, the literacy rate had increased from twenty-five to eighty percent. Although Botswana has some of the highest levels of income inequality anywhere, it is now an upper-middle-income democracy with a stable government and great aspirations.

Acknowledgements

My love and thanks to Chris Walls, my son, who as a young child shared my life in Botswana at Shashe River School.

Thank you to Dr. Bethany A. Reid, poet, writer, and teacher, for her gracious assistance; to Deanna J. Bell for our lively phone-chats; and to Sandy Jensen, neighbor and friend, for our restorative walks to the Bluff.

Thank you to my beta readers: Sharon Y. Stanford, Sarah L. Love, Christie Nelson, Judy Fallas, Dr. Jayne Marek, and the late Dr. Karen J. Reiber. I am grateful to my editors, Sandra Scofield, Dave King, Danylle Salinas-McCord, and Danielle Acee.

Eric Shilling, Alex Schmidt, and Michael O'Reilly shared their experiences in the U.S. military during the Vietnam War era. Greg Hertel provided information on weapons. Tom Stanford explained the use of ham radios. Dr. Poppy Fry, expert on southern

Africa, instructed me on the history of the region. Janice K. Case detailed her ideas on teaching. Ryan Walls provided technical support. Thank you!

Thank you to Andrea Furber, Lori Vanderbilt, Jena Hennessey, Bonnie J. Wilmot, Carla Shafer, Joy Fry, Krista Harris, Kawika Costa, Sharie Bowman, Gloria Young, Nancy and Jim Wadington, Lorraine Toly, Diane Inman, and Gail Hughes for their friendship and encouragement.

Requiescat in pace. Gitz Moreng, Trevor Newall, and Eugene "Hutch" Jenness, colleagues at Shashe River School.

Further Reading

Achebe, Chinua. *Things Fall Apart.* Fawcett Crest, 1959.

Declassified Secret Memorandum of Conversation: Henry Kissinger, Balthazar Vorster etc. Hotel Bodenmais, Germany. National Security Adviser's Memoranda of Conversation Collection at the Gerald R. Ford Library.

Capp, Carmena. *Pursuing Shalom: One Family's African Story.* 2020.

Cleary, Frederick. "The Anguish of Rhodesia's Lost Children." *Times*, 16 Oct. 1978, p. 6.

Denbow, James, Phenyo C. Thebe. *Culture and Customs of Botswana.* Greenwood Press, 2006.

Dow, Unity. *Far and Beyon'.* Spinfex Press, 2001.

Fuller, Alexandra. *Don't Let's Go to the Dogs Tonight: An African Childhood.* Random House, 2003.

Head, Bessie. *The Collector of Treasures and Other Botswana Village Tales.* Waveland Press, 1977.

Katz, Richard. *Boiling Energy: Community Healing among the Kalahari Kung*. Harvard UP, 1982.

Knipe, Michael. "More Africans Cross into Botswana." *Times,* 21 Feb., 1977, p.4.

MacManus, James "Rhodesia Says 400 Students Taken as Guerrilla Recruits." *Manchester Guardian,* 1 Feb., 1977.

Makgala, C.J., M.L. Fisher. *The Impact of Zimbabwean Liberation Struggle on Botswana: the Case of Lesoma Ambush, 1978.* B.A. Dissertation.

"Mission Students Left with Guerrillas 'Voluntarily.' *Times,* 10 July, 1973, p.6.

Mitchison, Naomi. *Sunrise Tomorrow: A Story of Botswana.* Farrar, Straus, and Giroux, 1973.

Moeng, Gothataone. *Call and Response.* Viking, 2023.

Morse, Eleanor. *White Dog Fell from the Sky*. Penguin Books, 2013.

Morton, Barry, Jeff Ramsay. *Historical Dictionary of Botswana.* 5th ed., Rowman & Littlefield, 2018.

No. 1 Ladies' Detective Agency TV Series. Created by Richard Curtis, Anthony Minghella. Timothy Bricknell, Producer. March 23, 2008. (Based on stories of Alexander McCall Smith.)

Oitsile, Boipelo W. *Botswana and the Liberation in South Africa and Zimbabwe: The Government and People Against White Racist Rule.* 2010. Trent University. 2010. M.A. Dissertation.

Ottaway, David. "Guerrillas Slay 12 at Mission School." *Washington Post,* 25 June, 1978

Praise-Poems of Tswana Chiefs. Translated by I. Schapera. Clarendon Press, 1965.

"Rhodesian Rebels Kidnap 278 at Mission." *New York Times,* 6 July, 1973. p.1.

Scholz, Christopher. *Fieldwork: A Geologist's Memoir of the Kalahari.* Princeton UP, 1998.

Scott, Robyn. *Twenty Chickens for a Saddle: The Story of an African Childhood.* Penguin Books, 2008.

Shostak, Marjorie. *Nisa: The Life and Words of a !Kung Woman. Harvard* UP, 1981.

Smith, Alexander McCall. *No. 1 Ladies' Detective Agency Series.* Penguin Random House, 1998-present.

St. John, Lauren. *Rainbow's End: A Memoir of Childhood, War and an African Farm.* Scribner, 2007.

United Kingdom. Amma Asante, Director, 20th Century Studios, 2017.

White, Luise. "Students, ZAPU, and Special Branch in Francistown, 1964-1972." *Journal of Southern African Studies,* v. 40, No. 6, p. 1289-1303, 2014.

Wittenberg, Colm. *Poison in the Rhodesian Bush War: How Guerrillas Gain Legitimacy.* M.A. Thesis. University of Leiden, NL. 7 Sept., 2018.

Treaser, Joseph B. "Twilight in White Rhodesia." *Atlantic Monthly,* May 1977, p. 63.

Yeats, William Butler. *The Second Coming.* Poetry Foundation. *https://www.poetryfoundation.org/poems/43290/the-second-coming*

Copyright (All in the Public Domain.)

Arnold, Matthew. "Stanzas from the Grande Chartreuse." 1851-52.

Handel, George Friderik. *Messiah*. 1741.

Housman, A.E. "How Clear, How Lovely Bright." 1880s.

Kalidasa. "Salutation to the Dawn." 2500 BC.

King James Bible. Isaiah 43:2, Proverbs 31:10.

Newton, John. "Amazing Grace." 1623.

Shurtleff, Ernest W. "Lead On, O King Eternal." 1887.

"The Dying Cowboy." Cowboy Ballad.

Williams, William. "Guide me, O Thou Great Jehovah."1745.

Yeats, W. B. "The Second Coming." 1919.

About the author

Francine Walls hails from the Pacific Northwest. She has earned her living over time as a waitress, motel maid, pineapple factory worker, laundry worker, secretary, portrait photographer, teacher, academic librarian, and library director. She holds master's degrees in English and librarianship from the University of Washington and a doctorate in education from Seattle University. A Pushcart Prize nominee, her poems appear in the writing handbook, *Writing Across Cultures,* the anthology, *Peace Poems* v. 2, and numerous journals. She authored two books related to librarianship as well as a poetry chapbook, *Waiting for Someone to Find Me.* She is a certified InterPlay leader, involved with InterPlay for over twenty years. InterPlay activities are composed of storytelling, movement, vocalization, improv, and just plain fun. (InterPlay.org).

In late 1971, she traveled to Botswana with her young son, Chris, to teach English and typing for a year at Shashe River School in Tonota, Botswana, near Francistown and the Rhodesian border. The Facebook Author Page for *Cradle of Lightning* is at "Francine Walls." You can contact her at Trilliumspring360@gmail.com.

Made in the USA
Columbia, SC
27 May 2024

35881470R00214